ELECTRIC CITY

Electric City

a novel

ELIZABETH ROSNER

COUNTERPOINT
BERKELEY

Library of Congress Cataloging-in-Publication Data

Rosner, Elizabeth.
 Electric city : a novel / Elizabeth Rosner.
    pages cm
1. Edison, Thomas A. (Thomas Alva), 1847-1931–Fiction. 2. Steinmetz, Charles Proteus, 1865-1923–Fiction. 3. City and town life–New York (State)–New York–Fiction. 4. Science–New York (State)–History. 5. New York (State)–Intellectual life–20th century–Fiction. I. Title.

 PS3618.O845E44 2014
 813'.6–dc23

                                        2014022623

ISBN 978-1-61902-346-8

Cover design by Rebecca Lown
Interior design by Megan Jones Design

COUNTERPOINT
2560 Ninth Street, Suite 318
Berkeley, CA 94710
www.counterpointpress.com

Printed in the United States of America
Distributed by Publishers Group West

10 9 8 7 6 5 4 3 2 1

for Carl H. Rosner
and all the other Wizards of Schenectady

I run with the blue horses of electricity
who surround the heart

and imagine a promise made
when no promise was possible.

—JOY HARJO

ONE

B EFORE THE NAME Electric City there were other names, and before those names there were no names at all. The river carved itself into the valley, remembering everything. Pines thickened and pushed against the sky. Autumn went dark, then ghostly, freezing into the hibernation of winter; spring resurrected the landscape and the creatures that filled it, painting the scenery back to life. Summers shimmered with wet heat until fall erupted into a riot. The story repeated and repeated, the same and yet not the same, year in and year out.

The Hudson was known as *The River That Flows Both Ways*, or Muhheakantuck, and sometimes simply *The River*, as though the only one. Tributaries were referred to by their outer banks, shadowed by the trees best suited for canoe making. There was Shenahtahde, *Water Beyond the Pines*, and also Andiatarocté, or *Here the Lake Closes*, later, much later, to be known as Lake George.

Seneca, Cayuga, Onondaga, Oneida, and Mohawk people braided themselves into a confederacy with the name Haudenosaunee, building longhouses beneath the Great Evergreen Tree. Making shelter under the deep-rooted pine—with its eagle hovering above—the collective of voices agreed to put down the weapons of war and let the waters wash them away.

Even when the Longboats watched the arrival of the Van Curlers, curiosity became regret only after it was far too late. Surely there were meat and fish and grain enough to feed all of them, enough flat ground for planting on, enough wide sky to worship toward.

We know you have arrived and are not leaving.

Tribal arguments were as old as the mountains, but those wounds always healed eventually, when tended with proper care, blessed and forgiven. Now these darker-skinned and lighter-skinned alliances gave way once again to wars, followed by burying of the innocent and the guilty side by side. Uneasily borrowing each other's language, awkward hesitations and gestures filling the spaces in between the mispronounced words, the Longboats and Van Curlers negotiated dividing, took turns being the teacher and the student. It was at first strange and then common to call places by the names of people instead of using words to describe nature belonging only to itself.

We know you have arrived and are not leaving.

The wampum belt depicted a hopeful coexistence: white-beaded rows flanking and separating the two purple-beaded rows, to show it was possible for vessels to travel freely in both directions. Shards of freshwater clamshells, purple and white, represented generations of voyagers. European ships and Iroquois canoes. Still, one truth told its story over and over: whatever the earth gave, it could also take away.

F RIDAY IN THE peak of autumn, 1919. Along the cliff edge of the Mohawk River, maples, sumacs, and chestnut oaks blazed red and orange, while pitch pines stood in their greenery. Pigeons wandered and flew off and returned. Somewhere far too high to be noticed, an eagle rode a current of air. And a fox slept inside a secret.

Charles P. Steinmetz steered his cherished Baker electric car until the cabin he called Camp Mohawk came into view. Last night's dramatic thunderstorm had given way to a sparkling morning, and he was eager to spend this weekend in his canoe, pine plank stretched across the gunwales to provide a space for his mathematical calculations. In that floating office, his mind felt as wide as the horizon, and his aching bones were lightened with buoyancy. Alternately paddling and gliding, he relaxed into the accommodation offered to his abbreviated frame and hunched back.

"Divine discontent," he called his condition, not only alluding to his physical state but also reinventing the equation of his life. A triumph of mind over matter.

Now Steinmetz clamped a fresh Blackstone panatela cigar between his teeth, shrugging off the recent headline in the Saturday *Globe* calling him "Wizard of Electric City." It might have suited him, admiration offered in a play on words, but he preferred irreverence. In any case, anonymity had never been an option for someone shaped like him.

Approaching the turnoff to his encampment, he often considered the fateful decision Thomas Edison once made to choose this verdant valley for his new company. He had claimed it for the way the rivers met here—the grand Hudson and its greatest tributary, the Mohawk. Like the confluence of time and space. Edison must have sensed that in a land of quartz, feldspar, and magnetite, he could make a city that would light up the world.

It took Steinmetz a few ungainly movements to clamber down from the high-seated car, and for a luxurious moment he stood to inhale the beauty of his simple refuge, this morning of birdcalls and the almost-imperceptible muttering of the river. Entering the unlocked house, he recognized the scorched smell alongside the visible residue of an unin-vited guest. Cracks in the blackened doorframe, an arc of burn marks below a window that was torn from its molding. Not caused by any human vandal, as he might have guessed had he still been living in Europe, not by thugs in pursuit of valuables or in belligerent destructive pleasure.

This was Zeus's handiwork. *Lightning.*

Stepping carefully around a large shattered mirror, he noted the way its rectangular oak frame still held a few shards, even as the jag-ged remainder lay on the dusty floorboards. What was the last image reflected here in its wholeness? A flash of someone's distracted face, the back of his own head as he walked away, the blur of a trapped bird searching for a way out?

Foolish to have kept a mirror in a cabin, he chided himself.

Instead of stooping in agitation toward the mess, wondering how to restore peace so he might work, Steinmetz felt the spark of an idea. Why not investigate this ordinary mystery? Find a way to harness nature's own extravagant power? In one pocket, his fingers curled around the shape of a book of matches; the skin on his forehead tingled and his jaw tightened around the still-unlit cigar. To start with, the damage left by this electrical visitation could be preserved with the faithful box camera he kept on a bookshelf by the window. He could gather evidence of the path of discharge. Track it like some wild animal.

His friend Joseph Longboat would surely appreciate the analogy. Together they had frequently marveled at the life beneath the river's opalescent surface, the coded language of geology and biology along the river's edge. Shale flaking down in a stuttering whisper as the two men strolled, often without speaking, companions staring at the water and gazing into the sky. They compared knowledge of currents that moved the Mohawk, waves that moved as light. Joseph shared tobacco and silence; Steinmetz mentioned Frankenstein and Einstein. Once or twice they had discussed Michelangelo's image of the gap between fingertips, animation touched into existence. When Joseph spoke of Spirit, Steinmetz knocked on flint.

Pausing only long enough to brew pot after pot of black coffee, occasionally remembering to chew on some stale biscuits and apples, the mathematician worked meticulously all weekend to reconstruct with patient exactitude the splintered mirror. Using two panes of glass to hold the pieces in place, he meant to build a map of the lightning's choreography.

"This silver puzzle is more than a man-made thing," he explained when Joseph made his usual Sunday afternoon appearance. "It's a portrait of infinity. The story of what we've loved and have lost."

Only with Joseph could he speak this way, about the world inside the world. "Bodies are energy fields," Steinmetz said, pointing at the place where his heart pumped along, faithful as ever. "Swirling patterns that we take to be our bones and organs, our vessels and skin." He stubbed out the remains of a cigar and reached for a replacement. "When we chart the course of a natural force," Steinmetz explained, "we find everything is as curved as my back. Even time itself!"

Joseph, the canoe maker, sat in a Shaker chair straddling the threshold of the open cabin door, so that he could survey the familiar layers of bedrock and sandstone, caves and sediment.

"You can look sideways through time," he said. "It's sticky like amber."

Both men could hear the nearby bridge with occasional cars clattering across. The only missing sound, it being Sunday, was the end-of-day work whistle from the downtown factory.

"Home is where you come from and where you choose to build it," Joseph said. "It's where the pieces fit together."

Steinmetz nodded, using tweezers to set the final splinters of glass into place. These two days had marked the beginning of a new game: erasures and incandescence, a mosaic bent by gravity. He believed in mathematics the way others believed in God. Notebooks lined every shelf, filled with scribbled formulas for magnetic reluctance and power surges, potential for control and its opposite. Several pages had been grabbed by wind and tossed into the river, but no matter. With equal parts perseverance and daring, a scientist could become a magician. Steinmetz had already experienced such a metamorphosis of his own, when he crossed from the Old World to the New.

In early spring, after months of bizarre explosions resounding from within Building 28, reporters from as far away as New York City were invited to witness the Wizard's latest creation. The theoretical experiment devised at Camp Mohawk had gradually expanded to fill the space of a downtown warehouse, its solid walls creating a container as vast as it was secure. The Company always provided Steinmetz with whatever component parts he required, no questions asked. Sheet metal and vacuum tubes, porcelain insulators and tungsten wire. Equations were being translated into light, into voltage.

Even Edison was here for the demonstration, seated on an overstuffed armchair brought in for the occasion. Increasingly deaf, he held his ear trumpet so as to capture whatever sound he could. When Steinmetz approached to offer a personal welcome, tapping in Morse code onto Edison's arthritic knee, the old man offered a rare smile.

"You always understand me better than most!" Edison shouted.

No need for amplification today, Steinmetz tapped. *Believe me.*

The rest of the selected crowd stood at a specific distance from the model village of Electric City that had been arrayed on a room-size platform. Balsa wood and painted paper buildings wore stenciled labels to identify which was the hospital, which was the grocer, the undertaker. The university's sixteen-sided Nott Memorial was graciously included, though its stained-glass windows were not as carefully detailed as the college president might have preferred. The marquee above Proctor's Theatre promoted a feature called *Modern Jupiter!* The curving boundaries of the Vale Cemetery had been sketched into place on a green-painted hillside with clay tablets for tombstones. Railroad tracks ended abruptly at the edges of the stage. And a blinking circle of light was suspended above a miniature version of the Company's headquarters.

Not counting Joe Hayden, the devoted assistant who had become Steinmetz's adopted son, only two of the guests knew what they were about to see. An eleven-year-old fair-haired girl whose nickname of

"Midget" had been chosen by her adoptive grandfather, "Daddy" Steinmetz. And Joseph Longboat, leaning almost invisibly against a far wall, casually but firmly holding on to the shoulders of the child. On both faces, matching grave expressions revealed nothing of the secret they had been sworn to keep.

"Artificial it may be, but like Nature herself, this will be loud and spectacular," Steinmetz had promised Midge the day before, gazing into her dark, serious eyes with undisguised fondness. Of the three Hayden children, she was his favorite and everyone knew it. "You might want to cover your ears."

The time had come. Steinmetz raised one hand in a sober request for silence, and with no further warning, the diorama was electrocuted by a generator's split-second emission of one million volts.

Trees became smoke. A church steeple burst into flame.

P ICTURE THE LOGO — you can still see it anywhere. A monogram of curling letters meant to look like someone's handwriting, adorning some appliance or other, your fridge or your stove, maybe a washing machine, a dryer. Now picture it huge, glowing neon white above the factory headquarters whose dull red facade shadowed a stretch of the Mohawk River. You could see it from the bridge, driving away from or toward downtown, with the river flowing dirty and despondent below. You could see it from all over town, and even in your dreams, hovering with incandescent power above elms and train platforms, above barns and telephone poles. Sometimes it seemed to cast a particular glow onto the mossy brick of the campus residence halls, the stately ones bearing plaques engraved with the Van Curler name. And sometimes it left an eerie sheen on the gravestones in the Vale Cemetery, that place where the living and the dead still met.

In a company town, everything wore the Company insignia. "Live better electrically!" the slogan said. Everyone believed it.

And yet, on an ordinary Tuesday afternoon, with autumn tipping into winter, when most but not quite all of the dying leaves were down on the frozen ground, when the vague but unmistakable smell of rotting pumpkins could be found in certain driveways and alleys, when the full moon had begun its slow climb into the darkening sky, when fathers all over town were driving home from work and mothers were preparing dinner and children were bent over their homework, the lights in Sophie Levine's house flickered for a few seconds and faded to nothing. The refrigerator and dishwasher were suddenly mute; the electric stove lost its orange-hot flare. Even the clothes dryer ceased its tumbling.

Sophie, alone in the family room, had been avoiding completion of a trigonometry assignment, puzzling over an echo from that morning's homeroom that wouldn't quite leave her mind. A classmate who had refused to stand and recite the Pledge of Allegiance was sent to the principal's office, and she couldn't stop wondering what his motives had been, what else would now happen to him. Absentmindedly flicking a nearby floor lamp on and off, on and off, she thought at first she'd simply burned out the bulb — or worse, had broken something in the wiring. But when she tried to turn on the television, that switch had no effect either, which had to amount to more than coincidence.

When her father's car pulled into the garage much more noisily than usual, she realized this was because every other sound in the house was missing. It was November 9, 1965, and Sophie was fifteen years old.

Tuned to WABC, the kitchen radio had just been playing "Everyone's Gone to the Moon," and it was funny, for a moment, to think that maybe this was what had happened. Everyone had simply launched into outer space. Miriam said the music was warping and wavering as though someone were holding a finger on the record player. "The electricity is slowing down!" the radio announcer said. "I didn't even know that could happen."

Even before her father had made it out of the garage, Sophie saw that her mother had already found matches and the box of white Sabbath candles, which she began lighting a few at a time. There was a decent flashlight in the broom closet, but its batteries were dead and Sophie was sent down to the basement holding a candle to see if she could find some new ones. Hot wax dripped onto her fingers and cooled just quickly enough not to burn; she stubbed her toe on the leg of a table in the hallway.

Sophie's father said, "What's going on?" when he met her at the bottom of the stairs.

"Good thing we have so many candles!" came the call from her mother in the kitchen. "Maybe this isn't what they're meant for, but still."

Sophie thought this was exactly what they were best for: pushing light against darkness.

"No luck," she called on the way back up, having found no spare batteries to replenish the flashlight. Returning, she saw her mother smile.

Sophie loved watching her mother light candles on Friday nights and whisper the blessing so quietly that no one could make out the words. Miriam didn't just close her eyes but placed both hands over them too, making sure to block out everything that might distract her from the intensity of her praying. Sophie had long suspected that she wasn't reciting the traditional Shabbat blessing but was instead making up her own words.

Tonight, her mother lit candle after candle, blowing out matches just before they burned her fingertips. Once again, Sophie didn't ask the question she always wanted to ask: *What do you whisper?* Instead she pulled aluminum foil off its tube and built makeshift holders; they had run out of candlesticks.

Sulfur from the extinguished match tips hung in the air, temporarily obscuring the other aromas of frying onions and meatloaf and dill on potatoes. In the moody glow, her mother looked wistful, as if she were listening for Sophie's older brother Simon's footsteps on the stairs. He was in his first year of college in California, and the three of them still weren't used to his absence.

Her father put his briefcase in the hallway closet and hung up his overcoat in the usual way. He loosened his tie but didn't take it off. "Let's see what happens now," he said.

The telephone began ringing and didn't stop for the next half hour. All of the Levine family friends were checking on each other, a kind of impromptu phone tree spreading its limbs across town. Reena and Irving, Magda and Daniel, Rose and Benjamin. The women were making the calls, and the men were testing the fuse boxes, but eventually it became clear that the blackout had spread all over the city, and much farther, beyond the northern border of the United States even, into Canada. Sophie's father's transistor radio was a source of information, but at first nobody could explain much about the vastness of the power outage. Electric City had gone dark.

M IDGE LEANED A hip against her kitchen counter, rinsing dirt from the last of the squash from her garden, to be chopped and combined with tomatoes she had canned the year before. A package of egg noodles was neatly poured into boiling water on the stove. She had only just turned on the overhead light minutes past the fading of sunset, because her favorite time of day was always this—savoring the glow of the sky and its reflection on the Mohawk, allowing it to seep under her skin and to be stored there through the gloom of winter.

From decades of observing the land, its creatures and plants, Midge knew that you could submit to the long frozen nights as though they permitted a welcome time of rest. Still, approaching sixty and with the steady ache in her joints becoming more pronounced, she also knew that sleep was no guarantee of waking up again. She stared at the back of her freckled hands as she held the zucchini under the flow of the faucet, noting how the bluish tint of her arteries took the shape of naked tree branches.

Moments later, she switched off the radio. It was unbearable, listening to the broadcast about what had happened in New York City earlier that day. The term itself was excruciating: *self-immolation*. A young

American imitating the Buddhist monks in protest against the Vietnam War. They said he wasn't expected to live, with 95 percent of his body burned. Midge covered her eyes with her hands but knew that the image of a man in flames would stay with her for a very long time.

The blackout wasn't obvious at first. It could have been a blown fuse, or some wind-wrecked power cable, but after investigating both inside and outside the house, considering the options, and drawing her own conclusions, Midge went in search of her emergency candles and the kerosene lantern she kept in her mudroom. Both the fragrance of the smoking wick and the quality of light itself brought her all the way back to the days with Daddy Steinmetz, those long summer weekends at Camp Mohawk, so close to town and yet as far as another world.

The cabin was long gone, and Steinmetz too, not to mention each of his beloved pets like Jenny the monkey and the Gila monster. All surrendered to the gravitational pull of time, the Big Sleep, *gone to graveyards every one.* Midge heard the tune in her head, then hummed it quietly into the hushed kitchen, forgetting the words. She drained the mostly cooked noodles and ate her solitary meal by lamplight.

The day of the man-made lightning exhibition came back to her now too, the opposite of this unilluminated moment, a flash of light so astonishing it seemed able to banish every darkness. Steinmetz had explained to her that he was studying the most invisible yet important power on earth, convinced with his characteristic optimism that nature's electromagnetism could be harnessed for the benefit of all beings—no matter how small, no matter how distant from one another, as far apart as stars.

Studying the sky before bedtime, monitoring the cycle of the moon and the movements of the constellations, Midge could occasionally feel his disembodied presence beside her, the way on brief summer nights they used to stand with their feet in the river while he talked about the vastness of the universe. He told her about his childhood on another continent, about the mother who had died when he was only one year old, about the mountains in Switzerland where he had studied as a young man. He taught her to swim in the river, shallowest among the reeds, and later in deeper water after the Erie Canal changed the shape of their own creek edge.

Steinmetz had died when she was only fifteen, but even now, forty-two years later, she had never met anyone else as kind, as silly, as smart. She missed him every day of her life.

She considered her own death sometimes, and her decision not to have children, and the question of who would be there to witness her departure. Her brothers gave forward momentum to the Hayden lineage in their own way, while her choice was yet another curious echo of her tie to Steinmetz. How natural it could feel to spend time with other people's children, connected not by blood but some other substance there was no name for.

And what did it mean not to be carried forward with an imprint of your own genes; what did it mean to Steinmetz to be the last of his family line? She was the one who chose to preserve the molecular memory of Steinmetz more than any of them, keeper of his canoe and his modified bicycle, his cigar boxes holding flakes of old tobacco like some atomic residue of the genius long departed. Joseph Longboat, who too was long departed by now, would have understood each of these thoughts, she felt certain. For a moment, sitting beside the subtle smokiness of the lantern, hands folded in her lap, she remembered the gentle pressure of Joseph's hands on her shoulders the day they stood together watching Steinmetz set the imaginary town on fire.

When the phone rang and Martin Longboat's voice was there, asking if she was all right and whether she needed any help, he could come right over, she smiled. Looking out the window that would ordinarily have shown her the distant beaming logo of the Company, Midge focused her gaze on the rising full moon instead.

"I've never really minded the dark," she said.

SOPHIE COULD TELL from the WABC announcer's voice that the extent of the power failure was unprecedented; he kept exclaiming over the way New York City looked so unlike itself, with ribbons of light from the cars in dramatic contrast against black skyscrapers under the moon. She couldn't picture it, having visited the city only a handful of times with her family when they drove the four hours south for a rare expedition to Radio City Music Hall. Mostly she remembered her amazement at the crowds and traffic and sea of yellow cabs in all directions.

"What about the elevators?" Miriam said suddenly. "Or being trapped in the subway! A tunnel!" The three of them stood in the kitchen together, tilting in the direction of the radio as though it were a television.

David shook his head. "Extremely strange that they don't seem to know what caused something this major." Sophie was reminded of how much her father loved to use his intellect, how frustrated he became when faced with other people who didn't enjoy problem solving quite as much as he did. "I'm good at locating what's wrong," he frequently claimed, and to Sophie this was altogether too much of the truth, even though she knew he was referring to what went on in the research lab where he worked. Unfortunately, it also happened to describe family life at home.

In that moment, she felt it more disconcerting than ever to have Simon living so far away, in a place where it wasn't even night yet. Until this past year, she'd had him as an ally of sorts. Someone with whom to share the blame, or at least a discreet rolling of the eyes.

"Is there something for dinner?" David asked, focusing on a more immediately relevant subject. Miriam, still wearing her apron, served three plates of meatloaf and potatoes that were already losing their heat. Arranged in their places around the Formica table, Sophie watched her parents' faces in the dim glow of the candles, sensing as usual her distance from the private thoughts they were keeping to themselves. David and Miriam even had a private language, Dutch, whose vocabulary remained a mystery to both of their children, a choice rationalized by their commitment to assimilation. Their accents faded year by year, although Sophie always heard the extra thickness in their throats when they spoke English. Adding that sound to their "eccentric" religious observances, Sophie was convinced they were the most Jewish Dutch people in all of Electric City.

"You know Daniel specializes in this kind of thing," her father commented between bites. "Electrical outages, I mean."

"Then I bet he'll fix it," her mother said.

The radio had been turned off to conserve its batteries, and as if on cue, three of the candles sputtered on the kitchen counter. In the near-silence, Sophie felt that the three of them were alone in the universe, dangling in concert but not quite attached to anything else.

"It's the anniversary of Kristallnacht," David said softly, and Sophie imagined that he was hearing the crunch of broken glass underfoot. She knew only a single episode of this story: her father as an engineering student wandering the streets of Hamburg, counting every synagogue and Jewish storefront that had been smashed to pieces. The nationwide outburst of organized violence had convinced him not only to return to the Netherlands but to leave Europe in haste altogether.

That brief tale always segued rapidly into the scene of his very first visit to Electric City, with the half-serious joke about how the car broke down on the way to his other interviews, and so he had no choice but to accept the job he was offered by the Company.

"I guess we were supposed to end up here," he said, each time performing the same shrug.

"Like all our friends too," Miriam said. "We were supposed to end up here together."

Arriving within the embrace of Electric City's glory days, all the men found engineering jobs offered up on the abundant waves of postwar productivity. To Sophie it was as though they'd all been seduced by the neon sign atop the Company headquarters. Yet she could also sense a tender inevitability to the group her parents gathered with, refugees from assorted countries but all from the same war, all Jewish and all homeless, looking for a place to make a living, buy a house, raise a family. They brought a handful of languages with them, but none of Sophie's generation spoke in the accents of their parents. On the phone and during visits over coffee and cake, she often heard her mother gossiping in Dutch and Hebrew, strains of Yiddish sometimes too. But when they were all gathered together, English was the only vocabulary they had in common.

"It's a full moon!" Sophie's mother announced, clapping her hands as though she had just been awarded a prize. "Let's go outside and enjoy it."

After clumsily stacking the dishes in the sink, Miriam pulled three coats from the hall closet and urged her resistant husband and reluctant daughter out the front door to sit on the steps facing the silent street.

Every other house looked abandoned both inside and out. Miriam hugged David with one arm and squeezed Sophie with the other. Instead of a Shabbat melody, her mother sang "Everyone's Gone to the Moon," just one line and nothing else. For a few minutes that seemed to go on and on, they watched their breath make vapors in the silvery dark.

Hours later, in the darkest part of the night, Sophie woke up in her bedroom, listening for familiar snoring down the hall. The last of the candles had long since burned out. When she parted the curtains and saw that the moon had set, Sophie pulled a thick chenille bathrobe over her flannel nightgown, slid her feet into slippers, and grabbed a wool blanket for extra warmth.

On the concrete slab making up the back patio, she held her breath to look up, where stars poured in profusion against a vast black bowl. The blanket was big enough to lie in folds on the concrete while also cocooning her shivering body. Sophie stretched out to watch the sky for as long as she could keep her eyes open.

This is what it's like in the desert, she thought, *or in the middle of the ocean.*

The sky lightened so imperceptibly it was the first time in her life she understood that the stars were always there, and it was only the brightness of the sun that blinded her to the other luminous bodies scattered throughout space. Only when her back was turned, when she looked away from her own bright beacon, could she see how magnificent all those others were—countless suns all around.

When she finally admitted that it was morning, and tiptoed back indoors, the first thing Sophie noticed was that the old sounds had been restored: the humming from the fridge and the faint but now noticeable buzz of the kitchen lights. She hung up her robe and climbed back into bed, waiting for her parents to awaken too.

The return of power was reassuring—a recognizable melody running through the house—but it also set off a strange sensation in the pit of her stomach. At first she thought maybe they'd been reminded that life without electricity was still possible, that they could manage perfectly well without it. Maybe they wouldn't need to feel so plugged in; alongside "living better electrically," they could rediscover what it was like to be dark for a while.

Why did it seem weird that the fathers would be heading back to work as they did every ordinary Wednesday, and the mothers making lunches for school? Sophie heard Miriam on the telephone spreading Magda's news: her husband Daniel was the engineer who figured out that the system put into place to prevent a blackout had instead caused the opposite.

"He fixed it," Miriam said to both David and Sophie, pouring orange juice into their glasses. "Just like I said he would."

Life was resuming as though nothing at all had gone wrong. But to Sophie everything seemed a little too bright, and yet not quite bright enough.

ALTHOUGH MARTIN LONGBOAT lived with his grandmother *across the river*—that is, on the side of the river supposedly outside the limits of Electric City—thanks to the complicated insistence of his father he attended high school with all of the scientists' kids, the school with an Indian name. It alternately amused and infuriated him that no one there seemed to wonder about the translation, casually using the Iroquois words as if they all assumed the meaning of the language no longer mattered.

Land of high corn.

Land beyond the pine trees.

These were the timeless place-names given by his forebears, the now-invisible ones. There were still plenty of pine trees, but the fields of corn were shrinking, year by year. He wondered often if he was the only one who noticed. It was nearly impossible to sit still in geology class, for instance, and hear the teacher droning about metamorphic terrain and postglaciation. How could they care so much about scratches and chatter marks on shale without knowing the histories of this land and of his tribe?

Whenever he stayed up late at night listening to his homemade recordings of elders speaking Mohawk, and considered the idea that the Electric City Museum ought to collect such things, he always ended up assuring himself that he was better at safekeeping than any museum could ever be. Even the battered trunk with a broken lock served as a treasure chest when it was draped with one of Annie's hand-made quilts.

He would have had to teach the basics of listening, and he had no idea how to explain the subtleties of telling stories by beginning with "you" instead of "I." On his high school English papers, that same "you" was repeatedly crossed out with red marks, replaced in the teacher's handwriting with her strangely detached "one." It would take more patience than he possessed to explain that in his own tongue, there was a "we" that meant *you and I*, while another word for "we" meant *he/she and I, but not you.* The language of including and excluding could be simple, but not easy.

Why share this legacy with people who owned too much already, and yet seemed oblivious to the value of preserving what they claimed. Not the land, not the river, not even the houses they built or the machines they made. The letters in the sky and the kitchen appliances and the things that came after.

In the faintest background of certain tapes, Martin recognized the cacophony of mayflies. Their singing so brief and urgent.

You know how to quiet everything down toward a center point, a place where even your breath is barely a disturbance, like the mirrored surface of a pond. Present to nothingness, you can be present to all, even as you stay off to the side somewhere, watching. The flight of an owl in the darkness, wings against air, silent.

You keep waiting to hear somebody tell the true story of the massacre at the Stockade. Instead all you ever get is the twisted history being told all wrong about who fought and who died. To refer to women and children as "combatants"!

You feel rage in your fingers; the muscles in your legs tighten with a confusing mix of defiance and helplessness. Who made up these words? And who claimed the right to use the names of your people for their street signs and subdivisions? The wrongs are everywhere.

Trapped behind your desk, in the angry voice you keep inside, you challenge the teachers to talk about American history in a different way. You dare them to learn the whole of what happened before they claim to know the facts. The inside voice threatens to erupt, especially now that massacres seem to be happening all over again, in jungles on the other side of the world.

Today, a November morning, you get in trouble for refusing to say the Pledge of Allegiance, sent to the principal for remaining in your seat with your fists clenched. You don't even bother to explain to the homeroom teacher why you will not say words that aren't true, won't even shape your mouth around them.

In the principal's office you mumble something about hypocrisy, about the lies of *freedom and justice for all* when you know better, know what it's been like for your ancestors and even now, for all the so-called nonwhite people, which really means the ones with no money and no power.

"I don't pledge my allegiance," you say. "I won't put my hand over my heart, not for this flag. You can't make me." You sit up straighter in the hard wooden chair. You don't want to get into any argument or negotiation.

Amazingly, the principal listens. Mr. Borden leans forward and keeps his palms flat on his oak desk. You are shocked to realize that this middle-aged freckle-faced man really does seem to want to understand,

and his milky blue eyes are fixed with great seriousness on you. He wears a tightly buttoned collar and a green tie with some kind of white bird printed on it, and you wonder if Borden genuinely cares about birds or nature in general, if he spends time with his children (there are family photos on the desk, turned so that both you and the principal can see them: the smiling blond wife and two girls, carbon copies of their mother but one shorter than the other and one missing a tooth). Does he take his daughters on camping trips, or maybe swimming? Does he teach them the names of birds and trees?

The principal says, "I want to suggest a compromise."

You remember a spelling lesson: "The principal is your pal." You hold your tongue, wondering if this is how it used to happen every time, the promise made and the promise broken.

But here is how it lands: you agree to stand wordlessly during the recitation of the pledge, hands by your side and staying loyal to yourself while acknowledging the rights of the others to speak their own truth. The flag will keep hanging in the corner of the room, where you do not have to look at it.

On the way home from school, you find out that on the very same day of your own small resistance, a young man planted himself in front of the United Nations building in New York City and set his own body on fire. He is burned beyond saving. The blackout that follows doesn't seem anywhere near as shocking as this piece of news, carried on radio waves into the very hollow of your chest. Exploding.

K ARL AUGUST RUDOLF Steinmetz waited in an interminable line with close to a thousand other steerage passengers on the deck of *La Champagne*. It was July 1, 1889, and the temperature so blistering that most of the passengers, wearing multiple layers of clothing, stood nearly paralyzed with heat exhaustion. One might have expected pandemonium, or at least a kind of restless excitement, but this was the last in a lengthy series of degradations to be endured, and there was nothing to do but bear it.

Steinmetz was still trying to stifle the cough that had wracked him for much of the two-weeks-long crossing from Le Havre to New York. He knew that the first order of business upon arrival at Castle Garden meant passing the medical inspection, and he had more than the average challenges to worry about. Standing slightly over four feet tall and with the same hunched back that disfigured both his father and his grandfather, he was all too aware of the innumerable physical ailments guaranteed for a twisted body like his. He had even temporarily forgone his greatest pleasure, cigars, in order to give his cough an opportunity to subside. Today, mentholated throat lozenges filled his pockets, and he slipped yet another one into his mouth as he watched for the line to inch forward.

Just ahead of him in the queue, a young yet gaunt-faced woman was surreptitiously breastfeeding, shrouding herself as well as the infant in a webbing of brown wool shawls. *In the name of modesty,* Steinmetz thought, *she is nearly suffocating the child.* He tried not to stare, resisted every impulse to suggest that she give the poor creature a chance to breathe some fresh air. But of course he had no idea what words she would understand. During the voyage he had counted at least thirteen different tongues, muttered and shouted and cried out in dreams. The sea of humanity astonished him. And here they all were, making way for a new land, carrying what they could on their backs.

"Look out there, you!"

"Move up, and stay in line!"

Directives in his new language flew all around him. He felt the press of those eager to reach solid land, while trunks and crates and baskets and satchels were hoisted onto shoulders and carts. There was altogether too much to absorb: light bouncing off the surface of the seawater; children wailing from hunger and weariness; smells of damp wool and unwashed bodies mingling with the stench of the harbor. And within shouting distance, Steinmetz could see several other steamships with their equivalent load of human cargo, waiting for the brutally slow processing to be completed.

The arrival building rose impressively at the dock's edge, its rococo style reminding him of Bavaria and yet also suggesting a reinvention, more modern, certainly cleaner and less ravaged by soot and weather. Two eagles sculpted in granite posed above the grand entrance, a symbol of this brave world. Not to mention the graceful countenance of the green lady in the harbor, her arm stretched toward heaven with a gilded torch. "I lift my lamp beside your golden door..." Something like that.

His peripheral vision again took in the masses of people pulsing against him. How many would be turned away for carrying visible signs of disease, not to mention for reasons of insanity ("caused by condi-tions on the ship," Steinmetz muttered to no one). How many like himself would be grilled in a vocabulary they didn't yet possess, asked to prove their capability for earning a living, told to name someone in the States who was willing to sponsor them, help them settle. Were they expecting to be penniless or did they vow to work hard like good Americans?

Like plenty of others, no doubt, he was significantly weakened from the journey—terrible food, little enough fresh water, overcrowded sleeping compartments, and whimpering youngsters at every turn—but he allowed himself a palpable thrill at being so very close now to the true beginning of the rest of his life. It seemed clearer than ever from this vantage point that neither Vienna nor Zurich could have made suit-able refuge for a Socialist such as himself; the political constraints he had fled from in Breslau met him there. His fellow mathematics student and friend Oscar Asmussen, a Danish American, had been the one to persuade Steinmetz to join him on this cross-Atlantic voyage. No matter that all he could afford was steerage class, while Asmussen would take his place on an upper deck.

"Would you prefer to end up in some Bavarian prison? Or dead?" Such were the simple equations declared by his friend, and Steinmetz had been unable to refute their logic.

Europe, for him, was over. He was about to step onto an unfamiliar shore, with its promises of renewal and freedom, and adopt it as home.

Inside the vast entrance hall, Steinmetz gazed upward to the curving ceiling and saw a pair of red, white, and blue American flags hanging limp in the hot air. Having been exhorted to leave behind all cases and bundles, trudging up a wide staircase along with his fellow passengers, he noted the team of medical evaluators peering down over the balcony, studying all of them for obvious signs of infirmity. Steinmetz imagined how pathetic he must look from their viewpoint, no way to hide his compressed frame, his uneven legs. But at least he wouldn't be seen straining for oxygen or raggedly wheezing like so many on the stairs above and below him.

On this second floor, with doctors scanning each individual in a matter of seconds, scribbling with chalk on dark coat sleeves and lapels, Steinmetz tried to present himself with as much dignity as possible under the circumstances. To be publicly examined by strangers was to be the finale of the humiliations, he hoped.

Just ahead of him, a powdery B and P were hastily sketched on an elderly woman's woolen shoulder; her cataracts and ghastly pallor couldn't be mistaken by even a layperson. Steinmetz observed adults and children of all ages being directed to one side or another, led toward clusters of those who would be taken to the island's hospital for treatment. He heard loud-voiced assurances that they would be seeing American doctors, not taken back on board.

"You are not being sent home," a hoarse young man barked over and over. Protests in multiple dialects were elaborately offered in return.

"You are not being rejected. Just need to get stronger first, that's all." The young man flexed his muscles as though to demonstrate or perhaps translate, but the gesture was met with baffled expressions.

Steinmetz felt his heart pounding in empathy, knew his own strength was a matter of doubt. Having traversed one treacherous ocean, this seemed to him yet another sea of distress, with feverish looks on nearly every face, even the ones who were passing inspection. The middle-aged woman to his right was wearing about seven or eight skirts, so much material it must have been like carrying around an extra fifteen kilos of weight. *What a clever inspiration*, he thought, and managed a smile. Why not wear everything you own instead of packing it into a suitcase.

His turn had finally come. He held out his passport, looked straight into the eyes of the medical officers, and waited.

The pair of sandy-haired doctors assigned to him wore similar mustaches; one wore spectacles and the other did not. Almost in unison, they jotted rapid notes on their clipboards and shook their heads. In mere seconds their stethoscopes revealed he was suffering from bronchitis, his eyesight was poor, and even a cursory glance deemed him a truly unpromising figure on all counts. A chalk mark on his sleeve was to be the inevitable result: *L* for *lameness*.

This was the moment when Asmussen shouldered his sizable frame through the throng and began waving a stack of paper bills toward the faces of the officials.

"This money," he sputtered. "All of this belongs to my friend here, Herr—I mean Professor Steinmetz. It's been saved for him especially!" Asmussen, having easily cleared each inspection as a returning citizen, stood in an impressive white blazer on the far side of a high oak desktop, fluttering the money again.

"And allow me to mention the most important thing. He's a mathematical engineer with a first-rate mind. A genius! An ideal American, I assure you!"

The younger of the two doctors squinted back and forth between Asmussen and Steinmetz, his chalk poised in midair. The older doctor adjusted his spectacles as if reconsidering the object before him.

Steinmetz stood patiently, *like a mule*, he thought, until they finally and wordlessly stamped his documents with their approval. Money had spoken. He would be allowed to disembark, set free to place his feet on dry land, accompanied by his single trunk and his beloved cigars.

But one thing would be left behind, drowned between the Old World and the New. From this day on he would call himself by an American designation, one that reflected his new identity, his determination to start over.

Charles Steinmetz.

The middle initial P. would come later, followed eventually by his full inclusion of what the letter represented: *P* for Proteus, the god of changing shape. His classmates had given him the nickname back in Breslau, a kind of teasing but without cruelty in it. They claimed it had to do with his mind's phenomenal fluidity, shifting from one intellectual pursuit to another.

He knew too that being called Proteus was simply an acknowledgment of what was impossible to ignore, his hump, his twisted frame. Quietly he maintained a conviction that this was as God-given as his mind, to be accepted without complaint.

Hardly anyone knew about the near-constant pain in his torso and limbs. There were few positions in which Steinmetz could remain comfortable for long, a favorite being perched on a stool like some exotic bird, to allow himself the possibility of rearranging his weight whenever necessary and also gaining some much-needed height when others were sitting nearby.

He would be his own invention, in this land decidedly famous for liberty of ideas and expression. Breslau would recede into blurry memories of forgotten faces, along with those of Vienna and Zurich. Unlike his grandfather and his father, he had already vowed never to marry, never to sire offspring doomed to carry the same deformity. He was perfectly sure of this, at the age of twenty-four, confident he had some other legacy to leave behind.

Finally on the same side of the gate, threshold of the New World, the two travelers embraced in triumph. Steinmetz, whose head was nearly two full feet lower than his friend's, gripped Asmussen around his thick waist.

"At last, at last!"

He turned his curving back to the harbor and the Atlantic Ocean, strode forward into the future.

I F IT WEREN'T for the annual Company picnic, Henry Van Curler and Sophie Levine might never have met. Their lives could have passed side by side without overlapping, the perfectly parallel lines of a railroad track, never touching except in the illusion of a painting. Though they were nearly the same age, and ordinarily might have collided in the hallways at school, that never happened. Henry went to a boarding school in New Hampshire, the same exclusive place that had graduated the men of his family for generations.

His lineage went back to the earliest Dutch settlement of Electric City, and his last name appeared on some of the oldest grave markers in town, the ones obscured by moss in the Vale Cemetery. The Van Curlers had resided in Electric City without interruption for some impressive number of centuries, a number Henry was always forgetting on purpose. Being "known" by way of his legacy, not to mention by way of the Tragedy, weighed more heavily each year of his life; he would have gladly shrugged it off like an old coat, a useless dead skin. So far, at least, that wasn't one of the options.

Within the past couple of years, thousands of families had been exiled from Electric City all the way to Virginia in the aftermath of layoffs and "relocations"; nevertheless, the simulation of a thriving future persisted. And though no one but Henry seemed to notice, the annual picnic was designed to fool everyone else into imagining Electric City comprised a single extended family. Abundant food on the Independence Day theme was provided by the Company, along with a seemingly unlimited supply of soft drinks for the kids and beer for anyone over twenty-one. Even Henry was unaware that one family among the many hundreds in attendance didn't eat any of the grilled hot dogs or hamburgers but instead discreetly loaded flimsy paper plates with potato salad and coleslaw and ears of fresh corn. A man muttered apologetically that he wasn't very hungry, rather than daring to explain that he was keeping kosher in the midst of so many non-Jews. Keeping a low profile was best, at least in certain situations in which it was easier to say too little rather than too much.

It was July 7, 1966, and people were still talking about the blackout from back in November. Off-color jokes were shared among the adults about the wave of pregnancies appearing in the aftermath of that night.

"Urban legend," someone scoffed.

Instead of smirking at the indirect mention of sex, the kids were more intent on passing around grim rumors about the Knolls Atomic Power Lab, sitting just a hillside away.

KAPL was squat and gray and ominous, set back far enough from the crest of the road that its structures weren't quite visible to anyone just driving by. Out front, a huge parking lot filled and emptied twice a day, and everyone knew without exactly being told that KAPL and its secrets compromised their safety.

"We're on the top ten targets for Soviet missiles because of that place," a boy with black-rimmed glasses said. In his yellow T-shirt and plaid shorts, he looked to be about eleven, but sounded both older and younger at the same time. Maybe it was the way the word *Soviet* came out of his mouth in between bites of hot dog going in.

"Duck and cover," another boy said, red-haired and pudgy. He pantomimed the routine as if it were supposed to be funny, but nobody laughed.

In Henry's prep school this past year, the students had obediently practiced climbing under their desks and tucking their heads beneath folded arms. He kept reflecting on the fact that the Dutch word for creek was *kill. How could that be anything more or less than coincidental?* Looking around now at the research lab scientists in their short-sleeved white shirts and skinny ties, their identical haircuts and pocket protectors, Henry thought they were all pretending that anyone could be saved.

Three-legged races were taking place in one of the wide grassy fields, and a softball game was assembling farther off. Henry wandered away from the duck-and-cover conversation to sit at one of the empty picnic tables draped in green-checked cloth. From there he could watch the action from the sidelines and remain invisible. In previous summers, he might have been out on the field swinging a bat, attempting to blend into the crowd by participating. But this year he had no choice.

He had broken his wrist in early May, stumbling during a track practice with hurdles and landing hard on his left side. *Falling down instead of leaping over.* The coach had been furious at Henry, as though he'd personally disappointed the entire team, and thus the school year ended on an especially sour note. When, after the first cast was removed, it was discovered that the bone had healed improperly, there was sobering news. Back home and "out of reach of those country bumpkins," Henry was faced with his father's insistence that their own physician break it again. This was the kind of thing Arthur Van Curler was particularly good at, Henry knew. Breaking things until they were made more perfect.

Sometimes, when he was surrounded by people whose names he couldn't easily pronounce, Henry imagined himself the child of Italian or Polish immigrants, people employed by the Company who lived in dilapidated houses full of unrestrained noise and spicy cooking. Feelings happened loudly in those kinds of families, he supposed. Maybe sons were expected to work in the family business too, but at least they seemed optimistic about their inheritance. All over town, storefronts with names like Petrocelli & Sons or Blesky Brothers gave Henry the convincing impression of pleasurable shared ownership among parents and siblings, while in his own case, he could only locate a disquieting sense of embarrassment. In a picnic setting like this, where the only obvious rules were the ones involving sports, Henry still couldn't wish away the uncomfortable secret of privilege. He knew exactly which side of the tracks he came from.

Daydreaming, vaguely observing the arc of the white leather softball, Henry was caught off guard by Sophie's approach. Sitting down at the picnic table, she said "Hi," at the same moment one of the players yelled "You're OUT!" The creak of the table under their shared weight became another voice from the game. Miles beyond the field, the Company headquarters sign managed to keep glowing against the backdrop of blue sky, even in the daytime.

"Why aren't you playing?" she asked him, and then must have noticed the plaster cast on his left wrist, covering part of his forearm and with his thumb and fingers protruding. He held it up as she said, "Oh, I see." He admitted he was just fine with being let off the hook for a while.

"What's your excuse?" he asked, and Sophie shrugged.

"I'm a girl," she said.

While Sophie picked at a scab on her knee, Henry used a small twig with his right hand to scratch inside his cast on the left. He couldn't help noticing the way Sophie's thick auburn curls glistened in the sunlight, heard his own small sigh of relief from the itch. Something began to shift inside his heart. Just like that.

D ESPITE THE PROBABILITY of Henry and Sophie not seeing each other again until the picnic the following year, if then, their summer worlds intersected the next day. Henry happened to be leaving the glassed-in foyer of his dentist's office just as Sophie pulled up on a bicycle with a package in each of her rear baskets to take to the post office next door. It was Monday. He recognized her first, and had a chance to study her while she was locking the bike to a utility pole, head down and concentrating.

She was wearing cutoff denim shorts and had a streak of grease on her right calf from the bicycle; a faded red bandanna tied back her hair, which Henry figured would have otherwise gone wild and tangled while riding. The day was hot and humid, already oppressive by 11 AM. Henry saw how Sophie's T-shirt stuck to her lower back, and almost-invisible rivulets of sweat ran behind her knees. He was embarrassed to feel relatively cool in his pale blue T-shirt and khaki shorts, as though he'd been recently washed and pressed.

"The dentist was air-conditioned, I bet," Sophie said, looking up to catch him taking a few steps toward her.

Henry gave her an affirmative with a lopsided grin, then pointed to his mouth. "Novocain," he slurred.

She nodded back. "Not a good time for conversation," she said, and he shook his head. Sophie's eyes were green, a new discovery.

He looked at his watch. "Ice cream?"

Sophie held two packages in her arms, and Henry found himself resisting the urge to wipe away the moisture pooling at the hollows of her elbows.

"I just have to mail these for my father," she said. "And then we can walk to Friendly's?"

Henry grinned again.

"By then your Novocain will wear off. And the ice might make you feel better."

Sophie looked at him gravely, as though she wanted to interview him for a job, then blushed while bending down to retwirl the combination on her lock.

Something about her hands fascinated him. It was the first time he'd ever felt that way—that looking at someone's hands could be like looking at their entire being.

Inside Sophie's packages were books intended for some unrelated Levines who lived in Chicago, people with apartment building addresses in a city she'd never seen. Henry waited outside, having found a patch of shade in which to lean against a tree and massage his numb jaw with his unplastered hand. Sophie stole a few glances in his direction while the postal clerk weighed the books, hoping Henry wasn't aware of her gaze.

When the clerk—whose receding hairline and acne-marked skin made her feel sorry for him—took her money, he raised an eyebrow. She guessed he had noticed her watching the boy outside. Embarrassed again, even though nobody said a word, Sophie stashed the change in her pocket and practiced acting casual on her way out the door.

"All done," she called out to Henry and bent down to untwist the bike cable, glad to have something to take her attention away from Henry's sky-blue eyes. He had his cast and now his slightly swollen jaw, and still Sophie thought he was the most handsome boy she'd ever seen. Their conversation at the picnic had stopped abruptly when the softball game ended, neither of them quite knowing how to say goodbye. Now that he was standing near her again, she decided his legs were exactly right for a pair of legs, lean and sturdy and just shapely enough to be compelling. His skin was just a little tan, with fine golden hair gleaming, and she surprised herself by wanting to touch him.

Far enough from the more exhausted and decaying parts of town, Friendly's was packed. Everyone was inside to escape the swelter, which meant no room to sit down, even on the red vinyl stools at the counter. Henry and Sophie ordered cones from the takeout window. When he opened his wallet to pay for their ice cream, she caught a glimpse of his driver's license with the Dutch last name.

Sophie couldn't help asking, "Isn't it strange that our families came from the same place in Europe?"

"Your family came from Holland too?" Henry said, worried he was about to lose his temporary anonymity. "I guess history has a sense of humor."

"I hardly ever think history is funny," she said. "Not ha-ha funny, that is."

"Good point. Religious freedom was a serious enough reason to cross an ocean."

They had found a small bench alongside the pharmacy, with a place to lean her bike against a brick wall. A sign said NO LITTERING, but someone had scribbled a G into the message.

Henry laughed. "What's wrong with glittering?"

Maybe it was the echoes of the picnic, and all the chatter about who worked where—maybe it was the word *glittering* that prompted Sophie to tell Henry that her father worked with magnets. He listened while she described her father's visit to her fourth-grade classroom, how he had accidentally-on-purpose spilled metallic shavings onto the floor. "I thought he was kind of a magician," she said, as proud and shy as she remembered feeling all those years ago. "He waved a magnet in the air and all the scattered pieces danced into place."

"Does he work at the research lab?" Henry asked. *Dangerous territory now*, he thought. But he felt unable to change the subject, not yet.

"Now he works with superconducting magnets," she said, nodding, realizing how many times she'd heard and even repeated the words without quite knowing what they meant. Her father's lab, where she had once been allowed to visit, was full of tanks and cylinders wearing stenciled nametags: LIQUID NITROGEN and LIQUID HELIUM. The gleaming enamel containers were taller than she was. In room after room, sterile and quiet, the shiny reflective walls and doors warned: DO NOT ENTER WITHOUT PROTECTIVE EYEWEAR.

Henry cleared his throat as if preparing to make an important announcement. If Sophie was going to dislike him sooner or later, he might as well get the worst over with.

"Here's the weird thing," he said, and held up what was left of his cone in an awkward toast to an invisible audience. "Your dad works for my dad."

Now it was Sophie's turn to be silent. She envisioned the glowing company logo hovering over the city at Christmas, temporarily red and green in honor of the holiday. It was an image that always reminded her of being one of the "other" residents of Electric City, the ones who didn't celebrate Christmas, the ones whose parents had audible accents and who were missing grandparents. Then she thought about the team of scientists her father worked with, how he might be withholding details about what he was doing, even from his own family. *Company secrets. Company man.*

"I love magnets," Henry said, testing the air between them. "I don't really know why."

"Opposites attract?"

They both smiled, relieved.

"How is school going?" Sophie asked, sensing that both she and Henry wanted to steer sideways from where they had been headed.

Henry told her about his out-of-state boarding school, saying it was the same place his father and his grandfather went, and generations further back than that.

"I bet some of the same teachers are still there," Henry said, which Sophie thought was a weak attempt at humor until she saw that Henry's face was utterly somber. He chewed on a corner of his upper lip. "You have no idea," he said.

"You're right," Sophie admitted. All she knew about private school was what she'd observed in Electric City: the Catholic girls in their plaid uniforms filing their way down Union Street; boys in stiff-looking jackets and ties. She knew of only one Jewish kid sent off to a neighboring town where there was a modified yeshiva.

Then again, she had to endure her own family obligations in Hebrew school. "Two afternoons a week," she explained to Henry. It had to do with her father's fervent commitment to all things Jewish, especially education.

"But you really don't look Jewish," Henry said.

She reflexively leaned away, startled by his words. Simon had told her that one of his college roommates had openly searched the back of her brother's head for horns. *Surely Henry wasn't* . . .

"Damn," Henry said, smacking himself surprisingly hard on his forehead. "I can't believe I just said that."

"Um," Sophie managed, getting up from the bench to retrieve her bike.

Henry leaped up too. "Why didn't you tell me to shut up?" he demanded.

When she reached for her wobbling handlebars, Henry put his hands on top of hers, his good one as well as the one wrapped in plaster. She noticed there was a navy blue drawing of a dog on the cast that hadn't been there at the picnic. His fingernails were bitten down to the quick.

"I'm not as idiotic as this all the time," he said. "Crazy from the heat."

He surrendered the bike to Sophie, and tried shoving his hands into his pockets, except that the one with the cast didn't fit. The fabric ripped a little but wouldn't yield.

"It's okay," Sophie said. "I figure you couldn't possibly mean it the way it sounded."

Henry shook his head, squinting up at the sky with a mournful expression.

"Okay," she said again, though she was not entirely sure that it was. Her hands tingled where he had touched her.

To Sophie this seemed the right moment to climb back onto her bike and skip past yet another potentially awkward goodbye. She was only half-surprised when Henry continued to speak.

"Hey, there's a sun dog," he said. "See?" He pointed to the huge radiant halo adorning the sun.

"Atmospheric ice crystals," Sophie said in her father's voice.

Henry exhaled loudly, as though given a reprieve. "Rain tomorrow," he said.

Instead of returning to the dentist's office where he'd parked his car, Henry chose a meandering route in the opposite direction. The upbeat mood at Friendly's yielded abruptly to a grittier scene: pizza parlor with dusty windows; two matching rusted station wagons side by side in front of the liquor store; a bakery with a padlocked front door and a handwritten sign announcing its farewells to the neighborhood: THANKS FOR YOUR BUSIENESS.

Though he usually avoided the place, Henry found himself turning several corners in a semiconscious daze, until he slowed down to face the still-majestic ivy-covered brick house where his family had once lived. An enthusiastic sprinkler blasted mist across the wide front lawn, and the spray of water looked so inviting, Henry imagined Sophie beside him, suggesting they make a dash through it.

Oh, I don't think so, he would have had to say.

The water aimed in staccato bursts against the trunk of a massive elm whose sturdy limbs reached out and up, almost dwarfing the house itself. Henry couldn't take his gaze off the branches, whose density seemed to pull at his attention with an irresistible force. At the same time, the weight of the day pressed down so hard he felt as though he might pass out. No matter that shade was spreading in a generous pool below the tree; approaching it was forbidden in a way he couldn't have admitted to anyone. When he detected the shadow of someone moving around inside the leaded-glass entryway, and felt the warning bass drum of his heartbeat, he rallied himself and turned away, sprinting in the direction of his car.

The next morning, a summer thunderstorm hit, with delirious sheet lightning and enough heavy rain to flood the drains and spill with abandon across the streets. The day was warm, but Henry stayed inside to view it all from the couch beside his living room window; he watched the sky grow purple and blue gray and fierce. Leaves turned inside out in the wind.

I N YONKERS, STEINMETZ discovered it was surprisingly easy to drape an imaginary black cloth over his own European backstory, and to focus now on the vivid outlines of an American existence. Asmussen had drifted away after helping situate his friend in the position of lowly draftsman for Rudolf Eickemeyer's machine shop. This left Steinmetz to fend for himself, to explore the intriguing streets of the Lower East Side, and to improve his command of English. The blending of Old and New Worlds was an endless source of fascination: matzo factories alongside hat shops, pickle sellers, and drugstores; Yiddish shouted from tenement windows, and streetcar wires crisscrossing overhead.

Who could have predicted that within three years, Eickemeyer's inventions would evolve from mechanisms for hatmaking to revolutionary modifications of electrical motors? Technical drawings made by Steinmetz proved not only his exactitude but his keen understanding of the intersections between groundbreaking mathematics and engineering marvels.

It was an introduction to Thomas Edison, the first one fully able to recognize the texture of the small man's genius, that forever changed the direction of Steinmetz's future. Determined to hire Steinmetz for his own newly established company, Edison was stunned to find that Steinmetz possessed not only a powerful will of his own but a deep sense of loyalty to his original employer. Not a man who tolerated refusals, regardless of justification, Edison purchased the entire Eickemeyer enterprise; Steinmetz was brought like a human trophy to the recently acquired location upstate. Edison exclaimed that they would join forces just the way the Hudson and Mohawk converged, a symbol for the power they were harnessing to transform everything in the world.

What Steinmetz wanted most was a laboratory, a space devoted to experimentation and accidental epiphanies. Inspired in part by his own body's perturbations, he could readily discern the difference between those mechanical considerations one could control or modify, and those that were fixed as givens. Soon he was constructing an oversize house on Wendell Avenue, among the newest mansions of Electric City, with an extension alongside the ground floor designed to meet Steinmetz's specifications and vision.

The cabin near the edge of the Mohawk was Steinmetz's other equally invaluable sanctuary: just far enough from town to bring him back into the embrace of nature, and yet close enough to be accessible each weekend. Joseph offered to build him a canoe. There was something redemptive about the way its adjustments at the water line referred directly and automatically to his weight and balance, not in contrast to any other person but merely in response to himself. He climbed in on one side and out on the other, the way its maker taught him.

The board that served as his desk was plain and unvarnished except when it began to show signs of water damage, at which point Joseph sealed it under a modified coat of the mixture he had used on the hull. Now the desk and the canoe appeared almost inseparable.

Steinmetz was only interested in fish when someone else caught them; he had no patience for the line in the water, preferring expeditions of the mind. Thus he was able to forget for hours at a time that his spine curved like a second cage around his lungs and heart, pushing one shoulder forward and reorganizing almost all the nearby bones to accommodate distortions. Thinking about electrical current while riding a river's echo was consolation enough.

Ideas about harnessing the Niagara coexisted in alignment with Steinmetz's fervent commitment to justice. The political arena that had summoned him in his youth, Socialist views that sent him into exile all those years earlier, further contributed to a seemingly endless hunger for change. It would have been ironic to come so far in the name of liberty, only to end up witnessing from the sidelines instead. Just as applied science had seduced him, he wanted to transmit the thrill of invention into the world of the real, to leap the space between invisible power and the palpable modernization of quotidian life.

When Electric City elected a Socialist mayor, Steinmetz felt reverberations of hope for a role of another kind—in the laboratory of the classroom. Not with the graduate students at Union College, or even the undergraduates, but on behalf of the youngest students, the ones at the beginning of life. He was elected president of the school board, recognizing a chance to interweave his love of youngsters and his love of discovery.

"Here is where the New World can truly begin," he proclaimed. "These children, raised in a climate of possibility and expansiveness, are the ones who will bring the highest evolution for us all. Orphans have the same rich potential as those born into privilege; humanity is God-given and equal at the start. Progress for all of us depends on this truth."

Joseph Longboat thought his friend was a wonder, not unlike the formations on the bark of injured pines, hardened resin lasting for millennia. Persevering in the face of so many obstacles, Steinmetz floated on the river the way amber floats on saltwater. The canoe was the finest Joseph had ever made.

"You have the disguise of a geode," he told Proteus one afternoon. "Misshapen on the outside, dazzling facets inside."

M ARTIN'S FATHER HAD followed the patterns of his ancestors, and of the natural world too. Always said he was coming home in the spring, after the thaw, when the ice on the
river broke apart and slowly, inevitably, thinned and disappeared.

"It's a rhythm you can count on," Robert said, "measured by opening your eyes and listening. Not the calendar pages, not the clock on the
wall. The earth will tell you."

Robert must have learned about paying attention from his mother.
Annie spoke of these signs to her grandson Martin, teaching him about the
texture of the softening world during their walks at the edge of the river.
Annie would reach down to touch the ice, then place her fingertips lightly
on both sides of his face, imitating the gentle pressure, the letting go.

That gesture always made him want to ask about his mother, who
had died shortly after his birth. Her name was like his, Martine, but that
was practically all he knew.

At home, when Annie knelt beside Martin, their paired hands worked
the soil in the half acre of land behind their barn-shaped house. Annie's
fingers were arthritic but strong; she separated roots as though untan-
gling her own long hair, made room for the growing things to breathe.

"Under the surface the crystals are dissolving," she explained. "The seeds waking up from their patient sleep. You feel it in your bones."

Martin told her about sensations that kept him awake at night, a deep burning at the center of his thighbones, as if he were being pulled from both ends of his body.

Annie smiled sympathetically. "When the earth stretches, it makes space for the sun to come all the way in."

The sun came closer just like Martin's father came closer, his heartbeat steady and palpable. Martin came to believe Robert was like a migratory bird remembering home and knowing exactly when to turn around. Except once his father had stayed away through three years, a cycle that broke the rules Martin wanted to be able to rely upon. Annie said that could be his own chance to grow, to keep standing on his own steady feet without leaning on anyone else. Martin hated the enforced self-reliance at first, but once he learned it he was glad. Now his father saw how they both stood solid and separate, the way men were meant to be.

"It's a good thing," Robert said, returning after all that time, gray threads in his hair. And Martin said in his new deep voice, "Yes."

Martin had no one his own age he wanted to talk to with any regularity. There was his grandmother, there was Midge, and there was his retriever, Bear. Although his cocked ears were smarter than anything humans could imitate, Bear often fell asleep while listening. Martin's thoughts often remained within his own mind: *What about the way we are and are not inside our bodies, or limited to our bodies — maybe that's what I mean. That we are held here by gravity and skin, but we extend so much farther, we vibrate and echo and outlast our bodies too.*

When he looked at certain photos of Charles Steinmetz that had belonged to his grandfather Joseph, he saw the scientist looking right back, returning Martin's inquiring gaze with questions of his own. "Why do I interest you?" the ghost wanted to know. "What does my life have to do with yours?"

And Martin wanted to say: *Because of being strange and almost overlooked. Because you persevered despite the odds stacked against you, physically and otherwise. Even politics, even oceans, even language and money. None of it stopped you; none of it broke you.*

It was true, the library books told the story, and Midge repeated the tale to Martin in her own way. Recently when he had walked all the way to her house and ended up helping with repairs to her roof, Midge reminisced out loud. When Martin was younger, she had climbed the ladder while he stood at its base. Now their roles were reversed.

"Even with a bent spine and asymmetries of form, even when he had to say a permanent no to a certain kind of love in order not to pass along this particular suffering, Steinmetz found a place wide enough to hold an entire family."

Martin let the words become part of his skin. Too shy to meet Midge's gaze directly, he preferred these conversations when they were both in motion, collaborative and purposeful.

"He adopted an entire household," she shouted up to him. "A clan."

Martin pounded a piece of tar paper into place, followed by a stiff segment of asphalt shingle.

Your mother loved you, he imagined saying to Steinmetz. *She loved your father, after all, his own hump undisguised when they met, when she had every chance to turn away and didn't. She died too soon, like mine did. But still she chose to cradle you, and your father allowed your mind to flourish beyond every known container, then released you into the world*

*in order to be free. Was he the one who taught you courage? Not to accept
the burden of other glances and fears. Until you knew how to stand up
straight inside your own heart.*

Martin's frequent visits to Electric City's public library were the counterpoint to his long walks through the woods and alongside the shoreline
of the Mohawk River. There were certain revelations he knew to look
for in fossils, and others he needed to find in books. Though the texts
never named him, Martin knew that his grandfather Joseph had been a
close friend of Steinmetz. Historians mentioned a coonskin cap and a
canoe, but no hints about the rest. When the time came for Steinmetz
to choose a family to adopt long after he'd made up his mind never to
have children of his own, Martin knew that Steinmetz chose a white
man, ironically also named Joseph.

According to Annie, Joseph Longboat taught Steinmetz the enig-
mas of the river, especially the mystical pattern of its flowing both ways.
Together they had smoked fancy cigars and swapped stories into summer nights, their feet side by side in the shallows of a cooling creek.
With Midge, he got to see the images of what remained: the canoe,
the bicycle, photos of the Hayden children being taught to swim in the
shadows of Camp Mohawk.

Martin would have liked to visit the cabin where Joseph and
Steinmetz had enjoyed each other's company, but it had been carted off
for display in a Michigan museum, a relic of the Wizard's abbreviated
life. Martin figured that they must have most of his photograph collection too, organized like all those odd creatures Steinmetz had loved
in their exotic perfection. Cacti, orchids, lizards. Precious and fragile

things that could be protected from the cruelties of the world, waiting through their dormancy to restore themselves in the summer, thriving somehow even in the midst of an Electric City blizzard.

The library was where Martin could be hidden by choice instead of the way he felt disregarded so often by other places, at least other places with people inside them. Electric City seemed content to use native names for streets and buildings, but otherwise any living presence of Indians was altogether avoided. Too dark-skinned, too dark-haired, too long-haired. Seemed like where most white people were concerned, Martin was always too much of one thing and not enough of the other.

He couldn't help feeling the unmistakable vibration of attitudes, brushing up against him with prickly heat or icy cold. He would have preferred to stay home or walk alone in the woods, sit on the river's cliff-edge and watch the silt-thickened movements of water. But there were times like now that he needed the books on these shelves. If he had to sit and walk and learn among the offspring of scientists, he wanted to make sure that he was still in charge of what details gathered in his mind, still able to select and examine the images and information that mattered most to him.

That's why he was in the stacks, reading about the Erie Canal and studying one of the black-and-white photographs of skaters on its frozen surface, with the credit naming the photographer as Charles Proteus Steinmetz, 1899. Martin carried with him the photo of his grandfather that used to hang black-framed on the wall, the one Annie said looked so much like him, from the shape of his eyebrows to the line of his jawbone.

There was one drawer of photos in his grandmother's house that had been taken by Steinmetz: images of his dog Sir, who was nothing at all like Martin's dog Bear; the cabin he'd built beside the river; a self-portrait of the hunchbacked man inside his dark wool overcoat and wearing a coonskin cap. *Did my grandfather make that for you too?*

Martin glanced back at the image of the skaters again, thinking about Steinmetz and his photos of his grandfather. Lately Martin had been trying to write down certain stories of Joseph's, before he forgot everything.

He did more than write them down. He had managed to record his now-dead grandfather speaking in Mohawk, telling the story of a bridge disaster, and tales older than that one. His grandmother singing, the melody she made up in honor of Martin's birth, the one that sang him into the world. When Annie explained how she'd learned to weave baskets or repair beadwork on a ceremonial headpiece, Martin held a microphone nearby, not wanting to disturb her, determined not to lose the chance.

Nowadays there was so much talk about Mother Earth and ecology in school, and sometimes Martin wanted to stand up and make them listen to one of his recordings. His people knew for centuries that the land underfoot and all around was sacred, full of spirit and power, with rights that mustn't be violated or taken for granted. Teachers lectured about pollution and clear-cutting and damming rivers and DDT in the bodies of dead birds. Martin could have played them just one of his tapes, just one, but he was sure they wouldn't recognize the sound of the truth.

Just then he felt something peculiar at the back of his neck, an electric warning, and in the space just wide enough between two shelves of oversized books he could see that the girl was watching him. It felt to him as if they had just bumped heads. He thought she was about to come over and say something, ask what he was reading. But she pivoted away and vanished.

S OPHIE WATCHED SIMON leave early each July morning in his used Mustang, off to spend his days perched on a high wooden chair at the shoreline of the public beach on Lake George. His back and arm muscles had suddenly defined themselves as proof of his adulthood, and he wore his LIFEGUARD T-shirt with thinly concealed vanity. Just when she had almost reckoned with his absences while away at college, he was home for the summer. All the same, Sophie felt he had only partly returned. More and more he maintained a separate life that kept him out of the house until night; he didn't even have meals with them anymore.

When Miriam announced that she would be attending night school to finish her long-delayed bachelor's degree, Sophie began to wonder if everyone, even her mother, felt like a different person inside versus outside their family. Paperbacks with philosophical titles began piling onto the dining room table, and she realized maybe for the first time that her mother had a mind that carried its own images and information. Both of her parents had grown up speaking another language, and yet now they were living inside their new American skins as if most of that past wasn't quite relevant anymore.

She thought of the woman her parents knew from the same ship that had brought them to America. In the story Sophie vaguely recalled, the refugee suffered such homesickness for friends and family in Europe that she booked passage on a return voyage almost immediately, and then didn't survive the war. Sophie felt haunted by the idea that you could make the wrong choice, that there was no way to be sure which instinct would save you: the one that led you forward or the one urging you to turn back. She understood almost nothing about the woman except her name, Masha Bernstein, and the barest facts of what had occurred. Beyond that, her parents simply said, "Nobody knew. And then, suddenly, it was too late."

With a part-time summer job at the library, Sophie stamped the books departing and shelved the ones returning, occasionally repairing their protective plastic wrapping or erasing pencil marks someone had left on a book's pages. She tallied the dates as they turned in their slow, inky blur; she tracked her hours by lining up the spines with their Dewey decimals.

Watching the bored faces of strangers day after day, she sensed an unbridgeable distance from everyone she saw. She imagined Simon feeling it too, squinting behind his sunglasses at the swimmers and the splashers, inhaling the weird aromatic mix of grilled hot dogs and cotton candy and Coppertone. Maybe even her mother was feeling it, preparing her own homework, trying to complete something for herself.

We're all waiting for something to happen, Sophie thought. She wrote the sentence on an index card, using first her right hand and then her left. Later, she crossed it out.

The day after meeting Henry at the post office, the second day after the Company picnic, the rain was so relentless Sophie had to ask her mother for a ride downtown.

"I just realized I forgot to make you lunch," Miriam said, as Sophie climbed out of the car.

"It's okay. I have some stuff I brought with me."

"Smart girl," her mother said and waved as she pulled away.

Something about the greenish tint of the clouds made Sophie think about the secret time she had looked directly at the solar eclipse, the way she knew you weren't supposed to, testing it out for herself and not going blind. For weeks afterward she wondered if she would wake up blind one morning anyway, as if the slow burning of her retina would catch up with her. She had stood on the street in front of her house, cupped her hands as a small shield against her forehead and looked up. She saw the black curve eating the edge of the sun. She felt the day change color all around her, felt afraid and brave all at once.

Now, the usual stack of returned books waited at the counter, the ones that had piled up in the drop-off box overnight. Sophie could still remember when she and Simon used to take turns shoving their books through the return slot, counting out loud.

Mrs. Richardson, the reference librarian, blinked her usual "Good morning," barely looking up from her desk. Sophie was certain she loved her job so much she didn't want anyone to know it, so she frowned most of the time and kept her bifocals pushed down at the tip of her nose.

The cart of BOOKS TO BE RESHELVED squealed a complaint when Sophie began pushing it toward the Science section. Behind that sound, she could hear the soothing tempo of rain on the library roof. Here were a few of the customers she saw on a regular basis, all taking predictable refuge from the vagaries of the weather outside. She made up private names for some of them: Mr. Wallace Street, who read every column of the daily newspaper; Father Time with his weekly magazine; Mother Goose with her dwarfs, who sprawled in the children's area and preemptively *shush*ed each time the librarian looked in their direction.

When Sophie started reshelving a series of books on astronomy, she noticed someone vaguely familiar: a brown-skinned young man whose face was mostly hidden by the curtain of his black hair. A stack of books perched on a small table next to his chair, and several piles stood on the carpet near his feet. It wasn't until she got a look at him from another angle that she recognized him from homeroom at school. She even knew his name, Martin Longboat. The Quiet Guy, she had already called him.

He always nodded when roll was called, but suddenly the memory that came to her was from the morning of the blackout, when he had been sent to the principal's office for refusing to recite the Pledge of Allegiance along with the rest of her homeroom. He had stayed in his chair, like some of the antiwar protesters now appearing more and more frequently on the news, the ones who sat in the street until being dragged off and arrested. Mr. Turner hadn't touched him, though. Just pointed to the door.

She saw it all again: Martin gathering his notepads and books and leaving the room, never looking at anyone on his way out. The students all resumed the routine of saying the Pledge, with various sideways looks at each other, and a few low-voiced curiosities muttered when the bell rang to mark the end of homeroom. When Martin returned the next morning, he stood up when it was time to address the flag, but Sophie observed that his lips never moved.

This memory stayed with her as she returned to the checkout desk, as her hands continued their tasks of opening books to the DATE DUE page and pressing the stamp into its box. She noted a certain satisfaction about getting the numbers perfectly lined up without smudging the ink, although she could see that the other library workers tipped the dates at various angles.

Martin, now coming out of the men's room, looked straight at Sophie and raised his chin very slightly. She felt herself reddening as she nodded back. Then he tilted his head to one side, regarding her for an uncomfortably long moment, and smiled.

As if that weren't confusing enough, Mrs. Richardson summoned her and pointed at the telephone, whose red light was blinking.

"A call for you," she said, frowning even more deeply than usual. "Don't forget to keep your voice down."

Going pink-faced all over again, Sophie picked up the phone and punched the blinking button, assuming it was her mother calling to say she'd be late. But it was Henry.

"Wow," she said, without meaning to.

"Is this okay?" he said. "I mean, calling you at work?"

During their talk yesterday, Sophie had mentioned her job, but it hadn't occurred to her that Henry was paying such close attention.

"I'm supposed to be whispering," she said.

He whispered back. "Oh, right. It's the library."

"You don't have to on your end," she said.

He laughed, and his voice came back at full volume. Sophie pictured his eyes again, blue as the sky. "Listen. I'm calling to ask if you want to see a movie with me."

Her heartbeat, already racing, picked up even more speed. She grinned into the mouthpiece.

"Tonight," he added.

Mrs. Richardson pushed her glasses a fraction of an inch higher toward the slight depression at the bridge of her nose, and Sophie could tell she was counting the seconds. A little blond girl and her mother were approaching the counter, each cradling an armful of books.

"That would be great," she said into the phone.

"Yes, glittering!" Henry said.

EFORE HER SHIFT ended, Sophie found herself unable to resist a peek at what Martin Longboat had been reading. The area where he had been sitting was empty of every sign of him except for one book, lying facedown on a stool he'd been using as a table. When she turned it over and read the title, she felt rooted in place for several minutes, losing track of what she was supposed to do with this object. She imagined she could detect Martin's fingerprints on the pages, as though he had been reading a text printed in Braille. *Modern Jupiter*, the jacket said. *The Story of Charles Proteus Steinmetz.*

And then Martin was standing beside her, though she'd been sure he had left the building. Fighting an urge to turn away, she looked into his eyes, dark as obsidian, pupils and irises merging together, and with a bright gleam that made her think of the last point of light at the center of a TV screen.

Sophie's eyes were green, flecked with gold. *Almost the color of the river,* Martin thought, and there it was, a miraculous current of intimacy. He scanned back to his earliest memories of seeing her, when they sat a full three rows apart in homeroom. He could picture the texture of her winter coat, the dark waves of her hair.

He said, "I used to watch you sometimes between classes. I've always liked the way you walk."

"How do I walk?"

He thought about the lineup of jocks at the high school, the ones who seemed to have nothing better to do than lean against the walls, ogling as the girls went by. Martin hated the idea that she might think he was one of them.

"Don't get self-conscious about it," Martin said, looking away. "Forget I said anything."

Sophie held the Steinmetz book and let her hands change the subject. "He looks like someone related to me," she said, pointing at the jacket photograph. "But I never knew my grandparents."

There was a thicker space between them now, filled by the nearby sounds of a mother shushing a giggling child. Sophie often wished the library could allow for more laughter.

"What about your grandparents?" she said, testing her courage. "Did they speak to you in another language?"

Martin didn't want to answer yet. He pulled a spiral notebook from his bag and opened to a pair of pages on which a half-constructed bridge was sketched across them both. There weren't any words, but the drawing was one of his favorites, filaments stopping in midair.

"Unfinished spider web?" she asked.

Martin shook his head, tucking the pages away and heading toward the exit. "Maybe I'll tell you some other time."

Carrying the Steinmetz book to the reshelving cart she had emptied, she saw it also held one more book, *The History of Mohawk Skywalkers*. A photo of construction workers sitting casually atop a giant steel-framed building graced its cover. Sophie promised herself she would study the book on her own, when no one was else was looking over her shoulder. *Bridges and skyscrapers. Modern Jupiter.*

The reference area of the library darkened behind her as she watched out the door for her mother's car streaming through the rain. On the way home, passing storefront windows along State Street and the heart of downtown, she was startled to notice so many empty ones with signs saying CLOSING OUT and EVERYTHING MUST GO.

Some disturbances were becoming impossible to ignore. Where every streetlight might have once symbolized new life, the future appeared to be turning upside down. Was this the promise of change made by that blackout, a warning of what else could go wrong? Electric City was flickering and dimming, right in front of her eyes.

T HE PORTABLE TV was on in the kitchen, and Walter Cronkite was reporting on Vietnam in his courteous grim voice. Sophie had to swivel around to see the small screen on the kitchen counter near the telephone, but the words came at her even if she didn't turn to listen.

There was a jungle war being fought on the other side of the world, and increasing signs of a war at home too, not just in her country but in her own household. A week earlier, Simon came very close to being arrested at an antiwar demonstration in front of City Hall, and his parents were pleading with him to stay out of it. They were genuinely afraid, Sophie could tell.

"War is about dying—if not you, then everyone you love," Miriam said.

"That's exactly my point," Simon replied.

Sophie chewed her chicken and realized this was the first time all four of them were having dinner together since Simon had been home from college.

When she rehearsed the sentences for telling her family about the date with Henry, knowing the way she had said yes to him without hesitating, she almost choked on her food. There was no question about her parents' ideas on the subject; they were both absolutely clear about wanting her to date only Jewish boys. Did Simon have a girlfriend hidden away somewhere, possibly even in California?

Maybe, Sophie thought, it would count in his favor to mention Henry was Dutch and leave out the rest.

Before Sophie was born, when they first came to Electric City, her parents had lived in a one-bedroom apartment in a cluster of identical brownstone buildings called Sheridan Village. Miriam and David joked that it could have been a fairytale version of Holland, with its miniature pretend windmill on the front lawn.

There was an L-shaped shopping area within walking distance, providing a druggist and grocery store and dry cleaner and shoe repairman, just enough conveniences to allow them to manage with one car. Sometimes Miriam drove her husband to work in their moss-green Chevy station wagon, dropping him off at the research lab with his briefcase and thermos to join a parade of men just like him in matching overcoats and hats. Then, like all the other housewives temporarily in the driver's seat, she turned the car around and headed back home.

The Levines had arrived in America in late April 1939, both sent as twenty-one-year-old emissaries to the New World by families with foresight. Leaving behind their extended family in the Netherlands, the newlyweds embarked to cross the Atlantic with one trunk apiece, carrying only the basics for beginning an American life. They stood waving from the deck of the ship called *Nieuw Amsterdam*, which turned out to be one of the last passenger ships to make it out of Europe before the Nazi occupation.

Sophie used to imagine her young parents holding hands and locking their knees, hopeful and terrified and of course unaware that nearly every single one of their beloved relatives and friends would—within a few short years—be deported, gassed, and turned to ashes. An ocean would stretch between themselves and everything left behind, and the newspapers would bury most of the terrible news in the fine print on page seventeen. There would be dwindling letters, cables, cryptic postcards, until finally, they were left with desperate, permanent silences. Her parents waited in vain for death certificates with black satin edges, though none ever arrived.

"When we left, we just had to hope for the best," David said to his children, on the rare occasions he spoke about the past. "I wasn't even the smartest of my brothers, not even the healthiest." He would pull a handkerchief from his back pocket and blow his nose, remarking on the persistence of his allergies, shaking his head.

"Life isn't fair," he said. It was a statement he repeated often, much more often than Sophie liked. Sometimes she tried to figure out what *American* fathers believed about fairness and "liberty and justice for all."

She was born on December 31, 1949. Instead of getting to call herself a New Year's baby, the first one born just after midnight in the new decade, she had come to enjoy saying that she was born on the last day of the '40s. Sophie Esther Levine.

Both she and her brother, Simon, had been named after relatives who were murdered. When she was four and Simon was seven, their mother had a third pregnancy that ended prematurely with a stillbirth, another daughter who would have been named Lily, also in memory of some ghostly person who now seemed to have died twice.

Not that Sophie understood any of this at the time. All she knew was that her mother's once-charming and vivacious spirit seemed to fade and disappear, at least for a while after the lost baby. Miriam would sit for hours on one straight-backed chair or another, weeping and pale, the kitchen empty of its usual fresh-baked aromas, the many kitchen appliances cold and unused. Friends came and went, filling the table and countertops with their signature dishes, the ones for which they often preferred not to share recipes. The music of their gentle condolences wafted everywhere, accents from long-lost pockets of Europe.

That must have been when Sophie first began to recognize that all of her parents' friends were immigrants, all with strange names they either did or didn't choose to Americanize for their new lives. They assimilated at various rhythms, proud of their own cultural backgrounds but wary of how much to show on the outside. With rare exceptions like that mention of Kristallnacht on the night of the blackout, and the brief account of Masha Bernstein, Sophie hardly ever heard any specific stories about the lost Old World. There appeared to be a tacit agreement among their tightly knit circle not to compare notes about what had been left behind.

Especially after the stillborn baby, Miriam's periodic and occasionally prolonged waves of sadness spoke louder than anything she might have explained about those losses. Her shifting moods alternately darkened and brightened the house like the movements of the sun on a cloudy day. When Sophie came home from school she became accustomed to testing the air when she walked in the door, wondering if she'd find her mother recovered and talkative, her hands and apron dusted with flour, or brooding on the couch, absorbed in a book of poetry.

"I'm home!" Sophie would call from just inside the front door, listening with all of her senses. "Where are you?"

In the seventh year of their marriage, when Miriam was pregnant with Simon, she and David had found themselves hosting a family very much like themselves who came as traumatized refugees from Holland to the United States, having survived not one but two concentration camps, and enduring half a year in a French displaced persons camp after liberation. The house was thick with conversations that didn't happen; no one able to say out loud what they had witnessed, and how lucky they were to be alive, penniless but saved.

This, Sophie was later told, was how good people behaved: you took each other in, no matter how marginal your own circumstances, and you shared what little you had. Her parents' couch became a bed, the baby (the refugees had one already) slept in a shelter of pillows on the floor, and at mealtime the table simply filled up with a little more food that stretched onto more plates and fed extra mouths. In fact, David's favorite admonitions against selfishness seemed to relate directly back to the years when he and his wife had survived on practically nothing. Miriam had worked as a keypunch operator while he finished engineering school, and then he found his first job in Electric City just in time for the birth of their only son.

Sophie couldn't resist it, sometimes, the impulse to peer down the path of an alternate universe. *If the car hadn't broken down on the way to that other interview, that other city. If the* Nieuw Amsterdam *had carried her parents to another shore, another continent. If David and Miriam had somehow managed to forge passports with new non-Jewish identities that would allow them to hide in their own backyards until the war ended, and to start over without leaving the Netherlands at all.*

Each of these crossroads would have created another Sophie, speaking another language, wearing a stranger's skin and clothing. Simon would be someone else too, along with an entirely new assortment of neighbors and schoolmates. There would be a landscape shaped by different hills or flattened altogether, a river with some melodious name, trees reaching higher and wider. She would be a girl calling somewhere else her home.

H ENRY WAITED WITH his convertible a few blocks from her house so that she didn't have to explain to anyone where exactly she was going. Life in a Company town meant seeing its initials everywhere, but this was new: the chrome letters spelling out MG on Henry's dark green trunk made no sense yet. Though it mostly went without saying that her parents wouldn't drive anything made by Germans, her father insisted that buying American was good for everybody. "We all have to do our part for this country," was how he put it.

Here she was, opening the door of a secret. Without being asked, Henry told her that the car had been a gift for his seventeenth birthday just one month earlier. It was a little embarrassing, he admitted, to own something so beautiful.

"Impossible to turn it down, though," Sophie said, stroking the cream-colored leather before taking her seat. This was the first time she'd ever been a passenger in a car without a roof, and already she felt torn between looking at Henry's profile or the indigo sky.

"What does MG stand for?" she asked, daring him to find her naive.

"Morris Garages," Henry said. "Which means less to us than it probably does to someone somewhere in England." He smiled at Sophie long enough for her to start blushing.

"Okay. Seat belt," he announced, sounding apologetic and fastening his own. "You're precious cargo."

Sophie laughed as she complied. *Precious.* All around her, the night felt illuminated and warm, gently wrapping a second skin around hers. The idea of being encircled by Henry's arms was for the moment a little too much to hope for.

Now his key was turning in the ignition; his plastered left hand rested on the elegant steering wheel. "It gets windy," he warned, and the engine began singing. She twisted a fist of curls into a knot at the back of her neck.

Their staccato conversation went from simple to silent as Henry steered them away from Sophie's neighborhood. Past the unlighted windows of Friendly's, past the post office where they had met, past the fragrant Rose Garden as they entered Central Park. They stopped at an empty parking lot for Iroquois Lake, where the almost-full moon gazed at its reflection in the water.

"I hope you don't mind not going to the movies," Henry said.

"It's lovelier here," Sophie said.

"We're now at the highest elevation in Electric City." Somewhere behind them, the logo floated out of sight. Henry turned on the radio just as the deejay announced the next song. Simon and Garfunkel, "Sounds of Silence."

They adjusted the seats and leaned back to gaze upward. Stars were starting to appear. Sophie thought of that cold night in November when she watched the sky lighten and the constellations fade away.

"Were you away at school during the blackout?"

Henry nodded; in fact the song had been reminding him of the same thing. *Hello darkness my old friend.* "We all thought it was a prank at first," he said. "And then after a while, people kept asking me what was going on, just because they knew I came from Electric City."

"*When my eyes were stabbed by the flash of a neon light . . .*" Sophie sang along with the radio.

"Someday this will be a place to get far away from," Henry said. "Don't you think? I mean, my family has been in this town forever."

"We pretty much just arrived," Sophie said. Moonlight gleamed on the chrome details of the car. Her hands were folded in her lap, waiting for Henry to reach for them. But he didn't.

"I can't imagine being new," he said. "Though I like the idea."

"We're sort of opposites that way," Sophie said, turning toward Henry enough to see that his eyes were closed. *We're different in so many ways*, she thought, unsure if this was a good thing or not. *Opposites attract; like forces repel*—such were the certainties in her father's world of magnets. "I don't know the feeling of belonging to a place," she said. "Instead of just borrowing it."

Henry opened his eyes and reached over to place his fingertips on her collarbone. "You belong here as much as anyone," he said.

Searchlights swept broadly across their faces just then, and they both flinched from the glare. A voice came at them, amplified by a bullhorn: "This parking lot closed at sunset," it blared. "That means YOU."

Henry leaned close enough to whisper into Sophie's ear. "I know somewhere else we can go."

There were always reasons for things. Being forced away from the lake was a kind of relief, since Henry had been worried about kissing Sophie. Whispering into her ear had brought his lips so close, though. And her hair smelled like apple trees in blossom.

The cooling night pushed its way around the windshield and behind their shoulders. Pensive during the drive across town, they saw few other cars even when they passed the hospital. Human life seemed to be missing from the scenery. Slowing down on Wendell Avenue, Henry parked near the bottom of a long driveway, and the engine ticked into silence. "Built by my grandfather," he said, pointing uphill to where the house loomed.

They both got out of the car to stand for a moment under a streetlight, one of the older style, a throwback to the days of gas lamps. Sophie was trying to make out the shape and size of the half-hidden Van Curler mansion, but Henry was watching the empty lot across the street, a grassy square framed by leafy oaks and maples on three sides.

"That's where Charles Steinmetz used to live," he said. Instead of porcelain sinks and overstuffed armchairs, the organic lushness of nature seemed so inviting. Maybe he could bring Sophie closer by going the long way around; he strode ahead and beckoned to her.

"I've seen pictures of him," Sophie said, hesitating. *Modern Jupiter.* She didn't want to admit to thinking of Martin with his stack of books.

"Really?"

"At the library."

Henry looked for her expression but couldn't read its details. She rubbed at her arms, which made him notice goose bumps himself. A cloud of moths rushed past, and cricket song rose as though some volume dial had been turned.

"The house got torn down," he said. Toward the back corner of what must have been a foundation wall, there was one low stone ledge surrounded by nothing. Henry used his good hand to sweep debris from its surface.

"What a loss," she said, catching up to take a seat beside Henry on the cool granite, their thighs just barely touching. "I would have thought—"

Henry took her hand and she squeezed his fingers in response. It was amazing to realize that such a small amount of contact could transmit signals like this, enough to cause such a commotion on the inside. "People save the wrong things sometimes," he said. "Then all of a sudden it's too late."

The arm with the cast felt heavy and muffled in contrast to the hand now holding on to Sophie. He could have asked her to sign the plaster, but that seemed foolish. It was coming off the next day. And he'd rather ask for something more lasting, a photo of her to take back to school with him. Or maybe he could give something to her instead.

The crickets paused, and in the unexpected silence, a small rustling sound drew their attention to a spot just at the edge of the property, lit by the partnership of moon and streetlamp. Later, Sophie would remember this moment as though she and Henry had invented the scene together, conjuring the visitation by way of their intertwined fingers. Behind their backs, the ghost of a house no longer casting shadows, the murmur of a creek beneath the tangle of bushes. Pulsing heartbeats signaling back and forth, skin to skin. And a red fox, poised so motionlessly it might not have been real.

It was the first time in her life Sophie had ever seen a fox, anywhere. But there was no mistaking its flame-colored coat and its bushy tail sticking straight out, almost as long as the rest of its body.

A *wild thing in Electric City!*

They instinctively held their breath, hands gripped together. The fox seemed to sense them anyway—but remained just beyond the row of pine trees, waiting.

Henry slid his hand along Sophie's waist, pressed his lips against her mouth, her throat. She closed her eyes and felt a part of her dissolving, a blurry wave that contained both something freezing and something on fire.

THOMAS EDISON BOASTED frequently of how little sleep a man actually *required*, as long as a habitual pattern of napping was incorporated into his daily routines. It was public knowledge that the great man kept a cot in his office for precisely this reason, and he evidently considered this method, like so many of his other predilections, a superior way of life. Steinmetz, in contrast, understood that individuals could possess preferences not necessarily ideal for anyone else, though he too imagined at times that alternating periods of so-called work and so-called play were most likely beneficial to the health and well-being of all adults whether or not they called themselves scientists.

Regardless of the fact that by virtue of size and stature he might have been mistaken for a child, at least from a distance, it was his childlike wonder and pleasure in the world that made Steinmetz feel most genuinely blessed. Adulthood didn't have to be a death sentence, nor even a time to "put away childish things." Steinmetz believed in jokes and games and even silliness, and perhaps this was why his recurring Dream seemed to him both simple and complex, not accompanied by numbers and formulas as some of his half-waking states might occasionally produce, but purely visual, whether in color or black and white, static or in motion. And most surprising of all was that this image felt comprehensible to him as a form of knowledge not discovered but already owned, reawakened from its daytime hiding place in much the way that stars kept themselves secret except when revealed by the night sky.

The Dream visited Steinmetz at least once every few months, sometimes more, often enough to feel like a kind of night vision and not merely a synapse-firing exercise carried out by his brain during sleep. The first time he ever had the Dream, so far as he could remember, was the night of the day he had stood alone on the frozen river of Breslau, trying to determine the constant of the territorial magnetism of his birthplace. One by one, his school friends had walked away from the river's edge, complaining of the bitter wind forcing them back indoors, while Steinmetz remained stubbornly bundled against the elements, transfixed with determination to complete his measurements. All these years later, the Dream hovered in his imagination like an inexhaustible light.

Blissfully freed from gravity, Steinmetz floats in outer space, somewhere in the vast distance between the earth and her singular, reflective moon. From this perspective he is able to observe the earth as an orb itself afloat in space, a sphere whose surface is dusted with translucent veils of white, landmasses saturated in greens and reds, surrounded by an astounding pattern of aquamarine blue. And in the marvelous two-thirds-watery surface of his own home, now seen from the view of a star man, weightless and wide-eyed, he understands what the Dream is trying to say.

It is the certainty of everything being connected to everything else, the entirety of the physical world comprising a single unit, an entity of one. Time sticky like amber. Images shattered and reassembled. Each a facet and a completion. Images existing and then disappearing. The same story and yet not the same.

And most elemental, most dazzlingly true: all the rivers and streams and waterfalls could join forces; their combined and ever-replenishing

hydroelectric power could be harnessed like some limitless radio wave,
repeating and recycling itself forever.

Joseph said the Dream was as ancient as the earth itself, and that
his own people never believed anything *other* than the idea of unity
when it came to the sky and the water and trees and animals; humans
were as much a part of the whole as any rock or bird, and it was when
you thought otherwise that the troubles began. With the arrival of the
Europeans, including the Van Curlers, who devoted themselves to crisscrossing the land with fences and roadways, to building countless dams
and canals, the inevitable result was a cascade of disasters.

Harnessing power from the waters was not exactly what Joseph
believed could save the humans from themselves. Reassured on the one
hand to see his friend Proteus captivated by embracing the natural world,
recognizing its inherent value, Joseph still found it disquieting that his
friend was nevertheless willing to sacrifice the freedom of water in the
name of human need. The miracle of existence in all of its interconnect-
edness also meant that poison in one place would end up everywhere.

"Our boats will travel side by side down the river of life," Joseph
explained one night, describing the two-row wampum belt. The two
men sat watching the moon and stars, energies emitted across immeasurable space.

"That each will respect the ways of the other. That together we will
travel in friendship, peace, as long as the grass is green, as long as the
water runs downhill, as long as the sun rises in the east and sets in the
west and as long as our Mother Earth will last."

"Fireflies are 95 percent efficient in producing light," Proteus said.
"We have a very long way to go with our own weak imitations."

ARTIN'S TAPE RECORDER had jammed again, which would not have been particularly worrisome except that he was involved in a delicate operation. Not messing around with any ordinary mix of music and voices, but repairing one of the oldest intact recordings of his grandfather Joseph. Martin had listened to this story more times than he could count, but it seemed on every playback to instruct him with some as-yet-unrevealed detail, like beadwork whose colors varied depending on the quality of light, like the river's surface dappled by an ever-changing touch of wind. With a pair of needle-nose pliers wrapped in sterile cotton, he managed to free the tape from where it was caught in the mechanism, grateful to have spared it from damage.

It was nearly midnight, and Bear slept in a heap nearby. Reaching for his sketchbook, Martin seated himself on Annie's sagging couch so that he could allow the sound of Joseph's voice to guide his hand.

Tucked between two of his pages was a sepia-toned portrait of someone Martin might closely resemble in another forty years. He turned over the photo to see the half-faded inscription on the back: JOSEPH LONGBOAT.

There were no photos of that day on the bridge in 1907, nothing except the long-dead eyewitnesses and the ladder of storytellers. Martin's sketchbook could carry the dust-covered past into the realm of the visible as well as the audible.

"Your great-uncle Miles Longboat was a bridge builder," Joseph said on the tape. "My brother. One of the first of the Skywalkers."

"Back in the early 1900s in Canada there was a cantilever bridge designed to span the Saint Lawrence River. They needed to plant the support structures on tribal land and promised to hire men from the reservation to do some of the menial labor. Instead, the Mohawk started climbing all over the structure like it was something they'd been doing all their lives."

Martin's black pen scratched across the white page, filling in the spaces. Lines back and forth, sometimes connected.

"The bosses realized these Indians had amazing balance, better even than their most highly trained ironworkers. So your great-uncle Miles was up there, on steel girders way up high above the water." Martin listened as though he could detect the sounds beyond the whispering of the tape: two huge sections of metal groaning apart, giving way to the pull of gravity. "Those pieces came tearing loose, bad bolts or who knows. And thirty-three Mohawk men died, all from that one reservation."

Lines back and forth across the white page, sometimes connected. Not a spiderweb at all. For a moment Martin saw his drawing through Sophie's eyes, full of bodies falling and falling. Together they watched for the terrible splash.

"After that, the Mohawk women vowed they would never allow so many men from one community to work on the same job," Joseph said.

If he started at the beginning, Martin knew that the story could go on forever. The time before there were human voices, only color and sound, birdsong and wind through trees. The rush of water, animals of all species calling to one another across great distances. The percussion of shale as it shifted, the music of ice creaking at the river's edge.

*H*OW DO YOU *decide where to draw the line?* Sophie wanted to know. Somehow she had gone from seeing the fox to kissing Henry on a stone wall. "We should probably go," she had said, uncertainly. For once, no one was telling her what to do, which made for a perplexing intersection of freedom and mystery. Her body had its own ideas, perhaps.

After Henry dropped her off, Sophie entered the house and went straight to the kitchen for a glass of water. Simon's car was in the driveway, but both his bedroom door and her parents' door were closed, no light leaking from underneath.

A stream of jittery sensations made her want to lie down on the back patio the way she had done on the night of the blackout, to calm herself by visiting with the constellations. She was about to go into the hall closet for a blanket to take outside when she noticed that the kitchen cabinet holding her grandmother's medicine bottles was yawning open. Even mild headaches and stomach ailments seemed to inspire her mother's eagerness to reach for these foreign drugs. Sophie had always made a point of shying away from them.

"People save the wrong things sometimes," Henry had said. For the first time, she wondered why her mother wanted to keep old medicine anyway. Didn't that stuff have an expiration date? She selected one of the brown glass bottles, running her fingers across the fading inky handwriting on the label. It was in Dutch, so she couldn't make out the words, but then she saw the signature with its European flourishes. Her grandmother's name, Sonja Ansbach, MD, was written on each bottle, some of which contained only a few pills, or none at all. *It was the handwriting she must have wanted to save*, Sophie thought. *The hand of my mother's mother.*

She replaced the bottles in their lineup and closed the cabinet. In an American history class last spring one of the students had casually mentioned being related to President Garfield. On another day, when the teacher asked how many could trace their families all the way back to the *Mayflower*, a surprising number of hands had been raised into the air. Sophie simply blinked her eyes in private amazement. Why hadn't Mrs. Nelson wanted to know how many in the room were first-generation Americans, starting their new story on this continent? And how many generations did it take to feel like you truly belonged? She had a feeling that the coming year's coursework in world history prom-ised more relevance to her own family legacies.

Simon hadn't ever said so, but maybe choosing to attend college on the West Coast was his way of claiming an individual place farthest from where David and Miriam had landed. She could do that too, Sophie supposed. Or maybe she would cross the Atlantic in the opposite direc-tion of the route her parents had taken, stepping onto a shore both strange and familiar.

Later, lying on the patio and inviting the touch of dew on her face, she thought again about how the blue sky hid so much. Night's curtain wasn't falling, but the other way around: being pulled back to reveal the stars.

THAT NIGHT, HENRY dreamed about *Sputnik*. Standing beside the elm tree in his old front yard, he could see the spaceship high overhead where it glinted quicksilver in the midday sun and moved slowly enough that he could make out Russian lettering on its outer shell. He had the distinct sense it was sending him a message, coded signals bouncing off its shiny surfaces and aiming back to earth. And then *Sputnik* began to spin out of its orbit, careening like ice crystals through the blue-black sky.

He woke up in a sweat, but found to his great relief that everything in his bedroom came swimming back in sharp outline and full color: the stiff linen curtains and heavy oak furniture, the bookcase with its array of leather-bound novels and massive dictionaries, his desk chair heaped with yesterday's discarded clothes—all reassuringly familiar. The vivid memory of Sophie's lips seemed like a kind of sunburn, stored heat pulsing on his skin.

A surge of energy catapulted him out of bed. *Running*, was what came into his head, or more specifically, into his legs. Forget the stupid cast—which would be coming off later today! Forget too the inner cartoon of himself tangled in a pile of hurdles, the unspoken but all too obvious disillusionment of the coach. The creaking house seemed even emptier than usual as he threw on his shorts and T-shirt; within half an hour he was out the door and accelerating to a comfortable stride, a sound that could have been *Sophie* panted on each exhalation. He felt his long muscles working harder than they had in weeks. The lush summer fragrance of cut grass suggested that green was something you could smell.

"Thank you," he said out loud. And then out of nowhere, or as though a siren had begun to wail on an otherwise perfect summer day, the realization came to him that it was his brother Aaron's birthday. He would have been nineteen.

Henry had planned to run in the direction of the Stockade, but now it seemed he had to decide what to do about the cemetery. That's where his mother was, alone with her bouquet of sorrow, just like every year on this date. Did she prefer it that way? His father would have been at work, and Gloria never asked either husband or son to accompany her for these visits. Henry had no idea if Arthur ever went to the graveside on his own, since he never mentioned it one way or the other. Henry himself hadn't gone in all of these years, but the Vale Cemetery was only a few blocks away from where he was now, jogging in place while waiting for a light to turn green.

Then a truck pulled up beside him, and Henry couldn't help reading it as a sign, pointing him in the same direction his dream had offered. DUTCH ELM SERVICES, it said. The opposite of a graveyard would be so much truer for honoring his brother's memory. Not to keep an agonized focus on the nightmare of a branch cracking and a nine-year-old landing on unforgiving earth. He ran on. By the time he reached the edge of the vivid lawn and crossed its moist distance, he knew that the tree wasn't to blame, nor was the boy. Placing one palm against the time-scarred trunk, Henry admitted with regret that the stubborn cast would make his own ascent of that elm impossible for now. But at least he could do this: instead of standing by the underground storage of his brother's bones, he could touch the place where Aaron had once been fully alive, climbing up into the generous air.

TWO

E NTERING THE LIBRARY, Sophie was surprised by two things: first, that Mrs. Richardson, who had habits like a metronome, was not at her desk or anywhere in the building; and second, that she found herself searching in all of the study corners for another glimpse of Martin Longboat. It occurred to her that he was the only Native American she'd ever seen in person, but then realized there was no way to be sure. Maybe the school bus driver was descended from Indians, or maybe the boy who delivered her family's newspaper every morning before sunrise. Could Martin be unique in a town framed by the Mohawk River? Where so many of the schools and streets and apartment buildings had names like Mohegan and Iroquois and Algonquin?

Wandering toward the place where Martin sat yesterday, she reintroduced herself to the empty chair: Sophie Levine, born in America, the last day of the '40s, when optimism was rising fast and nobody wanted to be caught looking backward. Normal life, here at last, and plenty of it. Her parents and all their immigrant friends claiming a safe place on the buoyant leading edge of the future, suitcases and pockets filled with salvaged memories. David Levine still insisted that America was the greatest country in the world, and winning the race to the moon was only one of its triumphs.

A local newspaper editorial had recently announced that Expo '67 was going to feature entire pavilions dedicated to the future, displaying visions dreamed up by the Company. "All that brainpower coming from right here," it said. "Our very own city lighting up the world." But underneath the bravado, Sophie knew the warning signs were all over downtown—broken contracts in the shape of too many closing storefronts, followed by empty windows and streets drained of life.

Maybe the Levines and the Longboats were accidentally similar, with long columns of spirits just beyond their shoulders, breathing into their backs, whispering them forward in spite of everything. She thought she understood about carrying fragments and threads of near-extinction. Electric City was full of place-names alternating Dutch and Indian, but for a Mohawk, this might feel like the reverse of remembering. More like proof of land lost, the dying of an entire race, a promise built on a graveyard.

When Martin appeared in the doorway of the library, wearing a white T-shirt and blue jeans, his black hair pulled back into a ponytail, Sophie felt as though they'd already been talking for hours. The conversations in her head felt as real as the television news.

"Martin Longboat," she said.

"Sophie Levine," he said.

They strolled toward his usual reading corner. When he asked her without warming up to it why Jews referred to their people as a tribe, Sophie started rambling about rituals and prayer shawls, dietary laws and holidays. But when she admitted that the rules often made her feel frustrated and confined, Martin frowned, seating himself in his wooden chair, tipping it back and forth. Sophie folded herself into position on the carpeted floor, half turned away.

"You're luckier than you realize," he said. "You don't know how disappeared things can get."

But I do know, thought Sophie. "My grandmother was a doctor," she said.

"Really?"

"Really. My grandmother was a doctor in Rotterdam. My mother still has a collection of her old prescription bottles."

"The difference between medicine and poison is in the dose, did you know that?" Martin asked.

Sophie considered this for a long moment. "What about the skull and crossbones? Isn't that just poison, pure and simple?"

"I'm not talking about the stuff that's supposed to kill you," he conceded. "I'm talking about cures."

"It's complicated," she said. Her hands pressed on her knees, as though pushing against the idea of standing up.

Martin was quiet for a moment. "You can make up a new song," he whispered, leaning toward her. "You can be the first of an original tribe."

Sophie could have sworn Mrs. Richardson was creeping up, glaring admonishment at the back of Sophie's head. But when she turned, the person standing there was Henry.

"Hi, Sophie," he said.

Martin and Sophie jumped to their feet.

"I'm Martin," said Martin.

"Henry," said Henry.

Sophie thought, *I must be the only one who notices that they don't say Van Curler or Longboat.* But she was wrong.

Henry pushed up a shirtsleeve to show off the missing cast. "Got it removed an hour ago," he said. The paler skin looked a bit bruised, but Sophie could tell that Henry was just glad to have his arm back.

"Liberation!" she said. Then she pictured him scratching with a twig while they sat together on the picnic table, and the insistent memory of last night's kissing brought back that wave of heat again.

Henry looked as if he might be reading her thoughts, but all he said was, "I wanted to let you know I'm taking off for a week or so. Heading up to Lake George. No parents."

She couldn't help noticing the way Martin's eyes lit up. Did he see her crimson cheeks too? Or was it something else?

"That sounds fun," she said.

"Yeah," Henry said, shrugging. "It can be." Sophie followed Henry's gaze to the stack of books next to Martin's chair. "Charles Proteus?" he asked.

Martin nodded. He knew all about the fox; he knew more than anyone.

That was when Mrs. Richardson approached the little group, standing with hands on her hips and looking exactly like a head librarian in full armor. Sophie felt a date being stamped on her forehead, as in, the Date of My Dismissal. But Mrs. Richardson actually managed to smile.

"I think your break is just about over," she said, more gently than Sophie would have imagined.

Henry and Martin and Sophie all watched her walk back toward the reference desk, and Sophie exhaled as though she had just been granted a stay of execution.

"To be continued?" Martin said.

Henry looked at Sophie, and she looked helplessly at the two of them. "No kidding," she said.

"Hungry?" Henry directed the question at Martin, who nodded.

"Most of the time," he said.

Martin and Henry wandered over to Castle Diner on Erie Boulevard, the place whose jukebox was filled with a mix of Elvis and Duke Ellington and Frank Sinatra. The waitress wore macramé bracelets on each of her wrists, including one with beaded letters that spelled PEACE. She waved toward an empty booth by the window.

Martin reached into his canvas bag, releasing the scent of sweet tobacco; even the waitress seemed to sniff the air when he sat down, and then she smiled, both flirtatious and pragmatic.

"What'll it be, guys?" she said, handing them menus and waiting two beats.

"Swiss cheese omelet with home fries and toast," Henry said, not even looking through the options. "I missed breakfast today."

Martin cracked part of a smile. "Burger, no cheese," he said. "Medium rare and hold the onions." As an afterthought, he added, "Thank you."

The tobacco pouch in Martin's hand looked so simple and ageless Henry couldn't resist asking to see it. In his palm he could feel the warmth of the soft leather, the way it had been worn to perfection.

"First thing I ever learned how to sew," Martin said. He didn't describe cutting a perfect circle of tanned deer hide that Annie had saved since his birth, using an awl to make holes for the leather cord, massaging the hide with mineral oil until it took the curving shape of his loose fist.

Henry handed it back to him. "I don't smoke," he said, "but that almost makes me want to start."

What Martin also didn't say was that now the leather held some of Henry's molecules too, along with those of the animal who had once lived inside it, all blending into the years of being cupped in Martin's hands. He rolled a cigarette for later, making sure to leave some flakes of tobacco inside the pouch, as if by mistake, yet specific as treasure. So that it never emptied.

They sat for a few moments without either one knowing where to look except out the window, which faced onto a parking lot; mirrored sunlight flashed every time a car pulled in or out. Martin ordered coffee while Henry excused himself to use the bathroom. The coffee was black and bitter but stimulating, reminding him of the way Midge liked to brew her own. By the time Henry came back to the table, their food was arriving.

"First time eating with an Indian?" Martin said with a straight face, letting Henry decide if it was a joke.

Imagining Sophie had to want it this way, Henry chose to keep it light. "My family showed up right before the Pilgrims," he said. "Or so I've been told."

"Okay," Martin chewed and nodded, then allowed himself a quiet laugh. "We're okay."

H IS GRANDMOTHER ALWAYS said, "You can't push the river." It was a direct translation from Mohawk, and for once Martin liked the way it sounded in American too. Annie said that Martin was stubborn, that he got it from his father; she also said that Martin's poetry came from her. "A good combination," she claimed, although that still left him pondering the elusive inheritance from his long-gone mother. Every once in a while, Martin tried to aim a question sideways at Robert regarding the ghost of Martine, but the sounds ricocheted against a tightly sealed wall.

You're both of them and neither one, he told himself. *You're you.*

Could that be true of everyone, he wondered, including people like Henry?

Of course they knew each other's full names, Longboats and Van Curlers already sharing an uncomfortable history for so long. Martin could see Henry's genetics as if spelled out in neon for all the town to see, and maybe Henry saw the same thing from his own side. Sitting across from each other in that booth at the diner, Martin had felt his skin turn a few shades darker by contrast, wondered whether white people paid as much attention to the variations on their own color. Sophie's was probably what most people would call olive, he thought, while Henry's was more like the inside of an apple. There were black men he worked alongside at the plant, and he'd heard them saying "brother" to him sometimes, the young ones at least, the ones whose skin was even darker than his own.

His older cousin Isaiah had been employed as a welder for the Company, working a full year before convincing Martin to get an assembly-line job there too. "Would you rather dig ditches all summer?" Isaiah asked him.

"Come on," Martin said, for once testing out the role of an optimist. He'd been the only one in the family singled out by the statewide motivational programs, targeting "underachievers" who could be rescued by extra math and science classes. "You know as well as I do that *Sputnik* changed a few things."

"Yeah, you might get a diploma from the white school," Isaiah said. "That doesn't mean you can actually use it to get anywhere." He slapped Martin on the shoulder as if to wake him up. "There's always hauling trash, selling shoes. *Enlisting*."

As an experiment for the summer, Martin took his cousin's advice. Now they nodded when they passed, holding their time cards for punching in and out. The *thwack* of the machine stamp and the nearly relentless din of the factory were the cancellation of every sound Martin loved and reminded him that the collar and leash he never used for Bear were on his own neck now, jangling with an ominous prediction of the rest of his life.

Men his age who were heading off to basic training didn't look to him like heroes in the making. And Martin couldn't ignore a kind of gray pallor spreading across the faces of his coworkers, a grim portrait of the inescapable. Assembly lines and lifelines, vitality draining off the way the factory floor was hosed off at the end of the day, taking a little of their sweat and blood too, all of it down the drain and lost for good.

Company men. Company town.

Working six days a week, he made a point of getting to the library every other day either before or after his shift. The second time he met Sophie among the stacks, their conversation had veered toward music, toward geography, toward poems. During her break, they sat side by side wearing headphones and listening to Robert Frost recordings or Dvorak's *New World Symphony*. When Sophie closed her eyes, Martin watched her lids tremble along with the sounds. *Someday*, he thought, *you can share Joseph's stories with her*. Someday.

The geometry of himself as well as Henry leaning toward Sophie rattled him as dangerously as a broken windowpane. He forced himself to imagine some collision in which all three of them could be friends without friction, a blending of ancestry and melody like the kind Dvorak wrote into his music. Some casual but perfectly synchronistic arrangement. And then it turned out that the river actually wanted to flow that way. Because of a canoe.

For three years, Martin's father had stopped returning to Electric City altogether. The way Annie tended her garden out back was the only true reminder of a reliable tempo now. If Joseph had lived long enough to teach him the craft of canoe building, maybe that would have been his doorway to an autonomous future, but there were already too many factory-made canoes coming from Maine and Vermont, not to mention the scarcity now of cedar and ash.

He had to do what was necessary to keep Annie's home repaired, the screen and storm windows alternating through the changes in season, the persistent supply of firewood for the stove. She braided rugs for the house's bare floors, using scraps of old denim and wool that had once made up Joseph's wardrobe, simple colors and textures to memorialize a well-loved utilitarian life. The ovals made from Joseph's shirts were the softest ones, placed on the floor beside her own bed and Martin's.

The other day, Annie had come in from the garden with an armful of tomatoes and squash, saying she planned to start canning early this year.

"Bounty now will get us through any kind of winter ahead," she smiled.

To Martin she often sounded like a mystic even when she was referring to vegetables. When he saw the altar in the hallway with a freshly placed scattering of marigold petals, he realized this was the anniversary of her marriage to Joseph. She confirmed it when he asked.

"Today is sixty years," she said.

Martin tried but failed to comprehend that amount of life shared with anyone. His parents had been together maybe three years, or four. Long enough to conceive and give birth to a son, but basically leaving him to become what they had woven together.

"You know there's his last canoe," Annie said, turning to Martin after preparing her stewing pots, wiping her hands on her rough faded skirt. "You have to take that one out onto the river to let it breathe, and then sell it. Joseph's spirit told me it's time."

Martin thought he heard a quiver in her voice, saw the tender gleam of tears at the corners of her eyes. Speechless at her request, he searched her face for an explanation that could make some sense.

"I could drop out of school to work full-time, you know," he said.

She put her hands on his chest, stopping him from saying anything else. "No arguing," she said.

When he reached out to hold her, the sudden frailty of his grandmother's bones surprised him. Had it been such a long time since he'd embraced her? The years were spinning faster now that he'd grown so much taller than she was. There was a bunch of lavender hanging upside down above the kitchen sink, and he breathed that in alongside the earthy scent of the garden beyond the open door.

He had planned other activities for his day off: changing oil on the truck, a long walk with Bear. But Annie's decision obviously belonged at the top of the list. After washing dishes from his breakfast and leaving his grandmother cloaked in a veil of steaming vegetables, he whistled for Bear and headed outside.

In the shed, the canoe had been patiently waiting. Unlocking the door, Martin's first glimpse took in the radiant beauty of his grandfather's handiwork. Air and light—streaming in from the windows and now the shed's open door—stirred up clouds of dust motes that reminded him of mica chips glittering in river water. Suspended from the rafters and bone-dry from lack of use, the birch-bark canoe still exhaled a kind of vitality, a living, breathing body. He reached up to touch the hull, caressing its hand-rubbed seams, silently counting its ribs, imagining Joseph's fingerprints on everything.

Ready now, he lifted the canoe free of the hooks and placed it right side up on his left shoulder, grasping the paddle from its resting place on the wall. Bear was bounding ahead of him on the well-worn path that led from Annie's land to the water's edge. Within a few minutes' walk, the smooth surface of the river welcomed the canoe's arrival—no, its return—now doubling its beauty. Martin removed his sandals and allowed himself to envision Sophie at the edge of the water alongside him, her bare legs reflected and rippling.

Still, it was right and necessary to be alone for this part of the farewell. Martin told Bear to wait; they would be leaving together soon. Holding the craft steady, he knelt inside its cradling shape, and pushed away from the shore.

Paddling, pausing, he saw how his own hands had grown to resemble what he remembered of his father's and grandfather's too, his younger skin merely awaiting the eventual imprint of a worker's tasks. In contrast, at least for now, the work of his hands was in the service of machines rather than boats or bridges. Joseph's calluses wouldn't be repeated on Martin's body. The one-at-a-time art form his grandfather had pursued was nearly obsolete now, and it saddened him to think there was probably no one else in Electric City who felt the loss. Midge, perhaps? He would have to ask her.

Martin's thoughts wandered further as he passed the place where Camp Mohawk used to perch on the cliff. Joseph would have known how to measure the distance between the river and the treetops, tracking the arc of hawk vision and the amount of moisture in the air. Even the soil held such memories, fossils buried by time. For once Martin wished he had a recording of Steinmetz to add to his collection, a conversation blending the past with the future. All these voices so as not to be alone.

He trailed his fingers in the soft water, imitating the wavelets made by a family of wood ducks nearby. There should have been fish, at least an occasional brown trout or smallmouth bass, but they were disappearing, yet more evidence of a disturbing trend of losses. Streaming through his mind were questions he never felt comfortable asking in his classes, whispers of his own heart.

Electromagnetism everywhere, long before we knew how to harness it. And then what happened? DC and AC, the terrible stories about Edison who was so sure of his convictions about DC that he was willing to electrocute animals—*dogs! an elephant!!*—to prove that AC was the "death current." He was wrong. This was the way science could make monsters or monsters could make science.

What about Oppenheimer and all the others willing to pretend it didn't matter how their science would be used, or who mostly avoided talking about the uses they couldn't control? "Destroyer of worlds," Oppenheimer said. Yes, but it was already too late.

Tesla, the genius whose troubled mind turned against itself. And Steinmetz, whose body was a kind of curse. But still he held the dazzle of mathematics inside him, and he knew how to love other human beings, even if he wouldn't allow himself to father any.

Lightning paints yellow white across the canvas of night, and it's the gods who are doing it, the ones who determine fate and food and famine and plenty. The ones who give symmetry to some and disease to others, beauty and failure, in equations that never quite balance.

The dreamers were speaking to him—not only about the skies but also about the human kind of electricity. Reminding him to rest in a trusted current, and to release what couldn't be held.

C HARLES PROTEUS STEINMETZ, dressed in suit and tie, stared straight at the camera with his arms neatly folded and a cigar resting between the fingers of his right hand.

And in Martin's favorite photograph: Steinmetz in his own birch-bark canoe. Joseph's elegant mastery, even though he was nowhere to be seen. Leaning intently over a plain board stretched across the gunwales, Steinmetz was wearing a white cotton undershirt, revealing rounded shoulders and tanned arms.

This photo was in black and white just like the others, but somehow seeing the man so relaxed and alert, as though he had just looked up during the space between calculations, always made Martin imagine the blaze of sunlight on the river, the heat-shimmer rising, colors he could have painted with his eyes closed.

Midge had told Martin some of what she knew existed beyond the edges of the photos. "Steinmetz kept piles of pebbles scattered on the bottom of the canoe, handy for weighing down his papers on a breezy day," she said. "Every once in a while they escaped, grabbed by wind and vanishing underwater. He used to tell me that the ideas retained in his mind's eye were the ones meant to be kept."

For his cigar, he always brought along waterproof matches, even if he just needed to feel the Blackstone clenched between his teeth, not for smoking but for concentration. His jaws were like his intellect:

determined and strong, chewing on whatever needed digesting. From the time he was in Zurich, all those years ago, he had more mental stamina than all of his friends; he wouldn't sleep until he had solved a problem, completed a formula.

And this river always reminded him to be patient and not give up. The camp he had built along the banks was home to several beloved pet crows and an ever-growing assortment of lizards and orchids and cacti, but mostly what he loved about the canoe was how he could be absolutely alone with the sky and the water and the silence.

"I was too young to understand some things," Midge said to Martin. Joseph Longboat was the only one who could visit with the emptiness.

"Feel like an adventure?" Martin asked when he met Sophie just outside the library doors. She was wearing a sleeveless green button-down shirt that made her eyes look like they were full of leaves. Seeing her bright face was the remedy for the loneliness he had begun to notice whenever she wasn't around.

"What kind of adventure?" she said. They followed the sidewalk, heading toward a small patch of freshly cut grass near the corner of Liberty and Jay Streets. The noon siren had just gone off at the factory a few blocks away. Martin brought a thermos of iced tea and a bag of potato chips; Sophie brought Swiss cheese and tomato on rye bread smeared with mustard.

"I've got to deliver a canoe to someone at Lake George," Martin said. He was planning to call in sick the next day, which was true enough if you counted his longing for fresh air. The lake was less than an hour's drive but usually felt like more.

"Let's get into my truck and drive up to see Henry," Martin said, having thought it through at least this far. All three of them next to a vast Adirondack lake could bring a wider view of what each of them held. Giving Henry the full benefit of the doubt could be easier if they were someplace removed from Electric City.

"Maybe we could even figure out how to stay overnight," he added.

White people aren't all alike, he heard his grandmother's voice murmuring with a note of hope. *You learn how to trust your choices.*

The audacious excellence of the idea made Sophie laugh out loud.

"Absolutely," she said.

IDGE'S HOUND DOG Zeus was the first to hear Martin's truck bumping up the road to the house, and he barked an excited warning. On her knees harvesting tomatoes in her vegetable plot, favoring her left shoulder, which had been sore since the previous morning on the golf course, Midge smiled even before she saw the pickup. Usually she resented intrusions, but this arrival was a welcome excuse to put down the basket and get to her feet. By the time Martin greeted Midge with an embrace, Zeus and Bear were already tussling in the grass.

"Lucky me," she said. "Two visits in one week."

Martin shrugged, pointed to the canoe strapped onto the truck. "I'm heading up to Lake George. Thought you might want to wish us well."

Midge immediately recognized Joseph's exquisite work, the harmonious curves and cedar details. In an instant, she was transported back to a sun-drenched summer day, splashing at the river's edge. When Steinmetz was absorbed in a private puzzle, drifting too far away from the cabin to be interrupted, she waited impatiently for his return. Since her two brothers always preferred each other for playmates, Midge saved her discovered treasures for Proteus alone. Fossils engraved like secret messages from outer space, skeletons of baby birds who had crash-landed, oblong stones perfect for skipping. During his longest absences, she built hiding places out of reeds and branches, arranged pebbles in the shape of constellations.

No matter how tired or hungry he might have been after hours of calculating, whenever he paddled back toward home, sunbaked and distracted, Midge cheerfully waved at him until the canoe scraped its landing in the mud. He would hand over his splashed papers and tuck a worn-out pencil behind her ear, promising a game of jacks before dinner.

Now, Martin was in front of her, not smiling at all. Even the dogs had settled into a quiet alertness, panting side by side in the shade. Her face asked the question without words.

"Annie sold it," he said. "Someone in the Adirondacks wants it for a private collection. The choice was hers, I guess."

He turned to squint in the direction of the garden and away from the truck with its captured prize. She could imagine his urge to untie all the ropes and call Annie, explaining that whatever agreement had been made, it could still be canceled. Martin must have tried to tell his grand-mother he wasn't yet ready to sell. Or wouldn't ever be ready. Maybe he was hoping that once Midge knew whatever price was offered, she could offer more.

"Do you have time for a cup of coffee? I baked a strawberry rhubarb pie, in case you need extra temptation. Being retired is bringing out the homemaker in me." She laughed and smacked her dirt-caked palms together.

Martin nodded with half a smile. "I've been told it's impolite to say no to pie."

While Martin reached for the garden hose to refill a water bowl for the dogs, Midge went inside to rinse her hands at the sink. She wiped a rag across the long kitchen table—one of the few pieces of furniture handed down from her mother, marked with scratches and stains from years of service to the Hayden clan. Countless dinners had been shared with Steinmetz, whose cigar ashes occasionally burned delicate, abstract patterns onto the oak's surface. Midge sometimes rubbed her fingers along the table edge where he used to sit, as though it might be possible to bring the smoky-sweet aromas back to life.

The pie recipe had been her father's favorite, but Midge couldn't remember if she had ever served it to Martin before. Someone at the golf club had told her that rhubarb was good for strengthening the blood. Or was it Annie who had said that?

He took a seat in front of the warm plate, bending to inhale its fragrance before piercing the crust with a fork. "Oh, excellent," he said, sighing. "You're good at this."

Midge sat down to eat her own slice in silence. Both Joseph and Annie had assured her she would know when the time was right to explain.

"Tractor doing okay these days?" Martin asked, wiping at the red stains around his mouth, shaking his head to decline a second helping, then changing his mind.

"Tractor Kitty is right as rain," she said, serving him a piece of pie even larger than the first. She had already told Martin about Daddy Steinmetz taking his bicycle onto the canal barge *Kitty* so that he could ride farther along the towpath. She was fond of borrowing his lexicon for her own uses. Even her golf cart was named Baker in honor of his electric car, though she kept it as an inside joke shared only with his ghost. It was because he'd been the one to teach her to drive, all those years ago, on the Wendell Avenue property and at Camp Mohawk too. No matter that she was twelve years old at the time.

Martin began washing the dishes while Midge remained at the table, studying his back. There was definitely something he wanted to discuss, maybe more than just the sale of the canoe.

"Are you going alone up to the lake?" she asked.

Still turned away from her, he leaned his hands on either side of the sink, tipping his head back to look at the ceiling, as if answers might be found there.

"Not exactly," he said.

Midge waited to see if there was more he wanted to add, watching Martin's fingers tap on the Formica. She tried to recall Joseph's hands, certain they must have looked a lot like his grandson's did now. She thought about how her own small hands had learned to wrap around a golf club for the first time at Pebble Beach during the family trip out west. How Steinmetz had brought them all on his long-dreamed-about vacation. Her golf trophies needed dusting like everything else in her house. Where did all the time go, now that she was supposed to have so much more of it?

"Is she someone from school?"

Martin pivoted and looked down at his feet instead of revealing his expression to Midge directly. "She's just a friend," he said.

Punctuating the conversation, Bear barked twice, and Zeus nudged open the screen door with his nose.

"I see," said Midge, making an effort not to press the subject. There was a mathematics of the heart that each person had to discover on his own. That was one of the few things she had grown certain about.

"It's all right," Martin said to her, unconvincingly. "There's a Van Curler involved too, but that's another story." He paused while Zeus leaned his full weight against Martin's legs as though to test the sturdiness of the young man's balance. Through the mesh of the door, Martin could see that Bear was standing beside the truck and ready to get back on the road.

"Okay," Midge said, agreeing to whatever unspoken request Martin had just made. "But can I tell you a story of my own first?"

Martin rejoined her at the table, choosing patience. Zeus stretched out beneath an empty chair. Beyond the screen door, he could hear Bear *harrumph* into a dusty pose.

"I was fourteen when Proteus died," Midge said. "Months later, we were still in shock, especially my father, who had worked alongside him for so many years. We'd inherited the Wendell Avenue house, but my parents had decided to move us somewhere else, a smaller place that would be easier to keep up. And nobody seemed to understand how much I missed him. Or maybe they just figured I was a normal teenage girl with better things to focus on than grieving." She laughed. "I was never normal!"

Martin smiled with her. Whatever *normal* meant, it was hardly anything he had aspired to.

"I didn't even catch a glimpse of your grandfather for most of that first lonely summer," she went on. "My brothers were always going somewhere else with their sports teams and friends and whatever. They had never been all that close to Daddy Steinmetz anyway, not like I had been. One weekend I just couldn't stand it anymore. I realized that even though it was a long bike ride on my own, I had to get to the cabin. To the river."

She traced some of the grain-sized burn marks on the table, remembering. In their house he'd had a special hardwood chair that was more like a stool for him to perch on, even while eating. These days it stood anonymously in the corner of her kitchen where it could receive the most light, holding a simple clay pot in which bloomed a pale yellow orchid.

"And that's where you saw Joseph," Martin said quietly.

Midge nodded. "I was overheated and breathless from my ride, thinking I would cool off in the water. And there he was, just returning with the canoe," she said. "Gliding in like someone in a dream, droplets catching sunlight on the tip of the paddle. You can't imagine how clear and beautiful the river used to be in those days."

Martin's hands were in his lap, folded like a prayer. *You were there,* he thought. *And now you are here.*

"Joseph didn't appear at all surprised to see me," she said. "And after he had carried the canoe to a dry patch of grass and reeds, we sat on the ground next to it for a while, our legs crossed. The red cedar glowed in the summer heat like something burning. Your grandfather told me that there was no reason to suffer about the death of our friend. That when the chambers of Proteus's heart had lost their ability to work in unison, it was time to return to the heart of the earth. 'They will become part of a new heart,' Joseph said. I'll never forget that."

Midge and Martin looked at each other for a while in silence. All he had been told until today was that the remnants of the cabin had been taken far away, and the canoe along with it. The river-drenched memories would belong with Midge, and with the details she passed to Martin. *Matter neither created nor destroyed.*

"The rest of the story is this," she said. "That canoe has been saved for you all this time. Not to worry about this other one going to a collector. We're keeping the treasure that matters most."

Sudden understanding poured into Martin's body as though he sat at the base of a waterfall. No wonder Annie hadn't allowed a single word of discussion, had brokered the deal as though his interests didn't concern her. No wonder Midge had always kept one of her sheds excessively weather-tight and locked even to him. She had another canoe, the one made for Steinmetz. The one saved just for him. *The treasure that matters most.*

Zeus clambered to his feet when Martin pushed his chair back to stand up. "Can I see it when I get back?" he asked.

Midge walked him out the door to his truck, where they hugged hard and let go. "Say hello to the lake for me," she said.

AUGUST HAD LANDED. Under-watered lawns were scorched around the edges; blotches of tar on the pavement softened during the day, trapping bits of gravel and chewing gum wrappers. There were bulky new air-conditioning units being installed in window frames all over town. The Company siren blared like a fire alarm every noon, as though the muggy heat demanded even more exaggeration. In the center of downtown, the moon-faced clock on the Electric City monument had stopped, its hands paralyzed at ten and two like someone in a state of surrender.

All too soon, Henry would be going back for his senior year at Exeter, to be further molded into the person his family expected and required him to become. He could feel the pressure around each evening's dinner table, when his father pulled attention away from the formalities of the meal just long enough to ask his son about preparation for the imminent start of school. There was perfunctory interest in test scores, college applications, but everyone knew the predestined outcome. Harvard was the family alma mater. There was only one university that anyone named Van Curler could attend.

At the house on Wendell Avenue, the whiteness of walls and linens and china, doubled and tripled in mirrors and polished silver, all provoked a tight buzz at Henry's temples. Just yesterday morning, he tried wearing a pair of Ray-Bans inside the fluorescent kitchen, and his father had said, "Those are ridiculous. Off." At which point Henry had elected not to attempt that particular battle.

Boarding school—despite its not-so-vague impressions of a tower favored by kings who needed a place to lock away their enemies until they could execute them—was located a few hours distant from Electric City. Though he'd been teased about coming from the source of black-outs, in his own mind he was far enough *away* there to be passably anonymous. In summer, the lake house at Diamond Point offered its own form of sanctuary, and though full from floor to ceiling with heirlooms announcing the Van Curler legacy, the place still waited for him like a friend.

"Please tell the gardener if you see him that he needs to do something about the gophers again," his mother had written in a note left where he'd be forced to see it on the small table by the coffee pot. "Love, Mother," she had signed.

It was difficult to imagine his parents even in their most intimate moments speaking of love to each other. As far as he knew, they still shared a bed, and might have had some rituals of comfort that were utterly private between them, as he supposed they should be. And yet, the ghost of their firstborn hovered between them no matter how fully they'd relocated themselves, no matter how much they pretended, even to one another, that they had moved on. Sometimes it surprised Henry that they wanted to keep him in attendance at boarding school after Aaron had died. Maybe it was easier to act as if both sons were still alive and simply away studying, easier than if Henry were around to remind them too much and too often of the one who wasn't there.

Just past dawn, packing almost nothing, Henry slipped out the front door before anyone could slow him down. Alone in his MG, top down and wind blotting out every thought of either past or future, he allowed himself a palpable longing for Sophie in the passenger seat beside him. He pictured her laughing, holding his hand even when it was resting on the gearshift.

Bugs splattered his windshield, and the northernmost edges of Electric City flew past in a pine-colored blur. Acres of cornfields waved their boundless blond tassels into the blue air. He sang the chorus of "Wild Thing" into the engine noise, head lifted toward the sky. What would his own wildness look like if he ever really tried it on?

As he approached the pullout for the Country Store, he debated about stopping for a cup of coffee or pastry, a few pieces of penny candy to relive some flicker of happy childhood a hundred years ago. When the family had been a foursome, they always picked up a bottle of maple syrup or an apple pie to bring to the house on the lake. Aaron and Henry were allowed to select one handful each from the seemingly infinite variety and cascade of sweets, the kind displayed in widemouthed jars or, better yet, filling the deep drawers of a wooden cabinet that were always open, always abundant.

His heart raced as though he'd gorged himself on sugar, and though he even felt himself salivating, there was also a bitter taste in his mouth, almost like bile. One of those family trips to the lake had been the very last time they were all together, but none of them had sensed anything different about it. Henry and Aaron had probably argued in the car over some trivial remark, or whispered bets on who would find an arrowhead for their collection. Gloria and Arthur would have been planning another game of bridge with neighbors, discussing the need for an improved ventilation system in the basement.

Why couldn't he recall now if they had climbed the white pine on that last visit to the lake house? Competed as usual about who reached highest and descended fastest? His palms were suddenly sweaty on the steering wheel. Memories could cut like glass if you rubbed at them too often, asked where the invisible line was crossed between before and after. Instead of turning toward the parking lot of the store, he gunned the engine and drove on, letting the wind pour through.

S OPHIE'S PARENTS THOUGHT she was on a Lake George trip with a school friend's family. She had never lied quite as elaborately as this before, but she couldn't think of any other way to make the journey possible. It would have been horrifying even to suggest that her two new friends were boys. Her father had tried convincing her as a small child that a blue dot appeared on her forehead when she was dishonest. She had believed him for many years, checking in the mirror to see if it was visible in the way he warned.

"I'm the only one who can see it," he insisted when she challenged him. Now she felt a strange nostalgia for the argument, puzzling over his willingness to be false in the name of endorsing *her* obligation to the truth.

Simon, remarkably, had come through with her alibi, assuring their parents he would keep an eye on his sister while she spent the weekend with Melanie and Alice at the lake.

"I'll be able to see them on the beach every day from my lifeguard chair," he told them. "And I'll keep Sophie out of trouble."

Whether his claims were a brother's bravado or generosity, she wasn't sure, because in his car together, he grilled her all the way to the appointed meeting place with Martin. Who *were* these guys, what exactly made her think she was safe with them, why wasn't she hanging out with those alibi-girlfriends anyway?

"They're gentlemen," Sophie told him, and Simon took a hand off the steering wheel to slap his thigh when he laughed.

"You're kind of old-fashioned for a kid," he said.

They parked on a stretch of gravel just east of the Mohawk bridge, where Martin and Bear waited. The streamlined canoe had been carefully strapped to the steel frame above the bed of Martin's pickup, just high enough to give Bear room to lie down on an old blanket underneath it. Simon gave a low whistle of admiration when he reached out to touch the curving wood. In contrast, Sophie was struck by the harsh reflection of the bridge's ugly underside, the way it seemed to double the river's metallic gray-brown sheen. It looked less like an invitation than a warning, a place where nothing would want to live.

"I'm trusting you," Simon told Martin, leaning against the door of his Mustang, tipping his mirrored sunglasses onto the top of his head and regarding him with a Serious Older Brother look. "No dangerous stuff, right?"

Sophie blushed and mock-punched Simon's muscled arm.

Martin returned the serious face, then pointed at Bear, who was wagging emphatically from the back of the truck. "Guardian of all virtues," he said.

With a casual toss, Sophie's paisley overnight bag rested against the rolled-up tent Martin had brought because he hated sleeping in soft beds and his dog loved the night air. Bear's chocolate-lab head was like a silk pillow; Sophie would have liked to stroke him for the entire trip.

"What does he do when you're at work?" she asked Martin.

"Grieves like an orphan," he said.

They sat side by side on the only seat of his truck, with Bear's majestic head leaning in through the sliding window. It went without saying that they would take the country roads rather than the newly built Northway, which would have been faster but not at all kind to the canoe or the dog. *So much better to stay inside the scenery rather than keep it on the margins of a blank concrete invention*, Sophie thought. Martin fiddled a few times with the radio dial but never quite found any station worth keeping.

"Are you okay with silent time?" Martin asked.

Sophie nodded. "Mm-hm." *The rhythm of truck wheels and visual music was soundtrack enough*, she thought. *And Henry at the end of the road.*

Dramatic clouds played catch with the sun, dappling the road with light and shadow. Signs for hamlets like Burnt Hills and Gansevoort passed one after another. Sophie wondered if Martin wasn't tempted to pull off in search of a place to dip the canoe in water, or at least invite her to climb out of the truck for long enough to splash their faces and arms. Give Bear a drink too. When she tried very quietly to pronounce Kayaderosseras Creek, he named it out loud for her, and then she repeated it the right way.

"What does it mean?"

"You'd call it 'the land of the beautiful lake of the winding river.'"

Saratoga Lake, Fish Creek, Lake Lonely. In the height of summer, birches, elms, maples, and oaks were all rejoicing in their glorious greens. The woods periodically yielded to scattered ranch-style homes and farmland, produce stands offering ears of corn and fresh eggs. A one-engine fire station, an elementary school. Cows. Bear went on alert every time he caught the scent of livestock or manure, lifting his head and sniffing energetically into the breeze. Martin smiled at the way he and Sophie were mostly limited to eyes and ears, while his dog's nose interpreted so much more of the world. Molecules in the air telling complicated stories of birth and death. Annie had built a chicken coop once, but after it was raided by foxes too many times, she finally gave up trying to keep the hens alive.

"Sometimes you have to declare someone else the winner," she had said.

Assuming Sophie had missed it, Martin pointed out the dense construction of a beaver dam just before they crossed into Adirondack Park. MOURNING KILL, the sign said. It was time to start looking for the turnoff to surrender the canoe.

Martin hoped the ease of the delivery in Silver Bay would be auspicious for the rest of the journey. Jonas Wheatfield, the buyer, waved the truck into his slate-paved driveway and handed Martin a check before they'd even unstrapped the canoe. Martin folded the payment for Annie into his deepest pocket.

Wheatfield looks nothing at all like his name, Martin thought, *more like a study in opposites.* His hair was dark and cut short like a Marine's, yet he wore cutoff jeans shorts and a T-shirt advertising beer.

"One of a kind," Jonas Wheatfield said, stroking the hand-polished frame.

Martin wanted to believe that the man understood its true value. Anyone collecting Iroquois treasures might be in it for the money—but something about the sincere gleam of appreciation in Wheatfield's eyes suggested otherwise. Without the reassurance from Midge earlier that morning regarding the preservation of the Steinmetz canoe, Martin might have wanted more proof that this particular sale wouldn't turn to regret.

Too late now to have insisted that he give up the canoe *after* spending a day with it on the silver surface of the lake. With Sophie.

Together, Martin Longboat and Jonas Wheatfield lifted the canoe down from its harness and deposited it on the patch of grass out front. The two men exchanged a nod and a handshake.

Sophie, after watching the transaction from a seat on the front steps, asked a bit shyly if she could go inside the house to use the bathroom. Even Bear had jumped down into the driveway for a chance to shake himself loose.

"Where are my manners?" Wheatfield apologized, holding open the screen door for Sophie. "Go on ahead. First door on your left, just past the kitchen. Can I offer you some lemonade? A soda?"

"Oh no thanks," she called back over her shoulder. "I think we're pretty eager to keep going." Once inside the house Sophie passed a living room with green walls hung with so many paintings it looked like a gallery. There were masks from around the world lining the hallway, and the kitchen cabinets had glass doors revealing marvelously colored dishware. Even the bathroom displayed sepia photographs and a couple of vintage opera posters. Jazz was coming from a radio or record player in some part of the house she couldn't see.

"She's right," Martin said. "Kind of you to offer, though." He gestured to the coiled hose near the canoe, which balanced gracefully on its side.

"Sure thing!" Wheatfield said, looking around for something that would serve as a water bowl. But Martin had already beckoned to his dog and cupped his hands. Bear lapped noisily for a while, and both men laughed at the pure sound of something so simple.

"At least let me get a couple of glasses for you and your girlfriend," Wheatfield said.

Sophie reappeared just as Martin was considering his reply; he couldn't tell if she had heard the word or not. "Water?" he asked.

"Yes please," she said, smiling.

When the truck steered back onto the lake road, it was only Bear who kept his gaze on what they were leaving behind.

Gandly three-storied with moss-covered stonework, a slate roof, and an architectural style Henry admitted he referred to as Old Money, the Van Curler house revealed itself at the end of a driveway guarded by elaborate wrought iron. While pulling open the gates for Martin's truck, he couldn't deny a twinge of jealousy at the sight of Sophie sitting right next to him in the cab. *But at least she's here*, he told himself.

Glittering! thought Sophie. Henry looked like a character in a movie, backlit by the Lake.

As soon as Sophie jumped out of the truck, Bear bounded off to explore. Martin busied himself with unloading his tent while Henry and Sophie stood hugging.

"Let's swim before we do anything else," Henry suggested, still holding Sophie in his arms.

Martin dropped what he was doing and started unlacing his boots. "Good idea."

Bear headed straight for the dock at the water's edge, as if the invitation had been meant specifically for him.

"Follow the leader," Henry said.

Lake George was so blue it almost hurt. Motorboat engines whined in the distance and bees droned somewhere nearby. The horizon of hills framing the water was a palette of pine and aspen and spruce. From time to time, the passage of a tiered steamboat turned everything into a hand-tinted postcard.

Bright wake billowing. A deck full of passengers traveling for miles. Red and black letters spelling out its name: TICONDEROGA.

"That one means 'the junction of two rivers,'" Martin said, but only after Sophie asked.

"Confluence?" Henry asked.

"Coincidence," Martin said.

Bear shook with abandon, sending water flying in all directions.

Combining provisions, they ate a picnic lunch on the dock and took turns with a round loaf of bread, tearing off fist-sized hunks and using Martin's knife for the cheese, the hard salami. They filled themselves with green grapes, carrots, soda. They had peaches for dessert that left juice pouring down their chins and onto their hands.

Bear napped nearby on the sun-bleached planks and chased something in a dream, his paws and tail twitching with the thrill of pursuit. Martin rubbed his sleek back gently with the sole of his bare foot and Bear relaxed again. Sophie wondered if it wouldn't be kinder to let Bear catch his prey first, let the dream win.

Lying on his back and squinting into the sun, Henry tried to whistle "Mellow Yellow," but kept losing track of the melody.

Martin started reciting the words to "Nowhere Man," in an exaggerated baritone.

"We can work it out," Sophie sang. They took turns playing air guitar for each other, and tapping rhythms on the deck with their hands and feet.

Sophie wished she could mention that Martin had the most extraordinary smile. When it appeared with such sudden brilliance, it almost took her breath away. Discreetly, she looked back and forth between

Henry's golden face and Martin's jet-black hair. If they were both steal-ing similar glances at her, she didn't allow herself to notice.

When Henry dragged some striped cushions from a distant region of the porch and threw them down on the deck, Sophie rolled their towels into pillows. There were three places to lie, side by side by side; she took the middle spot without even asking, and Henry lay down next to her. When their fingers interlaced so naturally, he was stunned to realize it had been years since he felt this happy, this released.

Bear barked halfheartedly as a family of ducks paddled past. Martin got up, encouraging Bear to relocate in a shadier spot.

Henry said, "Good move," and then worried it sounded like he was sending Martin away. Nobody said *Three's a crowd*, but it suddenly felt true.

"Okay," Martin said, "time out." He beckoned his dog uphill toward the farthest side of the house, telling himself this was another good rea-son he had brought his own tent. If he needed to, he could climb into the truck and drive to some other part of the lake altogether. Anytime he wanted.

Now that he couldn't be heard by Henry or Sophie, he sang quietly to himself in his family's language. The generous-limbed oaks and resin-rich pines seemed to lean closer. His bare feet traced patterns on the earth that spoke long love letters to a mother. He untied his hair, let it sweep across his shoulders like a mantle of black feathers.

Deep inside, he heard fragments of story his grandmother had told, preserved on a spool of magnetic tape. Adirondack was Ratirontak, porcupine, "eater of trees," which also mocked native people forced to consume bark and buds in hungry seasons. Eventually it became a term used by the Dutch to refer to the French and English behind their backs.

On the edge of the Van Curler property farthest from Henry and Sophie, Martin found his perfect climbing tree, as though it had called his name. The lower reaches of the white pine invited him into their arms, and before long he was high enough to see beyond the house, the dock, the rocky shoreline. He scanned for the half-hidden streaks of metamorphic rock embedded in the dense forests; he watched the day brighten and fade along the hip of the mountains.

On the branch he straddled, some notches had been carved into the shapes of letters. No surprise to recognize an *H*, but there was also an *A*, in knife-scratched lines side by side. No numbers. Martin placed both hands on the bark as though to soothe its scarred skin, returning his gaze to the horizon. Beyond the northernmost reaches of the Adirondacks, his great-uncle Miles had gone to Canada in search of a wife and had never come back. Those bridge workers must have climbed trees like this too, before making widows of all those women.

Bear naturally waited for Martin to return to ground, while Henry and Sophie either did or didn't notice how long he was gone. Loons consoled one another, back and forth, plaintive and eloquent. Sunset came slowly and doubled itself on the surface of the lake.

T HE SKY TURNED velvet, pocked with stars. Martin had settled on the wide front lawn in his tent, and Sophie was in one of the guest bedrooms: bird's-eye maple dressers and floral print everywhere, drapes layered in lace and gauze. She thought Henry seemed embarrassed by all these trappings, and so she pretended to be unimpressed.

Looking out her window, she noticed the glow from Henry's windows not far from hers, leaking gold into the darkness. As a kind of echo, she could see the lozenge of light inside Martin's tent, a lantern sketching the silhouettes of man and dog.

Although she had brought along a light flannel nightgown, she couldn't decide whether or not to put it on. She pulled off her sweatshirt and her T-shirt; unclasping her bra, she now stood with the nightgown in her hands, waiting for a sign telling her what to do next. The flannel was soft from years of winters, and didn't really make any sense here in the summer on the lake, but she'd imagined an unheated house, a cool night, the need to feel something comforting against her skin. The itch of having lied to her parents flared up like mosquito bites or poison ivy.

Listening with her breath held tight, she could hear Henry in the room next door, through the wallpapered wall they shared. There was a creaking closet door, tennis shoes tossed into a corner, a belt buckle dropping onto the hardwood. Then she heard water running in the bathroom sink, accompanied by the cascade of pee into the toilet.

Henry was humming now, a tune she didn't recognize. She guessed he was trying not to listen for sounds of her.

Brushing his teeth, Henry scrubbed hard as though to erase any chance of stale breath. He had kissed Sophie in the moonlit hallway, leaning into her so that the shape and fullness of her breasts under her clothes were unbearably clear. He had to make an excuse to pull away and say goodnight. Surely she could feel how much he wanted her. Was that going to frighten her away or draw her closer?

At boarding school, it was all most of the guys wanted to talk about, who had done it and with which girl, where and how many times. They boasted and exaggerated and probably lied outright to each other. He had "gone all the way" just once, with someone from town he'd flirted with after a track meet. Her name was Gail and she'd been the one to initiate sex, surprising him with her game attitude and apparent experience. Among the thousand ways he missed having an older brother, this was one of them: as a source of instruction about how to handle himself with a girl. No chance of such conversations with his father either. He was on his own.

Sophie chose a tank top over a pair of cotton shorts. There was no full-length mirror in her room so she didn't have to examine her legs to consider whether or not Henry liked them. She washed her hands and face and even rinsed her feet; she brushed her hair and waited with a surprising mixture of hope and fear for the knock on the door.

Trying to read a book, she remained stuck on the same page, unable to bring her focus back to the words. *Middlemarch*, a book her English teacher had recommended for summer, and Sophie had barely made it to page twenty. When the rapping on the door came, she threw the book onto the nightstand and leaped out of bed.

Henry stood there wearing almost exactly what she had on, except instead of shorts he was in jeans. Barefoot and with messy hair as though he'd been running his fingers through it, looking for ideas.

"Can I come in?" he said.

Henry thought about that one time with Gail and couldn't quite make the images fit with the feeling of Sophie in his arms. If he told her he had brought along condoms, which he had, would Sophie consider him crass or overconfident? Did he want to know if she'd had sex with anyone else? Somehow he was certain she hadn't, but did it matter? Would it matter to her to know he'd been with someone his classmates would have called a townie, dismissive and cruel except when they would have wanted to hear the details and then do it with her themselves?

Sophie whispered she didn't know what to do and what she really wanted to say was that she was insecure and terrified. They had removed their shirts and then Sophie's shorts but Henry kept his jeans on. The sight of Sophie's breasts in the moonlight (they had turned off even the reading light beside the bed) made Henry feel as though he might simply explode before he touched her at all. The texture of her skin when he pressed his bare chest against hers, the way her nipples rose like perfect berries into his mouth, all of this was beyond anything he had read about or heard in locker rooms.

He didn't want everything to happen all at once. He knew there was only ever going to be one first time for the two of them, and he needed to be sure it was all right with her. He found himself doubting he could give her enough of anything; he was going back to boarding school so soon, and would it be fair? Would it be better to wait and be more sure?

Sophie found she wanted to hear the word *love*, or to say it; she didn't know how to give herself without losing hold of safety. Henry would go away and she might not be able to stand it if they crossed this last, careful line; he could fall in love with someone else, and so could she, and then what would *this* mean?

They could wait, could allow time to bend around them and promise more of itself. Meanwhile, their bodies conversed in silence. All the words dangled electric and incomplete.

In his tent with Bear, Martin stayed awake and absorbed the night's harmonies of owls and wind. For a long time he lay on his back pretending the tent didn't exist so that he could look through the Milky Way, flowing with the curve of the universe. He forced himself not to think about the two of them inside the house. He was out here in the dark because he wanted to be, making his own choices.

I want UP, Martin sang silently toward the sky. *I can be a cloudwalker, an eagle nester, a treetop dreamer.* He was good at spotting raptors, especially from his perches in maples, oaks. His grandmother said he had hawk-vision.

But what about loving the ground? Lying with his face in the grass, ear turned toward the murmuring earth. He loved that too, the deep desire to climb underneath the grass, cover himself with a blanket of soil, bring his body back home to its origins.

I want UNDER, he thought. *I want roots at my fingertips, clay between my toes. I want the taste of earth in my mouth, the place the trees hold on to for dear life.*

Still, his prayer returned him to his recent place among high branches, echo of thrush music in the air. His bare feet had gripped the rough bark of the pine, his hands strong and true. He held on, even as the ghosts of falling men danced all around him.

I do not fall, he whispered to the leaves and stars. *I fly.*

I N THE MORNING, all three sprawled over a serene breakfast picnic under one of the widest oaks not far from where Martin had already unpitched his tent. The air was full of translucent butterflies and ricocheting grasshoppers; scarlet ladybugs landed briefly on Sophie's hands and she watched them explore the circumference of her wrists before flying elsewhere. In the distance, water-skiers careened around invisible corners, spraying rooster tails of foam into the blue.

It was clear that the previous afternoon they had spent too much time in the sun; both Henry and Sophie were bright pink at their shoulders. She tried wearing a hat, but it seemed reluctant to stay on her head. It was far too humid and sticky for the protection of long sleeves. By the time breakfast was over, Bear was panting in the shade, and even Martin felt drowsy with laziness. Henry said the only true remedy was getting onto the water.

"You mean into," Sophie said.

"That too," he said.

Martin wished again he'd kept the canoe just one more day. Sophie looked out at the *Ticonderoga* making its stately way across the middle of the lake. "You don't mean that kind of thing?" she asked, pointing.

"I forgot to show you the boathouse," Henry said. But he hadn't forgotten, not exactly. The *Sterling* was his father's pride and joy, kept in immaculate condition, as though new from the shipyard where it was built years earlier. A classic reproduction of the style popular in the '20s and '30s, when the lake drew visits from opera stars and gamblers. Ever since Henry had been old enough to follow instructions, his job was to towel dry every surface, removing every droplet that might dare to leave a murky shadow on the chrome or worse, stain the varnish yellow.

Praise for Aaron's skill at knot-tying had been one of Arthur's rare expressions of approval. And the only exception to his rules of spotlessness involved the annual tracking of his sons' heights on one support beam of the boathouse, dark inky lines with dates attached. They had, of course, stopped measuring after Aaron's death.

"Things can be so complicated," Martin said quietly, almost to himself.

"I know," Henry said. "So much better to paddle and glide. Right?"

Martin nodded, thinking of Jonas Wheatfield, and Joseph, and Steinmetz.

"My brother Simon is a lifeguard on the public beach," Sophie said. "Now that I know what it's like on private property, I vote for staying in this place the rest of the summer."

"Here the lake closes," Martin said, then spoke the phrase in Mohawk. He had told both of them about the ones who ate trees, about *Ratirontak*, and managed not to laugh when Henry struggled with the pronunciation.

Bear started barking with staccato joy at a platoon of ducks, as though reminding everybody to get wet.

"You're right!" said Sophie, and she ran toward the lake without looking back. Henry followed, and Martin did too, pausing only to grab a stick for aiming Bear's exuberance a little farther off. Otherwise the heroic dog didn't seem quite able to tell the difference between a splashing swimmer and someone in dire need of rescue. Sophie had begged Martin to call Bear away before he clamped onto the scruff of her neck in order to drag her to shore.

"Not drowning, waving!" she shouted, lifting both hands in the air. "I know you mean well, Bear, but this is beyond the call of duty."

"He's all right," Martin said, throwing the stick of distraction over and over.

"I'll save you," Henry said, pulling Sophie into his arms. Her eyes were the color of the tree-framed lake, a shimmering kaleidoscope of green. "You're glittering again," he said.

I'm all right, Martin thought, watching Bear paddling toward him with happiness gripped between his jaws. *Everything is all right.*

It was only when the dazzle of the lake threatened to set off a migraine that Henry explained he had to retreat into the shade again. No matter that being in the water with Sophie felt like some alternate universe; time slowed but didn't stop. She and Martin would drive back to Electric City and so-called ordinary life would reclaim them all.

"Doesn't seem right to stay here once you two leave," he admitted. They were on the steps of the porch, drinking lemonade and iced tea, collaborating on an early dinner. Henry hand-shaped hamburger patties while Martin placed half a dozen ears of corn onto a wobbly-legged grill. A trio of wet towels dripped on a nearby railing, and the truck was loaded for departure.

"You could follow us home," Sophie suggested. Her shoulders and cheeks were shiny with aloe for the sunburn. She sat on an Adirondack chair with her legs folded, slicing cucumbers and tomatoes on a cutting board across her lap. Without being asked, she had made up her mind to taste a nonkosher hamburger for the first time in her life.

"Caravan," Martin said, poking at the coals with Bear's fetching stick. "You got better things to do?"

"Good point," Henry said.

"I'd show you one of my favorite fishing spots on the way back," Martin said. "But then I'd have to kill you."

Henry laughed. "Thanks anyway."

"Simon will be waiting for me at the Mohawk bridge by dark," Sophie said. "Or else he'll kill you both."

"I think that's probably a good enough reason not to be late, don't you?" Martin turned the ears of corn until they were evenly singed. The hamburgers were spitting juice as they cooked, and Bear watched for anything that might find its way to the ground.

"Medium rare?" Henry said to Sophie. "Burned to a crisp?"

"Medium medium," she said.

"Same here," said Martin.

A breeze shivered across the lake while they were finishing dinner, hinting at the edge of summer. Before long there would be arrows of geese flying overhead, making a clamor of goodbye. Bear had wandered off to inspect the perimeter, discreetly marking territory.

"When was the last time you climbed that white pine?" Martin asked.

Henry reached for Sophie's nearby fingertips, astonished each time that such delicate hands could feel so strong. "Which one," he said, though he already knew.

Martin pointed.

"A long time ago," Henry said. "With my older brother."

"You have a brother?" Sophie and Martin asked at the same time. Even Henry felt a jolt of awe when he said the words out loud.

"He died." Sophie's hand held on and on.

Silence. Even the cicadas weren't singing, muted by the cooler air.

"He fell out of a tree," Henry said. "Ten years ago."

"Not *here*?" Sophie said.

"Back in Electric City," Henry said. "Another house. Another tree."

Martin saw his own hands on the limb of the pine, the meeting of lifelines underneath.

Sophie felt Henry lean all his weight in her direction as she wrapped her arms around him, pressing tight.

"I'm sorry," Martin said softly. And when his feet wanted to move, he stood up and spoke with his simple clear voice, to offer the story that had been waiting. It seemed right that there could be something that belonged now to the three of them.

"Here is the legend of Eagle," he began. "Whose life can be thirty-five years long, or seventy, depending upon this one rite of passage. Because reaching the age of thirty-five brings Eagle to the point where his beak and talons have grown so long and hooked that they no longer serve him as weapons of the hunt.

"After flying to the most remote of mountain peaks, Eagle must bite off each one of his talons, then smash his own beak against the rocks. Defenseless now, and with only his willpower to keep him alive, he waits."

Martin paused, remembering how the tape recorder hissed while his grandmother stopped and closed her eyes for a moment. Sophie and Henry were so intent he imagined they could hear the resonant echo of Annie's voice telling it. He went on, translating her words.

"If he can survive the growing back of his talons, the growing back of his beak, then Eagle is able to start over. He can fly out of the temporary dark and back into the wild blue. To exult in the second half—no, the second version, of his life."

S OPHIE RODE WITH Henry on the way back, with Martin's truck and Bear just ahead. The dimming light felt like something to grab with her hands, pull into herself like the strange flavor of grilled meat she could still notice at the corners of her lips. *Was it blood?*

Martin's story echoed for her alongside the hum of the car, his voice a kind of melody, a vibration. With the remnants of sunset looking like pale fire on the rim of the mountains, Sophie hoped Simon wasn't going to worry if she was late. She would have loved to take one brief detour into Saratoga to catch a glimpse of some jockeys and horses, even a groom or trainer, but there was no room left for anything else.

"Early mornings are best for that anyway," Henry explained. There was so much he could show Sophie next time: racetracks and betting windows, bandstands, mineral-stained drinking fountains. What about Martin's secret fishing holes—the places he wouldn't share, or couldn't? *How did you know when the second half of your life was going to begin?*

Bear in the passenger seat turned his head so often Martin was convinced he was still tracking the unity of his newly formed pack, making sure the other two were following close behind. The turnoff to Jonas Wheatfield's place pulled Bear's attention too, and Martin took a deep breath, remembering his plan to visit the stored canoe at Midge's. He would bring it back to the water with a prayer, a promise of buoyancy. As always, he would ask the river for permission to claim its fish, listening

with equal respect for the sound of yes or no. That practice was helping him now too, as he watched the faces of Henry and Sophie shining
together in his rearview mirror. Annie would say it with certainty, that
their particular happiness didn't take anything away from him. *There
was enough of whatever you needed. Always.*

If the sign had said OPEN, Henry would have chosen the very thing
he'd avoided while headed in the other direction: stop at the Country
Store. But all the lights were out and the parking lot was empty. *Too
late.* He swallowed the disappointment and kept driving south, allowing
himself a belief it would be possible, eventually, to layer new memories
on top of the old ones. Sophie would hold out her hands and he would
fill them with brightly wrapped sweetness, a taste of the lucky world
made new again.

S ATURDAY EVENINGS STEINMETZ could be found at his poker game, the one he called the Society for the Adjustment of Differences in Salaries. Forcing himself to clear space on the oval table that would otherwise have remained covered in notebooks and drawing paper, Steinmetz used the weekly gathering with friends and colleagues to joke about his Socialist tendencies. Of course all the players knew that these were serious convictions held since his student days in Breslau. If so-called Providence was typically credited or blamed as the source of this one's perfectly symmetrical face or that one's irreparable lameness, why shouldn't those born desperately poor be given the same rights and opportunities as those born into wealth?

From age five onward, Midge was allowed to sit beside him for the first part of the evening, since indulging her was almost as constant a pleasure as his cigar. Although Midge's mother Corinne frequently scolded Proteus for keeping the child too close to such adult preoccupations, he delighted in the way Midge seemed both fascinated and bored by the movement of cards and coins, the rambling conversation floating above her blond curls. He especially appreciated the child's intent concentration on practicing her letters on the same pages he used for graphing magnetite resistance and improving plans for an electric canoe motor.

Once she showed him a drawing she had made of Joseph Longboat in profile, a surprisingly good likeness. From time to time he would allow his focus to wander away from the poker game just enough to allow Midge to trace the outline of his hands, so that she could compare their shape to her own. He showed her how to draw objects in three dimensions, and she played tic-tac-toe using herself as an opponent. In these moments his ideas about women's suffrage and participatory equality became much more than abstractions—Steinmetz envisioned the day when Midge could be employed in any field she wished, following the inclinations of her own ambition.

By the time she turned eight, and with the election of a Socialist mayor in Electric City, Steinmetz had begun a more public role in political life. He stood on a small wooden platform elevating him to the proper height for the speaker's podium, so that he was able to address an audience without straining for visibility. The podium hid most of his twisted frame and thus allowed the attention of the crowd to remain fixed on his face, on the words coming out of his mouth.

"We are capable of greatness, each alone and all together. There is simply a need to recognize the fact of our brilliant capacity for more efficiency and less waste. We are able to see this in machinery; why not in our lives? Mathematics teaches us this. The best of us can be enhanced and the worst of us promoted to our highest ability."

Invited to broadcast his ideas by way of the recently launched local radio station, Steinmetz waxed eloquent. A four-hour workday could turn America into the true Utopia it was meant to be, a place where men spent more time with their families and among friends than toiling at their jobs, and the Happiness Effect would bring about such benefits for everyone, such an exuberant free-flowing exchange of goodwill and generosity of spirit, a current of alternating give and take, a place where needs were satisfied and talents used in the most collectively productive ways.

Day by day and week by week, his notebooks filled to overflowing with essays and mathematical formulations. Socialism and Invention. Disruptive Strength of Air. Relativity and Space. Educational Developments in Electric City. Not to mention the piles and piles of photographs in need of organizing. Corinne could at least be grateful that it was only a mountain of paperwork adorning her dining room table. Out behind the main house in his laboratory was where the truly messy explorations took place. While Midge was allowed to help tend to the lizards and cacti in the solarium, the laboratory remained generally off-limits. "Too many dangerous concoctions!" Steinmetz told her, even when she begged to visit. "I don't want to set your hair on fire!"

Meanwhile, out of earshot, Joe and Corinne worried about his painfully bent spine. Doctors warned openly that Steinmetz would have a shortened life. The compression of his organs and the cumulative burden on his damaged lungs would be especially costly. As for his own awareness, no matter that cigars might be accused of exacerbating his condition; Steinmetz didn't need to be reminded of his mortality.

The only unanswerable question was this: would he live long enough to see the realization of his most fervent beliefs? Escalated rumblings of a European war caused him to react first with disillusion and eventually with dread. To witness the interruption of those same young lives he tried so hard to benefit with unlimited opportunity, free education—*sending soft-cheeked boys to kill one another!* Again and again he devoted himself to explaining how the pure and elegant laws of mathematics could be applied to the turbulence of society.

Steinmetz drafted articles about the Company's dramatic contribution to the Panama-Pacific International Exposition in distant San Francisco. The Tower of Jewels was designed not only to attract people during the day with its cut-glass surfaces shimmering in the sun, but also to draw people throughout the night by means of artificial illumination. No fewer than fifty spotlights aimed their beams at the structure, with the aptly named Fountain of Energy nearby. Photovoltaic sources of energy promised to light up the planet in a perfectly renewable form. Everywhere evident and potent, a halo of the greatest of spectacular effects.

How daring, enchanting, and in every sense new. Electricity was both a servant and a provider of comforts, marvelous innovations releasing humans from drudgery, men and women both. Not to mention the resultant liberation of the human spirit.

Sitting with Midge on his lap, humming a resurrected melody from his own long-gone childhood, he dreamed of the day that everyone would understand. The pulse inside each body echoed the same current of the universe.

MEETING SOPHIE'S BROTHER Simon at the bridge had been more awkward than Henry imagined. He wasn't used to being looked at with so much mistrust, as though a Van Curler had to prove his own merit to a perfect stranger. But of course if he'd had a younger sister of his own, he would undoubtedly feel the same way toward someone turning up in the dark after an unsupervised overnight to a house by the lake. He hazarded a guess that Simon was evaluating the emotional distance between Martin's truck and Henry's MG, but maybe that was just his own wishful thinking.

"Sorry we're late," Henry said, pulling Sophie's paisley bag out of his trunk.

"Nice wheels," Simon said. "And if you were speeding I don't want to hear about it."

Sophie hugged Henry for a long minute before walking over to say goodbye to Martin. Even Bear looked disconsolate about the three of them going their separate ways.

"Thanks for everything," Sophie called out, waving in all directions. "That doesn't feel like nearly enough to say."

Henry and Martin waited inside their own vehicles while Simon's taillights disappeared uphill toward town. It wasn't clear to either one of them what was supposed to happen next. Henry considered inviting Martin to grab a milkshake or something at the Castle Diner, something to fend off his inevitable loneliness, but when he tapped his horn as a question, Martin started his engine and pulled away. The Company logo competed with the sliver of moon, same as always. Martin recrossed the bridge toward home.

The idea of going straight toward his parents' house on Wendell Avenue was more unappealing to Henry than ever. They'd be surprised to find him back early from the lake, and the last thing he felt like doing was explaining about having friends for such a brief visit.

All too soon, he'd be packing his suitcases for school, going back to the place where he was surrounded by people with roman numerals after their names, legacy upon legacy. He wished he had a nickname, some kind of identity he could truly call his own. He wished he knew his purpose.

Suddenly his mood couldn't find its way above the horizon. All he could think about was the looming dark of winter, cars in the black morning, snow in their headlights, snow in his hair, his nose staying frozen all through classes and his fingers and toes too. He felt himself bracing for the worst: cold snaps that happened fast and broke things. The sound of bursting pipes or the crash of icicles or cars sliding into snowbanks, the sound of tree limbs collapsing under the weight of the ice, branches unable to bear it.

He had held Sophie in his arms, touched the inside of her body with his fingertips. But he couldn't be sure that the memory would stay with him once they were all those miles apart.

SOPHIE DREAMED ABOUT riding her bike toward Lock 7, looking up at the innocent blue sky and becoming fixated on nuclear fallout. There was a roaring sound that might have been a siren, which, waking her, turned out to be the sound of a neighbor's lawnmower. She couldn't help feeling nostalgic for the delicate birdsong from just one day earlier.

"Looks like you forgot to protect yourself from the sun," her mother said, noting Sophie's reddened shoulders when she sat down at the breakfast table. Simon had already eaten his toast on the way out the door.

"Ultraviolet rays," her father said, not looking up from the newspaper. "They're stronger than you think."

"We had fun," Sophie said. "And the weather was gorgeous." She had experimented with braiding her hair, remembering that when she'd worn it that way as a child, the pediatrician had teased her about looking like Pocahontas. Maybe Martin would be offended.

"Your grandmother used to worry about skin cancer before anyone else had heard of it," Miriam said.

"That's a weird thing to be proud of, isn't it?" Sophie asked, pouring herself a bowl of cereal.

"She was ahead of her time," said David.

"I bet not a single one of your friends has a grandmother who was a doctor," Miriam said. "Am I right?"

Sophie noticed her father's suitcase in the hallway beyond the kitchen. "Are you going somewhere?"

"Los Alamos," he said. "I'm taking a business trip for a couple of days."

"Los Alamos?" Sophie repeated, stunned. "The place where they make atomic bombs?"

"I work at the research lab," he said. "With magnets."

"What do your magnets have to do with bombs?"

"Now you're going to start protesting the war too, like your brother?" her father said.

"So you really are connected with the war!"

"I didn't say that." He folded the newspaper and sighed.

"You implied it," she said.

"You'd make such a good lawyer," her mother interrupted. "Don't you think so? I can just see her in a court of law."

"*Mom,*" Sophie said.

"She can become whatever she wants," her father said. "As long as she works hard. That's the point."

"Please don't change the subject," Sophie said. The milk at the bottom of her cereal bowl looked gray.

"The Company has done a lot of good in the world," her father said. "And you have nothing to be afraid about."

"If you're getting involved with war research, we could all get blown up and not even know why!"

"Nobody's going to get blown up," her mother said.

Her father swallowed the last of his juice and shook his head. "My work has nothing to do with bombs."

"Do you really know that's true?" Sophie asked him.

He presented what seemed to her a wistful look. "I guarantee you," he said. "Scientific curiosity is our best hope for the future."

"But what about all those secrets at the Atomic Power Lab practically next door?" she said.

"Atoms are everywhere," her father said. "You could say we all consist of atomic power. Does that make us dangerous?"

"If the research weren't dangerous, they wouldn't have anything to hide."

"See?" her mother said. "A lawyer. I'm telling you."

Her father smiled. "This is America. You could even be president."

MARTIN COUNTED THE hours before he could end his work-day and head over to Midge's house. Getting acquainted with the Steinmetz canoe would surely help dispel the agitation left over from his return from the lake — the sound of the now-empty truck bed and the echoing space on his front seat where Sophie had been.

The night before, he'd returned to find Annie already asleep in her room. She had left a porch light to welcome him and a pot of soup on the stove, but he wasn't hungry. Instead, he sat cross-legged on one of Annie's braided rugs and stayed up past midnight rummaging through several of his most recent notebooks, pausing to touch slender strips of birch bark that had been inserted to mark particular pages. There were photographs of snow-covered trees and an abandoned pair of his father's gloves; a charcoal drawing of a broken ladder leaning against a gnarled apple tree; an ink drawing of an upside-down bicycle half-buried in mud.

As a last effort before going to bed, he made a note to remind him-self that the annotated list of recordings was overdue for an update, espe-cially now that the collection of tapes had overwhelmed his bookshelf and spilled onto the floor. Layers of sound piling up like shale. Mohawk voices and city cacophony. The noon whistle and the dripping of winter icicles. A pair of mourning doves at dawn. The sound of a canoe push-ing off from shore.

⊷❈⊶

Midge was still nursing a strained shoulder, grumpy about being unable to play golf for two weeks straight. While Bear and Zeus chased squirrels and dug random holes on the property, Midge gave Martin instructions about which of her several worm beds could benefit from some attention. Plunging a shovel into a compost pile and turning the layers of decay into something useful was highly recommended as a way to shake off the workday's residue.

"Isn't that soil looking good enough to make you want a big bite?" Midge said. She was standing nearby, resting one hand on the cracking dusty seat of an old bicycle; it looked like it was growing down into the dirt instead of emerging upward from it.

Martin laughed. "Annie always says, 'We eat the earth before the earth eats us.' I never thought it was quite so literal."

Midge muttered "Ouch" when reaching for a weed sent a streak of pain through her arm.

"My friend Sophie," he said, testing her name out loud. "She told me her father walks to synagogue by shortcutting through the parking lot of the country club. Have you ever seen him? Saturday mornings?"

Midge paused, looking for clues in Martin's face. "She's the girl you brought to the lake?"

He nodded, working the shovel with renewed vigor. "Her father's religious."

Midge thought of the occasions she'd steered her golf cart to avoid colliding with a man walking straight across the Mohawk Club's parking lot and dressed as if for church. *Saturdays. Of course.*

"I've seen him once or twice," she said. "We've nodded."

The earthworms gleamed among the cornhusks and shriveled cabbage leaves. Martin remembered the flicker of hope he'd felt when Sophie was riding in the truck with him, followed by the stab of letdown when they arrived at Henry's place.

"I'm sure the management hasn't recruited any actual Mohawks either," Martin said. He didn't blame Midge out loud for belonging to a place where people named Longboat or Levine weren't welcome. But the discomfort hovered between them.

Midge shoved hands into the pockets of her moth-eaten cardigan, wishing she understood more about the ways of the world, why people separated into groups identifiable only by last names and religions. Steinmetz used to talk about all human beings as unified fields of energy, like water. What kept that from being true, especially in a place called Electric City?

"Lost tribes," Midge said, though she honestly wasn't sure what the words meant. The phrase was something she had overhead in childhood, perhaps from Joseph Longboat or even Daddy Steinmetz, who people sometimes mistakenly thought was Jewish himself.

"We've waited for each other long enough," Martin said. "It's time for the canoe."

I T WAS HENRY'S idea to spend their last Sunday together playing tourists in their own town. He and Sophie met Martin at the boat rental shack on the edge of Iroquois Lake, the centerpiece of Electric City's Central Park. Sophie wore one of Simon's old baseball caps, fraying at its brim; the cumulative effect of summer sun had turned Henry's blond hair almost white. Martin wore sunglasses even though the day was overcast.

Deliberately silly in rented paddleboats, Sophie said it was better than bumper cars, though just barely. She and Henry sat side by side in a boxy yellow boat that kept their legs pressed close. Martin in a boat of his own bobbed higher in the murky water. Having chosen to keep the Steinmetz canoe at Midge's place after taking it on its first voyage, he smiled at the absurd gap between Joseph's craft and this plastic contraption. Maybe next summer he would bring the canoe to Henry's house on Lake George. Maybe everything would be different by then.

Aimlessly drifting, Henry and Sophie took turns resting while the other one did all the pedaling. Martin pointed out the way the swans were so graceful on the surface and yet with gangly black feet working hard underneath. Every once in a while the sun pushed through the heavy clouds, but mostly the sky threatened rain. This was nothing like the sparkling day they had all shared on the mica-saturated water of an Adirondack lake.

Sophie lost her baseball cap in the reeds while they were returning the boats to the muddy shoreline, but Henry managed a dramatic rescue, sinking in as far as his knees.

"Don't tell me about the percentage of swan droppings in this muck," he said. "Because I wouldn't do this for anyone but you."

Martin watched from drier land. *Swans mate for life,* he thought but didn't say. The idea was a little too romantic to believe.

Instead of a picnic they all went to the Castle Diner. Martin was disappointed to see no sign of Charlie the waitress, but realized she must have been taking night shifts. He had twice now, past midnight, brought a microphone hidden inside the sleeve of his jacket to sit at the counter, watching her. She didn't seem to mind smiling with apparent sincerity for each new table, switching herself on like generous neon. It wasn't that he objected to her role, or that he didn't sometimes wish she had some charm saved for him in particular. What surprised and intrigued him was her apparent way of choosing yes so much more often than no.

Sunday afternoon at the diner should have been packed, but the place was strangely quiet. In driving the few blocks from Central Park toward downtown, Sophie was struck by the number of nearly empty intersections they crossed through. Even the church parking lots looked deserted. She had a memory of the blackout music fading from the radio, "Everyone's Gone to the Moon."

When the check came, Henry insisted on paying for all three of their meals. "Our swan song," he called it. "Last Supper? Last Lunch?"

Sophie shrugged. "Great gesture. Wrong religion."

Martin laughed. "What she said."

The next stop should have been obvious, except that Henry was the only one of the three who knew it existed. Steinmetz Park, forty-five acres overlooking the Mohawk River and with its very own swimming pond and bathhouse. By the time they arrived, a thunderstorm had just begun, which meant that the few families enjoying the place were packed up and leaving. Two boys streamed past them on bicycles, wearing towels like capes, heads bent low against the hard rain. Martin parked his truck next to Henry's car where they had a wide view of the hillsides drenched in green.

"Perfect place to watch for lightning," Sophie said to Henry, then made jagged lines in the air with her hands so that Martin could get the idea through their closed windows.

He nodded, flashing his headlights in reply, just in time for a clap of thunder to reverberate overhead. Henry held up his fingers to count the seconds before the streak appeared, but it wasn't as close as he would have preferred.

"Better safe than sorry, I guess," he said to Sophie. "Are we having fun yet?"

After a few minutes it was clear that the storm was heading west and away from them, heaviest in the distance. Martin rolled down his window just long enough to suggest they move on.

"Pilgrimage to the Steinmetz house?" Henry said, leaning across Sophie, who had opened her window too. "The space where it used to be, I mean."

"I'm surprised they didn't build a shopping center on top of it," Martin muttered, unable to help himself. He was glad they weren't aiming toward the Stockade, where his own history and Henry's collided in too many complicated ways. Not least because of the tribal burial grounds covered with parking lots and warehouses, while the homes of the Dutch settlers had been preserved with careful respect. *No bitterness for today*, he told himself. *Even the land keeps changing its story—solid ground scooped into ditches and canals, seasoned with water, then ice. Filled in again to make a boulevard.*

Sophie tipped her head out to look up at the clearing sky. "It's rainbow weather now," she said.

By the time they reached Wendell Avenue, the storm had fully passed and steam was rising from the pavement, though dripping trees made it sound as though the rain hadn't yet stopped. On the cracked concrete footpath down the center of the Steinmetz property, puddles glistened.

Martin grabbed something from inside his glove box and handed it to Henry. "I thought you might take this back to school with you," he said.

A thick envelope held photos of Clinton's Ditch before it was full of canal water and then during and then afterward, a hundred years passing in a photographer's flash. Water, mud, mules and barges, canal paths, the straining of muscles and the sweat of man and beast, the churning of muddy wheels and muddy water, stench and slap of feet and hide and all in the name of moving things and people from here to there, upriver and down.

"Steinmetz took these," Henry said, amazed. He flipped through the collection of images while Sophie and Martin looked on. Here was the man-made river after it froze solid and could be skated upon, Erie Canal as a dance floor of white ice.

Progress, thought Martin. *The future.* Until it was the past and some other future was pressing down hard, filling in the drained ditch with gravel by the tons until it wasn't even a wet ghost anymore, and the name Erie Boulevard didn't make anyone think of water.

Sophie thought about the way the words sounded in her mother's mouth, the way it came out *Bull Var* like some vaguely French animal, heavy-footed but elegant in its movements, its steady forward motion. She guessed that Henry envisioned Paris, streetlamps illuminated with gas in the dusky night, softening everyone's edges, even the church spires gleaming beautifully. Her mother said *Eerie Bull Var* and Sophie thought it was a song, a lullaby to help her fall asleep.

"I'll consider this a loan," Henry said, tucking the photos back inside the envelope. "They belong to you."

"We can share them," Martin said, and decided this was the moment to leave the two of them alone. Easier to preempt the awkwardness of a threesome yet again.

"Bear is waiting for me at home," he said, by way of explanation.

"Are you sure?" Sophie asked. "Not about Bear, I mean. About leaving."

Henry took her hand. "We just got here."

"I know," Martin said.

Somewhere in its den out of sight, the fox was staying dry and warm. Sophie felt an urge to tell both of them about her father going to Los Alamos, about her dream of nuclear rain. She wanted some kind of reassurance that Henry's departure the next day was just a natural pause, like the changing of seasons. A page being turned.

Henry let go of Sophie's hand to shake Martin's, but Martin grabbed him for an embrace instead. Then they slapped each other on the shoulders, grinning.

"See you soon," Henry said.

"See you sooner," Sophie added, putting her arm around Henry to watch Martin drive off. She told herself that Martin could never again be the Silent Guy, now that she had seen him laughing in the middle of a silver-blue lake, now that he had told them the story of the eagle. Back in school together, they could reminisce about the summer. It was her own goodbye to Henry that she still didn't know how to say.

END OF AUGUST 1966, and the elms were dying. Disease had spread onto nearly every block in Electric City, through the center of town and along all its arteries. Almost overnight, Central Park was entirely under siege: bark curled and peeling away, deformed leaves turning black. Martin wasn't sure if it was an attack from within or without, but experts said that either way the plague was incurable. Driving his battered truck up and down the silent streets between midnight and dawn, he memorized the canopy of trees disappearing overhead. It seemed a bizarre coincidence that a lunar orbiter was taking photos of the surface of the moon, mapping it in preparation for the Apollo landing mission. On nights when even the constellations seemed to be missing, he stood at the base of a suffering tree, placed his palms on its rough skin, and prayed.

For the first couple of weeks after Henry went back to boarding school, Martin waited to see if Sophie would call him. Although they had a physics class together, it was scheduled so early in the morning that they hardly ever found time to say much more than hello. She seemed distracted when he saw her in homeroom, and he felt reluctant to approach her when other people were around.

Henry's absence wasn't especially noticeable until he sent a postcard mentioning that the Van Curler Hotel was going to be demolished, asking Martin to take a photograph or two before the place vanished.

"I'm not obsessed," Henry wrote. "But Aaron and I used to ride up and down in the hotel elevator. I wasn't tall enough to push any of the buttons except the one that closed the door."

Martin wanted to get close enough to the building to record the sounds of its destruction—or at least what it sounded like right before the tearing down began. He considered inviting Sophie to come along, but this was still an unshared practice, his secret eavesdropping on strangers. Maybe he would tell her about it once he knew what soundtrack he was creating—a story that wasn't even his own.

Luckily, when he showed up at the service entrance of the Van Curler Hotel, a construction worker who knew Martin's cousin Isaiah said it was all right for him to duck inside for a few minutes. Browsing mildewed hallways and peering into vacant bedrooms, Martin thought it might be a portent, an emblem of Henry's lineage being pulled back into the earth. The carpet was threadbare at the center of each stair; varnish on the banisters had long since cracked and peeled away to nothing. A sign on the ornate elevator door read PERMANENTLY OUT OF ORDER.

Martin dangled the cord of a microphone into the stairwell, letting it absorb the absence of footsteps; then, for Henry, his camera clicked its own Morse code. Walking back to the truck, he sensed Electric City's dust in his hair, on his skin. It smelled like cigars, and rust.

SOPHIE PROMISED HERSELF that while Henry was gone, she would focus on schoolwork, privately savoring the way he had said, "When I get back for the holidays, we can pick up where we left off." Every night she went to sleep holding on to the belief that there was someone in the world who found her beautiful enough to love. When she told Melanie and Alice about the trip with Henry and Martin to Lake George, giving them only enough details so they could corroborate her story, she felt relieved to be keeping most of the experience to herself. It was like owning a treasure hidden from everyone else's view, some shiny thing that she could turn over in her mind like a jewel.

Martin was in on the secret too, of course, but at first she couldn't quite decipher the altered shape of their friendship. Although she and Martin shared a particular connection of their own, without Henry around all of the particles collided in a different way. In theory, he was the person they had in common, but sometimes she imagined he was also the person standing between them.

Riding the half-empty bus to school in the early light, she noticed the autumn colors flaring with life in stark contrast to the entire swaths of neighborhoods resonating with decay and desertion. It was more than the dying elm trees that worried her. There were vandalized storefronts and fractured sidewalks no one was bothering to repair; OUT OF BUSINESS signs proliferated, especially in the heart of downtown. Though she had learned like so many other children to hold her breath near a cemetery, as if to keep from swallowing exhalations of mortality, the living in Electric City could no longer pretend to outnumber the dead. Illness didn't respect brick walls or evergreen hedges. You could travel all the way to a new continent and yet still find death waiting to greet you. Now that she knew about Aaron's accident, even passing by Henry's old house and gazing up at a broken branch could scrape open a wound.

Everyone was entangled. When her physics teacher Mr. Woodman talked about subatomic particles, she looked across the room at Martin, trying to catch his eye, wondering if he too was thinking about how they were all just like those quarks.

"Even at great distances," Woodman said, "on different sides of a continent, when one is interfered with, the other gets agitated too."

She wrote out the sentence on the back cover of her notebook, scratching the words into the cardboard as though carving a message into birch bark. After class, she stood in the hall until she saw Martin, canvas bag on his shoulder, as always.

"Were you thinking of Henry in there?" she asked.

He gave her half a smile. "My great-grandmother could feel it when her son fell from the bridge. Like she was losing her own balance and tumbling through the air."

Sophie thought about how many science lessons she had absorbed all her life, in school and at home too. Her father, his magnets. Her mother, the messages written on the brown prescription bottles. Simon was all the way on the West Coast, stretching threads of the Levine family even farther across the map. She considered her Dutch grandmother the doctor, and how her mother's education had been disrupted by the war, waiting for resurrection all these years later. Maybe that was the first time she envisioned herself attending medical school, a delayed reprise of her genetics. Her future seemed so inevitable, sometimes. A line drawn in space, pulling her, naming her. *Sophie Levine, MD.*

T HE WEEKLY POKER game convening in the dining room on Wendell Avenue had left Steinmetz more exhausted than usual. For once he couldn't recall precisely who won and who lost, only trusted as he awakened in the predawn light that the Society for the Adjustment of Differences in Salaries had performed its task according to the applicable laws of chance and entropy.

He shifted uncomfortably in bed while the sky gradually brightened and his bedroom windows framed a late October morning. Soon enough, beloved granddaughter Midge would tap at the door with a tray carrying his morning glass of tea, sweetened the way he had instructed her, and he would wait for his strength to come back. If it would.

The entire Hayden family—*his* family: adopted son Joe along with wife Corinne and the brood of children—had recently returned from a monthlong excursion across the United States, all the way to the West Coast and back again. The trip was his idea, a long-postponed wish to visit some majestic places on the other side of the continent, an adventure he'd never quite given himself time to enjoy.

To be fair, his cabin at Camp Mohawk had always provided countless opportunities for relaxation; it wasn't as though he'd denied himself a relationship with Nature and her wonders. But the calendar said 1923, which meant thirty-four years since arriving in America, twenty-seven years since becoming a citizen; no more waiting to broaden his vista. His years if not his days were numbered, and without much explanation he had insisted that Joe arrange train travel for the whole family. Their multiplied delight in the trip was how he enhanced his own happiness too.

Now it was all behind them: the cathedral of redwoods north of San Francisco; the astonishing scale of Yosemite with its granite edges and exuberant waterfalls; the gleeful meeting with Douglas Fairbanks. The latter was a nod to Corinne's starstruck request but a surprising treat for him too, and his own delight glimpsing the flat scenery behind the actors — magic tricks of Hollywood laid bare.

He fumbled among piles of photographs stacked on a bedside table to find the one of Fairbanks posing with all of the Haydens, undisguised pleasure on all of their faces. Beneath that, a jolly image of himself posing at an ostrich farm. If doctor's orders were to remain in bed, he would use the time for sifting through folders of papers he intended to label and organize. Here were birth announcements for Joseph Junior and for Marjorie Hayden. Joseph Hayden's graduation program, Elmer Avenue School, 1920. War Savings Army Certificate for Marjorie "Midge" Hayden, appointing her "Corporal." Joseph Hayden's certificate of promotion to high school, 1920. His own membership certificates to the National Marine League, the National Conservation Association. Citizenship papers, 1896, from the County Court of Electric City.

Here was a draft of the last letter he had written to his father in Breslau, the last one before the old man's death. It slid down to the braided rug beside the bed, but he was too weak to pick it up. *Later.* And here was a bill authorizing this Wendell Avenue home as a historic site. Reassuring to understand that there would be generations willing to carry his work forward. So many unfinished blueprints and plans not lost or abandoned but merely allowed to pause, as though his death were merely a railway station like those he had passed through during those thrilling days crossing an ever-changing landscape. Plains giving way to mountains and then desert; nights where the rocking motion of the sleeper car was a calming lullaby.

He had entertained Midge with stories about the game of "Going to America" he'd played as a child, featuring a red trunk and a faded watercolor map.

"How lucky," he said to her, "to have been born here already."

Upon returning to Electric City, he told Joseph Longboat it had been the trip of a lifetime, and a reminder not only of the humble place he occupied in the Universe but a full reckoning with the choice he made so long ago to traverse an ocean and build a new life.

That scene of arrival so many decades ago had blurred a bit, but it had never been forgotten. The lady in the harbor. Her lamp. The disturbed doctors who had to be persuaded he was fit to enter. Asmussen's welcoming embrace, and the taking of a name to match his metamorphosed identity.

Meanwhile, the European drama he left behind was being further extenuated by rivers of blood. Not just the brutal devastation of the Great War and its aftermath, but the interminable migrations of refugees wandering in every direction. Impossible not to regard with a certain longing what might yet come of the Russian Revolution and its promises for a Socialist utopia. Here among the papers was a signed photograph from Lenin, thanking him for being one of the scientists unafraid of the proletariat! But who could be sure what Stalin was capable of?

Joseph Longboat wisely warned that so much power in the hands of anyone, even an idealist, could turn destructive. Steinmetz worried that such darkness remained the fundamental flaw at the core of human nature. He had seen it proved out again and again, despite his optimistic wish for redemption. *Idealist to ideologue.* The forces for good pulling and pushing against the evil of resistance, like magnetism having its way with the world, invisible and immutable.

And yet, without his own willingness to change, he would certainly never have met Joseph, or paddled a canoe, might never have learned to read a river's movements or an eagle's wingspan. Instead of Europe, he had a son and grandchildren related not by blood but something more complex and poignant: his heart's choice.

Sighing, he held one wrist to let the fingertips count his own faint pulse. Ever since the return from California, the current state of his biology was causing alarm in the physician's office. The same doctor who had consistently joined him at the poker table—the one sharing his love of cigars and brandy—in sterile daylight apologetically explained that Steinmetz was showing all the signs of imminent organ failure.

"A common cold might be uncommonly deadly," he warned.

Exposing the frail chest of his patient, Dr. Rollings had attached electrodes in an equilateral triangle, measuring the pulsing energy beneath Steinmetz's gray-tinged skin. A slender ribbon of paper recording the map of heartbeats was suddenly as clear as the story of his entire life with electricity: jagged lines like fragments of Camp Mohawk's broken mirror, the lightning path, its musical notation, its symphony.

Someday, Steinmetz thought, waiting for Midge's visit with his cup of tea, *someday electricity will save the world's heart.* He will be a long-gone ghost by then, a Wizard no more. Only the name of someone who believed.

Now the knock at the door was like a drumbeat from far away, a rhythmic voice from the little heart he loved best.

"Come in, Midgie," he said. "I'm right here."

Without a family of her own to corral into place, Midge celebrated Thanksgiving at the Mohawk Club, inviting as her guests a handful of college students too far from home. In truth, she would have preferred serving meals in a soup kitchen or an orphanage, wherever the need was greatest, but every year the Holiday Committee claimed they couldn't manage without her. Donning a starched white apron and a pair of Corinne's simple pearl earrings, Midge played multiple roles as local farmer, head cook, and substitute mother.

The students (almost always nineteen- and twenty-year-old boys) showed up with their jackets and ties, scrubbed faces and shined shoes; accustomed to insatiable appetites, they offered effusive gratitude for the heaped servings of turkey and stuffing, squash and cranberries. Between courses, watching the plates wiped clean, she told stories about Daddy Steinmetz—especially his love of practical jokes and the way he shocked first-time visitors to his home with a mild electrical jolt upon shaking hands, using a delicately wired contraption concealed inside his coat sleeve.

It saddened her to notice that as the years passed, fewer students knew who he was, vaguely acknowledging the identity of a mathematician whose numerous patented designs for electric motors appeared in small print alongside the much grander claims of Edison's. It was the

Company logo they all recognized, glowing above the factory and displayed on countless shiny appliances. The curling insignia of nobody's name.

Worst of all, plans for preserving the house on Wendell Avenue had fallen through during Midge's brief absence from Electric City, especially her two-year experiment living in San Francisco. By the time she returned, the Steinmetz/Hayden house had been torn down without her knowledge, leaving a mournful empty space at the center of a tree-framed lot. Her brothers Joe Junior and Bill seemed entirely unconcerned about this disappearance, as though memories of a childhood with lizards and canoes could now be easily relegated to scrapbooks on a dusty shelf.

This Thanksgiving, 1966, she was fifty-seven years old, and she marveled that Steinmetz hadn't lived past fifty-eight. She tried to imagine this being the last year of her own life: the last round of golf, the last time walking her dog or driving her car, harvesting tomatoes for one final season. It seemed impossible that such an abbreviated life as his could have left behind so many groundbreaking transformations—not least of which was the very concept of a Company-sponsored research laboratory. And yet here was a group of college students in Electric City who barely acknowledged the originality of his lightning generator, his work on alternating current theory, his law of hysteresis.

Even the most extraordinary people end up with as little residue as anyone else, Midge thought. *A gravestone in a cemetery, a name on a plaque among the pines. A home dismantled and then erased.*

MARTIN REALIZED THE irony of carrying an extra-sensitive mechanism for listening when he wore earplugs at the plant to shield himself from the deluge of machine-made noise. The visible world didn't always match up with its audible counterparts; sometimes the frame couldn't hold the view.

During lunch breaks and with increasing frequency, Martin heard coworkers at the plant swapping stories about GIs who had begun to question the war out loud. He noticed in particular that black men were calling it a racist war led by a racist army. Someone had printed up a poster crudely calling for black mercenaries to help in killing off other oppressed peoples. SUPPORT WHITE POWER! it sneered. TRAVEL TO VIETNAM, YOU MIGHT GET A MEDAL!

"Body count" was being used to measure success against the Vietcong. Then came the words "enemy combatants," offered up in headlines, and the familiar sound hit Martin like a well-aimed blow to his solar plexus. That terrible term from the centuries-ago massacre of his own people, labeling innocent women and children so that history could repeat itself on the other side of the world.

Meaning: the wrong color of skin or shape of eyes, the wrong language, the wrong god. Phrases used as dirty weapons with the same twisted purpose as before, the same genocidal effect. All at once, he couldn't escape images of young men burning their draft cards, shouting in unison, "Hell no, we won't go." On the news, there were crowds marching with signs outside the Dow factory where napalm was being produced, bombs to be dropped on yellow people just like in 1945, Nagasaki and Hiroshima, always in the name of someone else's idea about freedom and justice. Martin endured standing while everyone around him at school recited the pledge, but soon even this would be the last form of participation. *No more.*

Each fall weekend, on his way to and from the plant, Martin walked beside a defeated-looking fence high enough to make a complete mystery of whatever lay on the other side. One November day the faded wood, there as long as he could remember, suddenly displayed a splash of white paint, followed a day later by more paint in the shape of a large rectangle, half the size of a refrigerator. The next day, a word was stenciled in black at the center of the box: BROTHER. And the day after: BEWARE.

A week passed with no change, simply *Brother Beware*, a pair of words creating a drumbeat in his head, his footsteps, disturbingly mimicked by the machines in the factory. *Brother Beware. Brother Beware.* And then a second white box appeared with a typewritten note stapled so that it was white on white, small words he could read only by standing close: THE MAN IS COMING FOR YOU NEXT TIME, BROTHER. IN THIS WAR OF AGGRESSION, THE STRANGER AT THE DOOR IS YOU.

When Martin lifted the bottom of the page away from the wall as though finally understanding that it was meant exactly for him, sure enough there was a symbol he recognized from readings on Steinmetz: the Greek letter omega. *Ohms*, he thought, *unit of electrical resistance.* Next to that simple insignia was a local phone number written upside down in blue ink. He committed the number to memory, knowing the message would now disappear from the wall, and knowing that someday soon, with a draft card in his pocket, he would need to make a call.

ENRY'S ANNUAL THANKSGIVING weekend in New York City with his mother's side of the family was usually a treat; since his three cousins were older, all married and with young children, he managed to spend most of the time out of the limelight. Someone, after all, needed to take the Dodge family corgis for walks several times each day, and someone was always needed to run down to the corner store for more ice (there was never enough) or olives (never enough of those either). Although his grandparents had plenty of staff to prepare elaborate meals and maintain the huge and fastidious apartment, Henry actually enjoyed being the designated supplier of missing ingredients. He welcomed the chance to see how long he could delay returning to the eighteenth floor, knowing that cocktail hour started especially early on holidays, and lasted late into the night.

On the other hand, staying away from Electric City was a newly discovered frustration. Sophie explained in one of her letters that her family had never quite figured out how to celebrate such an American event, and that it seemed to her an excellent time to take an offshore vacation. Although Martin had sent him the requested photos of the Van Curler Hotel, the envelope contained a note saying, "Wish you were here." Henry hadn't felt comfortable enough to ask Martin what he did for Thanksgiving, assuming that the very idea of the holiday was annoying at best and possibly reprehensible at worst.

"I'll call you from my grandparents' place," Henry wrote back to Sophie. "And we can make a definite plan for seeing each other in December."

Arthur and Gloria picked him up at school in their cream-colored Mercedes and the three drove to Manhattan late on Wednesday night. Henry stretched out on the backseat, claiming exhaustion from mid-term exams, but mainly attempting to avoid conversation as well as to keep whatever distance he could find from his father's chain-smoking. His mother either didn't mind the fumes or was choosing as usual to endure her circumstances in silence.

When the morning's radio news issued dire warnings about air pollution, and the announcers quoted medical professionals urging anyone with asthma and other breathing ailments to remain indoors, both Arthur and his father-in-law, similarly dedicated smokers, glanced out the window and then back across the breakfast table at each other.

"Looks like we're going to have to quit one of these days," Arthur said to Cleveland, who laughed and coughed on cue.

"New York City air has hardly ever been good for anybody's health."

The panoramic view from the Dodge living room windows indeed showed a cityscape heavily shrouded in smog, skyscrapers wearing dense gray shawls as though someone had draped them there for dramatic effect. Henry's grandmother, Constance, determined to focus every-one's attention on the elaborate midafternoon meal, enlisted help in setting the table and teaching the younger children how to fold napkins in the shape of swans. Henry was assigned the job of selecting music for the stereo and making sure his grandfather's ashtray didn't overflow onto the silk carpets. *Frank Sinatra. Barbra Streisand. Rachmaninoff. Mozart.* Thanksgiving dinner was served.

Various topics carefully avoided at the table included any reference to the fact that the Dodges' kitchen boasted a new refrigerator with an in-the-door icemaker manufactured not by the Company but by its major competitor. And also: the past summer's ten-year anniversary of Aaron's death. Only if you looked closely at a few of the older photos in the hallway near the guest bathroom, black-and-white shots from weddings and birthdays that included two young Van Curler boys, would you ever know that there was one child absent.

The cousins left in a flurry of activity soon after pumpkin pie had been served and inhaled, climbing into taxis heading uptown and downtown. The children were cranky and tired. Cleveland turned on the television in time to hear that upwards of two hundred people had died from respiratory failure and heart attacks due to the record-shattering smog. Gloria proposed heading back upstate to Electric City before things got any worse.

"More driving will just add to the problem," Cleveland said. "And anyway, the smoky stuff will clear up overnight. We just need a bit of rain."

Henry watched his mother's inscrutable face to see if she might be forming a reply, but instead of arguing her point, she reached into a drawer for a deck of cards and began playing solitaire on the marble coffee table. Constance was in her room down the hall, nursing a migraine, and Arthur was reading *Time* magazine, sipping bourbon.

Henry found himself imagining his brother Aaron the way he might look at nineteen, sitting beside him on the couch and deliberately ignoring the news. Nudging him in the ribs and working up a strategy for convincing the doorman to let them out for a walk after the rest of the family had gone to bed.

"The city that never sleeps," Aaron's ghost whispered.

When the remembered sensation of kissing Sophie poured through his body, Henry pictured her beside him, instead of Aaron. The two of them in his grandparents' apartment in Manhattan, grown-up and independent and happy.

Next year we will all be somewhere else, Henry thought, surprising himself with certainty. *I don't know where, but not here.*

FROM SOPHIE'S POINT of view, her family treated Thanksgiving as though it were a kind of anthropological experiment, designed either to defy understanding or perhaps to be gradually comprehended over a period of decades. This year, since Simon had insisted on staying in California for all of the holidays, starting with Rosh Hashana, she hoped that her parents and their friends would tighten their already-close-knit circle without suffocating her in the process. All of their children were old enough to be away at college or else married, and Sophie was the only one still young enough to live at home.

A secular celebration such as Thanksgiving gave Miriam, Magda, Rose, and Reena a rare opportunity to collaborate on their inspired interpretations of American food, turning the Levine kitchen into a communal space for the entire day.

"I'm doing something extra special this time," Miriam had announced on the phone to each guest the previous morning, already eager to welcome her friends into the house with their arms full of ingredients. "We're having duck!"

Sophie didn't have the heart to explain that turkeys were intended to be the main course. She was both amused and fascinated to realize that this menu was framed by an immigrant story far different from that of the Pilgrims. Irving didn't enjoy the taste of duck, so his wife prepared his favorite beef and cabbage stew. None of her parents' friends liked pumpkin, so the pie would be Reena's elegant apple, to be offered alongside Rose's signature coffee cake, known as babka. Sweet potatoes didn't make any sense when potatoes were much more flavorful (and familiar); no one made stuffing (what for?) but Magda brought homemade challah that contained no milk products (since David and Miriam were keeping kosher and therefore didn't combine dairy products with meat). This also meant no butter on the table at all, not even for the potatoes. And dessert could only be served three hours past the end of the meal, so as to allow the meat to be fully digested before any consumption of milk.

Daniel, Irving, and Benjamin all took their places in the living room to await the serving of the feast, while David served and refilled small glasses from the Levine liquor cabinet, the one Sophie knew had been holding the very same bottles for years. They snacked on bowls of tuna fish with chopped celery, herring in sour cream, cucumber salad, carrot salad with raisins, sliced tomatoes with red onion. They swapped jokes in lowered voices so that Sophie couldn't quite hear and critiqued the national economy in their accented English.

At one point, a reference was made to the previous year's blackout, giving Daniel a chance to repeat yet again the story of his starring role in restoring power to the entire Northeast.

Sophie leaned against the open doorway to the kitchen, polishing her mother's favorite silver candlesticks, inhaling the tapestry of aromas filling the air. She watched the men clink their glasses and give Daniel the congratulations he deserved.

"Someone had to fix it," he said, smiling.

And in that moment she had a powerful wish to have Henry standing next to her, wanting him to see how her own family and their friends had so carefully and earnestly woven their lives into the fabric of this

Company town, this electric America. There might be a duck in the oven and some colorful misunderstandings about the meaning of the day, but there was no mistake that one choice to live here had brought them all together.

Sophie looked back at the quartet of women in their flower-printed aprons. Her mother was arranging the duck on a platter garnished with sprigs of parsley, its crisp skin decorated with thin slices of orange.

"A masterpiece," pronounced Magda.

Although it wouldn't be eaten until much later, Rose was sprinkling powdered sugar onto her cake so that it looked as though it had been dusted with snow. Reena dipped a spoon into the pot of stew she had made especially for Irving, offering a taste to Sophie.

"Delicious?"

"Yum," Sophie said. It was.

MARTIN HAD ONCE again politely declined an invitation from Midge to join her annual gathering of "holiday orphans" at the Mohawk Club. He knew she meant well, and that she would have sincerely cherished including him as well as Annie around the extravagant table overlooking her favorite golf course. But there was simply no way he could manage the irony, expecting Annie (and himself) to serve as "real live Indians" on display. Working a night shift with double-pay overtime at the Company seemed a far preferable alternative, giving him the excuse of needing to sleep all of Thursday.

As Wednesday night wore into day, it occurred to him that Sophie was the only person he could imagine capable of relating to his attitude about the so-called holiday. She had recently told him of her respect for his refusal to recite the Pledge of Allegiance, and then shyly asked if he had noticed that she no longer spoke the words? He hadn't. But now their silent solidarity touched him more than he dared to admit.

Annie told him when he arrived home exhausted that a girl named Sophie had called but didn't leave any message except her number. He slept a few hours with a bandanna tied over his eyes to block the daylight, and then took a walk along the edge of the river with Bear, sorting through his thoughts about returning her call. Knowing that Henry was out of town somewhere with his family, Martin wrestled with the idea that he was Sophie's second choice, her backup plan. A part of him was tempted to drive over to the Castle Diner and see if by some long shot the place was open. But when he was back in Annie's kitchen, he picked up the phone.

"Interested in an all-new and not entirely American version of Turkey Day?" Sophie wanted to know. "I should mention that the main meal is already over, but we had to take a break before dessert. There's pie." The sound of her voice made him inexplicably happy. He held the phone away from his ear and looked toward Bear, who was wagging his tail. *Yes.*

"What does someone like me bring to something like that?" Martin asked.

Sophie laughed and Bear wagged even harder. "I was kind of hoping you would bring your dog," she said.

Although Bear was instructed to stay on a folded-up blanket near the front entryway to the house, Sophie had managed to make up a foil-wrapped gift to send home with him, sneaking a few small pieces of beef from the stew, along with a bit of burned duck that her mother had scraped into the trash. She introduced Martin to the group of women, first her mother and then the others, all back in aprons with their now-smudged lipstick and pot-scouring gloves. The dishwasher was full and the stove was empty.

It felt good to say his name out loud, *Martin Longboat,* and to see their slightly puzzled but nonetheless warm expressions as they repeated their own names in return. *Magda Rosenthal, Reena Selinger, Rose Hollander.*

Miriam was the one who pointed to a chair, asking if he wanted "both a slice of pie and also a piece of the babka?" Martin nodded, grinning.

A coffee percolator was puffing on the counter; Sophie carried cups and saucers into the dining room, where the men were once again seated. Ties had been loosened during the relaxed pause between the end of dinner and the start of dessert. David was offering schnapps. *It's like Passover*, Sophie thought, and then she was amazed at the correspondences, realizing why she had suddenly felt compelled to include Martin. A ritual meal with symbolic foods, commemorating a passage through a narrow place; a celebration of freedom, shared with a stranger at the table. A feast to honor the sacredness of enough.

Seated beside Sophie, Martin waited for questions that never came, the ones about his Indian name or his long hair, the ones about his skin. He wondered if Sophie had told them about his grandfather being a close friend of Steinmetz, and which of the men would ask which division employed him at the Company. Something about the way she studied him in sidelong glances made it clear that Miriam was trying to sort out if Martin was Sophie's boyfriend. David, on the other hand, was doing everything possible to ignore him. There was a stretch of reminiscing about growing up in Holland, about canals and ice skating and stockpiles of firewood for the winter. Daniel and David took turns predicting the newest scientific discoveries that were about to change the world, the room-size computers that could calculate the distance between stars in a matter of seconds.

When Irving said that the diseased elm trees were just one of the warning signs for the future, Martin cleared his throat and told them what he'd heard on the truck radio while driving over.

"There's been 'killer smog' today in New York City," he said. "Breaking all records."

Sophie immediately thought of Henry, there with his family and caught in what she imagined to be a choking soup of air. Maybe while trying to defend against the dangers of nuclear fallout, scientists like her very own father had forgotten to pay enough attention to what was right in front of their faces. If only Henry would call and tell her he was all right. She didn't think she'd be able to sleep without knowing.

"And here?" Miriam asked. "What about our city?"

Martin looked around at the concerned faces, embarrassed to be the bearer of such grim news. For years now, much of his life, he'd been watching his beloved river turn more gray and filthy, losing its shorebirds and its fish, growing a sickly sheen on its surface. Every time Annie heard from Martin's father in California, she worried out loud about Los Angeles, where the dangerous air was given ratings on its degree of difficulty to breathe. Perhaps a day of "killer smog" could wake people up before it was too late. Maybe the messages would be unmistakable now.

"Progress has its price," David said, with nods around the table. "Every time we create a new problem, we get to find a new solution."

Martin remembered what Sophie had said about her father's religious observances; now he could see where else he placed his faith. The echoes of Steinmetz were so palpable Martin was about to say his name, but that was when David rose to his feet and suggested they go to the den for the evening broadcast.

All the chairs were pushed back at once. Plates could be stacked in the sink while the dishwasher hummed through its cycles. Unable to catch David's eye even for a moment, Martin thanked Miriam for dessert. Sophie whispered that now would be a good time for them to slip away, take Bear for a walk, or better yet, a drive. She told Martin what a relief it was, that her father wasn't performing his usual interrogations.

"Because I'm Indian?"

"Because you're not Jewish."

Martin heard the television volume being turned up in the den. "I still don't get it," he said.

"If he expressed actual interest in you, that would be equivalent to endorsing your being part of my life," Sophie said.

He started to laugh but saw that Sophie was perfectly serious.

"That's what a tribe means to *him*," she added.

She grabbed her coat, wanting to be out the door quickly and yet worried about missing Henry's promised phone call.

"I'll be back soon," she shouted downstairs.

Being in the truck with Martin was so different than it had been just a few months before; the season of freezing darkness was upon them, with much worse yet to come. Bear sat between them on the cracked leather seat, radiating his body heat in both directions. Sophie suggested driving out to the airport, to a place Simon had once shown her after buying his used Mustang. She relished the idea of taking Martin to discover a pocket of home he didn't already know.

"Thank you for sharing the pie," Martin said.

Between Bear's enormous head blocking her view and the dim light of the dashboard, Sophie couldn't make out his expression. "Did you like it?"

"Yup."

"I usually don't invite anyone over," she admitted.

"You mean Henry hasn't been there yet?" He couldn't help asking.
Sophie sighed, almost groaning.

"They're just a clan of people who want the best for you," he said.
"What *they* think is best."

"Easy for you to say," she said.

"Not really."

They parked on a dirt road and tiptoed onto the dead yellow grass
near the farthest end of a runway. Sophie was shivering until Martin
stretched out a musty wool blanket for the two of them to lie on, and
a second, softer one to cover her up. Stretching into the distance, the
neon blue of the runway lights seemed an electric version of Henry's
eyes. Martin had no intention of wrapping Sophie in his arms, no matter what.

In another few minutes, there would be thunderous engines, the
shrill pitch of wings cutting air, the harsh skid of brakes on the tarmac.
They weren't passengers going anywhere yet, but someday, who knew
how soon, they would travel. Even Martin, who had been in Electric
City for so long; even Sophie, who had just arrived. The ground held
them but it didn't have to. When a plane roared in overhead, so close it
seemed they could reach up and touch its silver-white belly, their voices
poured together into the sky.

M ARTIN LOADED A camera with black-and-white film, focused on the silence of ice-coated branches and snow-drifts. He studied vapors made by his breath, envisioning the fox asleep in its den, nose tucked under its flame of a tail. North of town, the architecture of a beaver dam on Mourning Kill pulled at his attention, though the creek had frozen solid and there was no sign of the builder. Standing a respectful distance from the dense tangle of branches, Martin aimed his lens but wasn't quite fast enough to catch the flash of a woodpecker's departure from the scene, the back of its head marked in red like a bright winterberry.

All those expenses for developing and printing meant he needed to work extra hours just to stay even. As Christmas neared, he asked Annie what he could give, but she shrugged him off.

"Keep me stocked with firewood, and that's all I need."

Arthritis was making it harder for her to open jars, and Martin noticed her wincing when she reached back to untangle her hair. His wandering father had sent a postcard from Western Canada, no longer bothering to hint he might come all the way back. Bear slept longer and deeper.

Before the snow, Martin had placed green-tipped stakes at the corners of Midge's vegetable garden, promises of a distant spring. She gave him four different kinds of preserves to share with Annie, decorated with multicolored strands of yarn.

"If I don't give these away, they'll just explode in my basement," she chuckled. "You're doing me a favor."

"Would you mind if I shared them with a friend?" He held the jars in both hands, looking at the handwritten labels instead of meeting Midge's curious gaze.

"I've got more where these came from," she said. "Any friend of yours . . . well, you know."

Martin grinned. He trusted that one of these days she'd meet Sophie, though he had no idea when it would happen. For now, he gratefully carried Midge's prize out to his truck.

"We eat the earth before it eats us, right?"

She was quoting Annie. "Right," he said.

Martin Longboat's photo series, late December 1966:

Midge's preserves, lined up on Annie's windowsill in weak winter sunlight.

Silhouette of Bear standing in the back of the pickup, blur of his tail in motion.

Sophie half out of the frame, reaching toward something beyond view.

Annie's braided hair, woven tight.

A pair of hands woven tight: Henry's and Sophie's. *Welcome home.*

The Company's neon sign, suspended in a moonless sky.

For all of Christmas Day Martin sat with his grandmother and helped sort through scraps of fabric for her rugs; she was braiding a special black-and-gray oval to echo his photographs. Variations in wool and cotton: interlocking patterns of faded stripes, checkerboard, houndstooth. Annie had been collecting material for decades, longer than he had been alive. Martin watched her swollen hands while she folded and twisted the cloth tight.

When he stepped into the cold with Bear to leave deep footprints in the snow, the only sign of life was in the pines, pushing with green determination from underneath the weight of winter. Then he recognized chickadees and nuthatches chattering on a high telephone wire. Smoke rose from Annie's chimney and disappeared among the clouds, where the absence of color made everything converge.

As though making up for a late start, this winter felt as frigid as Sophie could remember, with sub-zero gusts making storm windows moan all night. Simon was confessing his plan to stay indefinitely in California, and she couldn't really blame him. Instead of letters, he mailed small boxes filled with lemons that had grown in his backyard. His version of a Hanukkah gift.

Cleaning up the breakfast dishes with her mother, Sophie could see from the kitchen window that nearly every neighbor's yard boasted at least one evergreen with Christmas lights, some of them twinkling even during the day. This made it easy to spot the rare Jewish homes, by way of what was missing. Her father liked to deliberately place their menorah in the window during Hanukkah, especially on the last night when all the candles were lit. It was a variation on David's practice of walking to synagogue through the parking lot of the country club. *We are here.*

"Is something wrong?" Miriam asked Sophie, who was holding her hands under the hot water.

"My joints hurt."

"You must be having a growth spurt," her mother said, and then tilted her head. "No, that wouldn't be right. That's for boys, isn't it? I think it's probably hormones."

"Great," Sophie muttered.

"Being a woman isn't always a picnic." Sophie noticed the faint etchings on her mother's wide forehead, the crows' feet and frown lines.

"Would an electric blanket help?" Sophie asked.

"Not with everything," Miriam said. On the kitchen counter beside the television, a basket of clean laundry was about to spill onto the floor. Sophie bumped into it, then scrambled to retrieve the fallen towels, still warm from the dryer.

"Fold these?" she asked.

"You read my mind," Miriam said.

"Fair enough," Sophie said. "Since you're so good at reading mine." She started unfurling bath sheets, holding the dissipating warmth of the cotton against her cheek, and then allowing the folding to become a kind of dance. Miriam watched her daughter with a smile that continued to widen.

"There's a boy in your heart," she said.

Sophie looked at her mother's expression, took a deep breath for courage, and was about to plunge into the forbidden sentence when her mother said the words herself. "And he's not Jewish."

They both looked around to see if Sophie's father was within hearing distance. Though David would have preferred spending the day at the research laboratory, pleased by the holiday-related vacancies, even his security clearance wasn't enough to unlock the doors on Christmas Day. But the TV was on in the family room, loud enough to cover their low voices.

"The boy you brought on Thanksgiving?"

Sophie blushed. "No. He's just a friend."

"It's always good to be friends first," Miriam said.

"There's another boy," Sophie began, more heat rising on her skin. "His name is Henry. Van Curler."

Miriam placed another folded sheet in the basket, then sat down with a sigh. "Life would be a lot easier around here if you chose someone from synagogue," her mother said.

Sophie nodded, then shook her head. She watched Miriam's gaze travel around the kitchen, where the Company logo seemed to wink from every surface: TV, dishwasher, fridge.

"Are you angry? Are you going to tell Dad?"

"Let's see what happens," Miriam said.

A FTER DAYS OF being ensconced within the family barricade, Henry called Sophie. It was the afternoon before her seventeenth birthday, the day before New Year's Eve. There were special occasions yet to be endured, but if he couldn't get away, at least she might come to him. Sophie explained that on her side of town, Hanukkah had been over since the middle of the month. The silver-plated menorah had already been returned to the glass-fronted display case in the Levines' dining room.

"Can you handle a dinner?" he asked over the phone. "I know the House of Van Curler isn't exactly your thing, but at least you'd get some champagne for your almost-birthday."

Sophie told herself she was about to get an up-close view of one of the oldest families in Electric City. Henry had already told her that his parents "dressed for dinner" every night, holiday or not. She imagined four forks on the table next to each plate, each with its specific purpose.

"Do I need to practice first?" she was only half joking. "Or attend finishing school?"

"You'll be fine," Henry said.

"I don't even know what finishing school is," Sophie said.

Henry laughed. "That's exactly why I'm inviting you." There was a pause while Sophie considered how rude it would be to ask what was on the menu. *Do they eat ham on holidays?* Henry jumped in to mention they were going to have halibut.

"Fish is a relief," she said. "But will you promise to kick me under the table if I do something stupid?"

The next trick was what to tell her parents about where she was going, and with whom. Moments after hanging up the phone, as if a benevolent deity was offering assistance, Miriam told Sophie that she and David were on their way to a dinner party at the Rosenthals'. "You don't even have to come along," she said, seeing Sophie's distressed face.

"You look beautiful, Mom." She reached out to touch her mother's necklace, shifting it slightly so that the amethyst pendant was restored to center.

"Happy almost-birthday, Sophie." Miriam left a lipstick kiss on her daughter's cheek, staying close long enough to whisper in her ear. "Just get back home before we do."

Sophie concluded it was a good thing she hadn't been given more than an hour to prepare for meeting Henry's parents. Without the luxury of time, she made the simple choice of her favorite sea-green sweater over a black wool skirt with black tights underneath. By the time Henry was walking up her front steps to ring the bell, she had already been waiting at the door with her coat on, self-conscious about inviting him to see where she lived. With Martin, the chaos and noise of the meal had enabled her to forget he was seeing inside her family; all the activities were a kind of camouflage, blocking the particular view. Now, she felt shy and overexposed.

"No need to come in," she said. "Nobody's home."

"Goodbye, Nobody," Henry called out, then took Sophie's elbow and guided her down the recently shoveled walkway.

At first the MG seemed as cold inside as the air outside; Sophie's wool coat and tights weren't doing enough to keep her warm. Henry reached into the back well and yanked out a faded quilt he had stashed there, tossing it onto her lap.

"I think I'm more nervous than cold," Sophie admitted.

"You're brave to say that," Henry said. "Most people would rather pretend. At least most people I know."

Sophie hugged herself with the quilt. "That's what I mean. As in, I'm not the people you know."

"I'm getting to know you right now," Henry said, turning to grin at her. "Lucky me."

As they drove, heavy mist made haloes around the streetlamps, and in a surprisingly short distance they were turning into the Van Curlers' driveway. Curving up and around a snowy hill, Sophie thought the property looked different in winter, with the now-naked trees revealing much more of the house than she recalled. *Not these branches*, she reminded herself. *Not this house*.

Arthur Van Curler was graying at the temples; he was dressed in a three-piece suit that looked more expensive than anything Sophie had seen in her father's entire wardrobe. Gloria Van Curler was wearing an off-white cashmere sweater with a pearl necklace and pearl earrings; her pale blue skirt draped itself impeccably. Sophie could easily imagine feeling underdressed around this woman no matter what she was wearing. At least her own unpolished fingernails were trimmed. She surreptitiously rubbed her shoes against the backs of her calves, hoping for a dull gleam at least.

With the four of them seated in neat formation around the rectangular dining table, Henry felt as blank as the tablecloth. He tried to guess how his parents looked from Sophie's point of view, as if they were strangers to him too, focusing on their classic profiles and posture, the way they held themselves upright so precisely. Even he couldn't help straightening his own spine when standing or sitting near them. It was weirdly comforting to concede that they might have that effect on everyone.

Once the napkins were unfolded, Louise in her gray-and-white uniform pushed through the swinging door to deliver the soup for inspection before serving.

"Lobster bisque with saffron," Mrs. Van Curler said approvingly. "I love the color, don't you?"

"It's very pretty," Sophie agreed and gave herself permission to taste lobster for the first time in her life. She waited inside the collective pause before they all picked up their spoons in unison. Henry was suddenly grateful that no one in his family said grace.

As promised, champagne was carefully uncorked and served in delicate flutes.

"I hear it's our chance to say Happy Birthday," Henry's mother smiled, her sky-blue eyes twinkling. She tapped the edge of her glass against Sophie's so that together they made a resonant note. "Please don't tell your parents we serve alcohol to minors around here!"

We are glittering now, Sophie thought, briefly catching Henry's gaze. He had his mother's eyes exactly.

"Cheers," he said.

There was a chandelier with more crystals than she could count hovering above the oblong table, casting refracted light everywhere. The silver shone as if it had never tarnished, and there were ancestral-looking oil paintings on every wall. Henry stole discreet glances at Sophie, who seemed to be studying everything as though she were visiting a museum.

She doubted she took a full breath throughout the entire meal, convinced she would break an irreplaceable goblet, or spill something onto the Oriental carpet. She dabbed at her mouth with a napkin just as often as everyone else did, keeping half her attention on the taste of things and the other half on tracking the protocols.

The conversation was polite and almost entirely lacking in intrusiveness except for the inquiry about where her family came from.

"Do you speak any Dutch, then?" Arthur wanted to know.

"I'm afraid not," Sophie said.

"Not exactly a useful language here in the States," Henry said.

"English is certainly useful all over the world," Gloria added. "Aren't we fortunate?"

It was more and more disturbing to imagine bringing Henry to meet *her* parents. The very idea was enough to make Sophie twist her monogrammed napkin into knots in her lap.

"He's out of the question," her father would say. "We don't even need to discuss the reasons."

"An extremely handsome boy," her mother would say. "But still." No matter what kind of temporary support Miriam might offer, she would in the end side with her husband.

Glancing at Mrs. Van Curler, Sophie was surprised to find a tender expression on the woman's face instead of the disapproval she had been imagining. "Enjoy being seventeen, my dear," Gloria said. "I hope you'll remember this as the best year of your life."

After angel food cake and whipped cream, after tea and coffee and *thanks so much for the delicious meal,* Henry and Sophie were excused from the table.

"Come upstairs for a minute," he said, leading the way. Ascending the wide staircase, she did battle with the static electricity making her skirt cling to her tights. Below, muffled piano music began to play on a stereo, and she pictured Henry's parents gliding into the living room, lighting up their cigarettes, holding brandy snifters. She imagined them contemplating their opinions of her.

"Here's the library," Henry said, pointing through an open doorway into a dimly lit room full of wall-to-ceiling bookshelves.

A vase of perfectly formed white roses was centered on a square glass table. Their fragrance made Sophie think of the Central Park rose garden, and then about the anemic bushes at the corner of her own front lawn. Her family could never quite seem to maintain them, though they didn't expire fully either, just hung on bravely through the casual negligence.

Except for minor variables like patterns on the living room rug or the art on the walls, Sophie's parents' furnishings weren't very different from the furnishings of all of their Jewish friends. Everyone had a couch and a coffee table, a few upholstered chairs and side tables, a magazine rack, lamps, the dining table with expandable leaves, the chairs arranged neatly in case of company.

"We're going up one more flight," Henry said.

His bedroom was on the top floor of the house; a hallway separated his from his parents', which he referred to as the Suite. Sophie suddenly remembered that she hadn't seen any martinis or gin and tonics being served at the dinner table, and wondered if all of that happened behind the closed doors of the Suite before she arrived. It never occurred to her to notice whether Henry's parents might have been drunk or at least tipsy by the time dinner was served.

All she knew was that the champagne made her feel like someone special, and she wished she could have another glass in her hand. She couldn't help smiling to herself at the contrast between the Friday night Manischewitz bottle and all of the crystal on the Van Curler dining room table. What a martini tasted like, she had no idea.

Unlike the bedrooms at the Lake George estate, Henry's room here was spare and unadorned. Above a substantial mahogany bureau there was a painting of a clipper ship on a storm-tossed sea, and a simple arrangement of felt college pennants covered one of the walls. HARVARD was what they all said, white on crimson, like flags from a small but important nation.

"Guess where I'm going to college," he said.

Pulling the leather swivel chair from its place beside his desk, he offered it to Sophie, while he took a seat on the bed. The surface of the desk was neatly protected by a large green blotter, and a massive diction-ary was lying wide open on a cushioned window seat. The clock on his nightstand said it was 8:00, which meant they had stayed at the dinner table for almost two hours. No wonder he was exhausted. He leaned back against his pillows and exhaled as though he'd been holding his breath all night.

"You too?" she said.

"It's like there's never quite enough oxygen to go around," he said.

Sophie laughed and took the chair for a little spin.

"Nice ride," she said.

"Speaking of which," Henry said, sliding off the bed with a burst of optimism. "Let's get out of here."

He took Sophie by the hand and propelled her through the door-way. It was a smart move: spending any time in the bedroom down the hall from the Suite was never going to be anything but ridiculous.

They were down the stairs, grabbing coats and closing the door before anyone could stop them, or ask where they were going.

Spaces between the houses became wider, opening to snowfields hiding fenced pastures and hibernating crops. Sophie felt as though the MG was riding the current of the invisible river; at every curve, she leaned toward or away from Henry, both held separately by the straps across their bodies. Dips in the road brought them gradually lower, yet still the Mohawk remained obscured. The air temperature dropped even further as they pulled into the parking lot at Lock 7.

Sophie was well aware that this was where couples went to make out. Henry's gloved hands on the steering wheel looked like a stranger's, and Sophie felt guilty for huddling under the blanket on her own. Trying not to tremble, she borrowed his right hand from the wheel and clasped it between her two hands, sharing the little body heat she could offer.

"Personal heating," she said. "Okay?"

"Better than that," Henry said, smiling. He parked but left the engine running, so the heater could stay on and the radio too. Tuning in to a jazz station from the college campus downtown, they heard Billie Holiday's blurry, sexy voice.

Sophie wanted champagne again. She wanted Henry to kiss her.

And then, he did. Reaching behind her neck with his suddenly gloveless hand, he pulled her face toward his own. All those kisses of late summer seemed to cascade forward like the closing of a circuit.

For several minutes, they tasted each other. And even though Henry's hands stayed on Sophie's neck and shoulder, her entire body felt like it was melting, with sensations that dazzled and tingled from her feet to the top of her head.

"Everything all right?" he asked. When he touched her lips with his fingers, lightly, she could feel how swollen they were.

"Very," she said. The gearshift was keeping them from pressing their entire bodies against one another. The MG didn't have a backseat, just a space barely large enough for one. Even Bear wouldn't have been able to fit.

Nearby were a few other cars with their steamed-up windows and muffled laughter. On the far side of the lot, a car revved noisily and pulled away. Henry and Sophie watched the red taillights disappear up the road and into the pines.

"It's getting kind of late, isn't it," Henry said. The dashboard clock said 10:09.

Get home before we do, Sophie was thinking. "Yup. It's late."

"How about tomorrow?" Henry said. "Birthday?" He looked intently into her face, reminding her of that first time in front of the post office. She still felt unskilled at this part, being studied; her eyes closed in spite of her willing them to stay open. He leaned into her with another kiss, reviving a current of heat, even after he pulled away and put the car into gear.

"Birthday," Henry repeated.

"Right," she said, and rearranged the blanket to cover her ankles, which felt cold all over again.

"Do I get to take you somewhere? Do you have to do something with your family?"

The headlights swept across the tree trunks as he pulled onto River Road. They cruised past house after house festooned with Christmas lights; reindeer and plastic snowmen cavorted among soot-covered snowdrifts on both sides of the road. It occurred to Sophie that aside from a wreath on the front door and poinsettia plants in the foyer, Henry's house was remarkably undecorated.

"Didn't you have a Christmas tree?" she asked.

"We always take it down before New Year's," he said. "My mother's allergic to pine needles but hates artificial trees. She endures her symptoms for about three days before the whole thing has to go, lights and all. Until the next year, that is."

Sophie imagined a room piled high with gifts, a page of the fairytale childhood she used to long for. Hungry to be like everyone else.

"What about it?" Henry asked, "Tomorrow, I mean?"

She reminded herself that winter solstice had already passed, which ought to mean that the worst of the dark season was behind them. *More light, coming soon.* Tomorrow would be the last day of 1966.

"It would be great," she said, "to do something with you."

He reached for her nearby hand in the car's dark space and squeezed. With her right index finger, she traced the outline of her lips, felt an electric pulse at her core. Was his body singing like this too? She didn't know how to ask.

O N THE NIGHTS Martin couldn't easily fall asleep, he sat in an old rocking chair and tuned in to the college radio station, one deejay in particular whose smoky voice reminded him of Joseph's when the years of breathing sawdust had finally caught up with him. It was the texture of his sentences as they slipped into the airwaves, smooth on one side and rough on the other; that was the way Martin tried explaining it in his notebook. But the thing was, you couldn't describe the sound in words. You had to feel it work its way inside you, both a prelude to the music coming after it and an echo of what had just been played.

The night before New Year's Eve was one of those long nights of listening. He played one of his oldest tapes: Joseph telling the story of the bridge disaster in Canada. Martin knew every pause, every sigh. The next day was Sophie's birthday, but he had no idea what to offer a girl when her heart aimed itself away from him.

Never mind, he told himself.

Maybe he could become more like his dog Bear, train himself to locate the notes too high for ordinary human ears, or too low. Maybe he could decipher how far away the source was, could tell if someone was sad or lonely just by recognizing the vibration underneath the song.

Awake in the dark, Martin vowed to be in love with the world and not any single being. He could be bigger than the place he came from, bigger than Electric City, bigger than America even, permeable and free. Something like the life that Steinmetz chose. Not an individual partner but a kind of connection to everything.

Stroking Bear's head, he leaned the chair back until it creaked in protest, sipped a beer in the after-midnight solace of his grandmother's house. Imagining he could hear the river moving even though it was miles away, imagining he could hear the scrape of branches let loose by the sharp December wind. And the fish breathing deep under the ice.

FORTIFIED AGAINST THE morning elements with long under-wear and wool pants, bundled into layers of down and fake-fur linings, Sophie told Henry she felt about as graceful as a hockey player.

"But at least we're outside!" he said, laughing. He drove them to the edge of the river where they would be meeting up with Martin, Sophie's privileged birthday request. He couldn't decide whether or not there was reason to feel jealous of the time Sophie and Martin spent together without him; Sophie's letters referred to the way Martin rarely said anything to her at school, but maybe their friendship was some hidden valuable shared only partly with Henry. Aside from the photos he'd requested, Martin's intermittent postcards sent to the boarding school address consisted of album recommendations listed in alphabetical order, printed in block letters. This may have been some kind of coded message, but Henry kept forgetting to ask Martin for the translation.

Hard to believe this place had been so drenched in green just a few months earlier, now that snow had disguised everything into anonymity. There were vague cartoonish lumps where bushes used to be, and ice-tipped trees shivering up and down the street, as though embarrassed to be so close to the blinking lights on so many evergreens.

Arriving early to have some time alone, Henry and Sophie sat in his car, parked along the curb and facing the frozen Mohawk. Lacelike patterns covered the windshield, especially at the edges, and every time Henry thought about kissing Sophie, he felt like an overheating battery. After asking her to take off her gloves, he placed a small white box in her left hand, fitting it inside her palm.

"Happy birthday, Sophie."

When she lifted the lid, she saw translucent white tissue paper gleaming with gold sparkles, delicate as fresh snow under sunlight. Folded into the tissue paper was a gold chain, fragile inside fragile. The delicate strand of links was so fine that when Sophie held the necklace up to her cheek, Henry saw how it shimmered and nearly vanished.

As if she were a gift box too, he unwrapped her scarf and touched her collarbone, the hollow of her throat.

"Can I?" he asked and fastened the clasp as though he'd been rehearsing this gesture all morning.

"It's beautiful," she said.

"So are you," he said and placed his mouth on hers, which opened with so much welcome he suddenly realized how closed the world had felt to him before now.

Once the long kiss ended, Sophie took both of Henry's hands and held them gently. That was the way they were sitting when Martin appeared carrying a huge branch of bright red winterberries posing as a bouquet of flowers. He smiled his stunning smile and planted the branch in a snow bank.

Henry and Sophie stumbled giddily out of the car, and Martin kissed Sophie on both cheeks while he retied her scarf around her neck.

"Foxes have been known to eat these," he said, pointing.

In his peripheral vision, the berries looked to Henry like drops of blood against the snow.

"Where to now?" Henry asked Sophie.

"Woods?" Martin said.

"Movies?" Henry said.

"Ice skating," she said. "Central Park."

"Iroquois Lake," Martin said. He said it twice.

AN HOUR LATER, after collecting what they needed, all three of them sat in the warming hut beside the iced-over lake at the center of Central Park, trading their boots for skates. Henry's were black and new; Sophie's were beige and many times renewed with polish to obscure the scuffmarks. Martin's were brown and double-bladed, salvaged a year earlier from the Army Navy store downtown, a remnant from someone else's discarded hockey season.

On the scarred wooden bench, Martin was quickest with the laces, tightening and knotting; ready first, he stood up with his arms outstretched for balance. Out of habit, he whistled for Bear, but then remembered the dog was at home with Annie, curled by the stove.

When Sophie stood, she could tell that one skate was still too loose; Henry reached over to tighten it for her, and she steadied herself with hands on his shoulders.

"Better now?" he said.

"Perfect now," she said.

He drew her close enough to touch her lips with his own. Just a light kiss; they were both self-conscious in front of Martin, who was circling nearby, vaguely paying attention. The rasp of his blades was both harsh and sweet, a kind of winter music.

Sophie thought that they could pretend to be in a movie about Flatlanders, a stiff breeze pushing against their blurry layers of wool, their gloves and hats. Cutting arabesques on the thick opaque surface of the lake.

"Let's dance," Henry said, releasing one of her hands and pulling slightly on the other. They were awkward together, and Martin laughed at them; then he skated backward and stopped with a flourish, head thrown back to admire the sky.

"You two can go ahead," Sophie said to both of them. "I need to practice a little on my own."

"You sure?" Henry asked, letting go of her, gesturing widely.

Sophie nodded, serious about the wobble of her ankles, preferring to fall without any witnesses. Martin glided off one way and Henry did a quick hopping run-on-ice in the opposite direction. Sophie turned her back to the open space and concentrated on her own balance. *Slow and steady*, she whispered to herself. The wind was picking up.

Martin's cap had earflaps he could pull low, shutting out voices and muffling even the knife sound of his skates. This was not something his ancestors would be doing. More likely they'd be wearing leather-strapped snowshoes, trekking among the pines. He thought of the hooded eyes of his grandmother and the suggestion of a smile on her otherwise somber visage. No matter the season, his parents stayed distant: Martine's face had long ago become impossible to conjure and Robert's was fading year after year. The tribal features he carried forward from Annie and Joseph would be passed on to someone, someday, and he would become an ancestor himself. This was a flickering hope.

Meanwhile, from an increasing distance, he stole glances at pink-cheeked Sophie as she struggled, and at Henry, who was already a dark silhouette against the trees. *We could be anywhere, anytime,* he thought. *We could be anyone.*

THE SETTLERS IN Shenahtahde were wrestling through a terrible winter, using every available fur and burning all the chopped wood and knowing the winter would still keep coming.

"How do the Indians do it?" the women asked each other.

Yet even in the midst of all that bitter cold, they shared nostalgia not for the abbreviated nights of Holland's summer but for the long nights of skating, the entire village out together in the deep dark but not minding, lanterns and a fire at the edge of the canal for warming afterward, and the ruddy faces and the laughter.

Man-made land reclaimed from the sea, metamorphosis from water into something solid enough to hold you up, becoming a place to plant potatoes, tulips. *Oh, Flatland,* where cities could be built below sea level and protected by walls, dikes, systems of control holding back the ocean. Well, holding it back most of the time, not always.

How mystifying to see that everything in the New World could be the same and not the same, children dying young here too, and women in childbirth, inescapable mortal cycles of the influenza, and yet they all struggled on. Pregnancies one after another, like the relentless revolving of seasons, life bringing itself back to life.

If it's a boy she'll give him the name of Henry. A good way to take the old name of Hendrik and make it a new name in a new country.

His lineage will become part of this other landscape, full of eccentric mountain ranges and virgin forests and wild water. She had seen the Indians come into town for trading, the faces unsmiling but not without curiosity. They were serious but not in the stern way her family was, and the women carried their babies in such a comfortable-seeming way, those obsidian eyes and wide cheekbones, the intricacy of beadwork reminding her of the lace her grandmother used to make with such patient care all through the long nights of winter, lit by kerosene lamps and candlelight until her eyes failed and she worked by feel.

And she knew this, even with a husband on yet another mission far from home: eventually, inevitably, spring would arrive all over again. There would be sweeping. A kind of pragmatic meditation, to pray at the same time as cleaning, to erase and make the surfaces an open horizon of possibility, like a sky free of clouds, thoughts flying like dust particles too small to matter, until they settled and got swept away again.

The world turning on its tilted, eternal axis.

One of the faces hanging on the wall of a long dark hallway in a forgotten corner of Henry's house looked so much like him it could almost be a fake, a ruse. Except this was real: the way features can insistently repeat themselves across generations. Missing only a beard, Henry knew he could have been mistaken for any of them, even now as he bent over his knees to touch the steel that felt colder than ice.

The face in the portrait belonged to Arendt Van Curler, after whom Henry's brother Aaron had been named. And whenever Henry thought about that, the storm clouds inside gathered until everything was gray and fierce and rattling his ribcage.

Here was the man who purchased the vast acreage that would, in a few hundred years, become Electric City. The man who brought his Dutch sensibility and passion across the Atlantic; the man who traded with the Iroquois and shared a common consideration for crops and animals and children and trees. His youngsters and his wife were living in an almost-finished house at the edge of the Stockade, and their dog had had its first litter; the fall harvest was so promising and the firewood had been well stacked to prepare for the coming winter.

Aged thirty-five, Arendt was on a trading journey in Canada, one of the last trips of the season. He missed his wife. He had a terrible cough that kept him from sleeping through the night; his boots needed repair and so did his gloves. He loved the wild beauty of this northern countryside, its jaggedly uneven horizon so much more provocative than the Flatland he memorized as a child. But the canoe in Lake Champlain was no match for this thunderstorm. Torrential freezing rain caught him completely by surprise, and it was impossible to change course, no one close enough to help.

Arendt capsized and drowned.

Henry felt like a figure in a painting by Brueghel, the one whose scarf ends fly behind him as he bends forward to pick up speed, hands clasped at the small of his back. *Imaginary Dutchman on Ice*, he thought, and his breathing found a syncopated rhythm.

In another minute or two he would circle back to gather Sophie into his arms, press their bodies together, and say the words he'd been practicing in his sleep.

I love you, he would whisper into her ear. *You, I love.*

ALL THOSE YEARS ago, Annie had showed Martin her favorite serpentine walking paths along the edge of the still-frozen river; at certain points, after slipping out of their shoes, Annie reached down to press her hands beside her own bare feet and Martin's too.

"Notice when that hardness gives way to something else, gets softer and wetter and more forgiving," she said.

But it wasn't anywhere near spring. It was the coldest part of December; it was the day before the start of a new year; it was Sophie's birthday. So Martin didn't take time to study the ice, to make use of what Annie had taught him about the texture of seasons. He skated away from Sophie, away from Henry.

By the time he realized something was wrong, *off*, he was on the far circumference of Iroquois Lake. *The frozen almost frozen lake.* He turned to look for Sophie first, to wave her back toward the safe embankment. But then he heard as much as saw the rupture where Henry's blades broke through, knew in an instant the deadly jolt of that urgent water, blue black and ravenous. The weight of Henry's clothes, his skates and all that gravity.

Moving low and fast, Martin got as close as he dared before lying down on the ice just the way he was supposed to; he snaked toward infinity on his belly, and it took much too long for Sophie to get there to hold on to Martin's legs with her own not strong enough why not strong enough arms.

Henry disappearing at the edge of the world.

HENRY'S FAMILY HAS a mausoleum at the Vale Cemetery, dove gray and solid, already sheltering the ghost of a dead child, though not a single person dares speak of this, especially not now. An elaborate carved angel graces the oversized doorway. Her serene face is looking up, not down; she seems so calm and unconcerned. It's a good thing, this marble house of the dead, because the ground is too frozen to dig open.

For the funeral, Gloria Van Curler wears a black veil over her face so Sophie can't see her eyes. But she already knows what they look like.

The ice is everywhere, everywhere.

THREE

THE FIRST MONTH of 1967 became Sophie's very own black-out. She fell mute, just like the televisions and stereos and every appliance up and down the Eastern Seaboard all the way back in early November of 1965. An eternity ago. Spending entire days curled in the corner of her darkened bedroom, Sophie couldn't find any language for her grief.

Although her daughter had told her so little about the boy before the accident, almost nothing, Miriam read Henry's obituary in the *Electric City Gazette*. There was discreet mention of an older brother who had died, years before.

Both of Sophie's parents remained patient in the silence. Miriam brought tea, toast, and broth. But after a week passed, she gently urged Sophie to consider going back to some of her classes, give her mind a place to focus.

"The guidance counselor authorized an extended absence, but maybe too much time away will do more harm than good," Miriam whispered, sitting on the edge of Sophie's bed.

David stood in the doorway of the room. "Shivah lasts seven days for a reason," he said. "I'm not saying you have to bounce back. But little by little, life goes on."

It's too late, Sophie thought, *too late to explain anything.*

Her mother reached for Sophie's hand under the heavy winter blankets. "You'll rediscover love," Miriam said, her voice gentle. "It doesn't seem possible right now, and you probably don't believe me. But your father and I are proof. You can lose your entire world and still, eventually, you can be happy."

Sophie kept her eyes closed, forcing herself to listen.

Her mother's hand held on as she spoke. "The heart is the most resilient organ in the body."

David could believe in a formula for mourning, but even science had its limits.

Sophie remembered Miriam talking about her best friend Greta Meyer who hadn't made it out of Holland during the war. She admitted this was the one person—aside from relatives—she found it impossible to get over losing. Every October 11, on what would have been Greta's birthday, Miriam lit a memorial candle and wept.

What about Greta Meyer? Sophie wanted to ask her mother, who was claiming that happiness was out there ahead of her, somewhere.

The answer seemed obvious, and irrefutable. *Certain deaths stay with you forever.*

Senior year had resumed in early January, but Sophie only managed to return by the middle of February. When she received her letter of admission into Union College's premed program in March, she read it with so much detachment the welcome might as well have been addressed to someone else, a stranger whose name she didn't recognize. That person had applied in some earlier lifetime. She was nobody Sophie knew.

Conversely, the public library felt too familiar, too much like a story she simply wanted to erase. She begged Miriam to call and tell Mrs. Richardson that Sophie wouldn't be coming back to work. The only possible source of comfort for Sophie was exactly the person who felt most remote, off-limits as though he were composed of the machinery inside her father's laboratory. If she allowed herself even a thought of leaning into Martin's arms, in the same instant, a pounding in her temples began. No matter her certainty the two friends had never been rivals competing for her, not overtly. The very image of being consoled by Martin over Henry's death struck her as the ultimate betrayal.

Occasionally, catching a glimpse of herself in the mirror, she tried to see if she could recognize the hollow face staring back. It even seemed that her eyes had turned a browner shade of green, her inner flame extinguished.

One morning in late March, with a burst of momentum, she decided to volunteer some hours every week at Ellis Hospital in a candy striper uniform. Perhaps this minor introduction to life inside the world of medicine would restore her, or at least allow an alternate version of herself to begin again.

She delivered food trays and took them away, offering rehearsed comments on her way in and out of the patients' rooms, giving herself the illusion that she was needed. The new routines brought a degree of ballast: stainless steel carts and bright fluorescent lights; the way someone was always sitting at the nurse's station, no matter the time of day or night.

"You're such a steady girl," Susan Yates said to her one Monday afternoon. She was the head nurse in the Department of Internal Medicine and the one who organized Sophie's schedule. Around fifty years old, without a wedding ring or any other jewelry, dark-blond hair pinned neatly away from her face, Susan was the kind of shapeless person whom Sophie could never picture wearing anything besides that blue-white uniform. Her existence outside the hospital was unimaginable, and she never asked Sophie anything about her life, her family, or her schooling. She had no idea that Henry had died. That Sophie was in a state of barely manageable grief.

Somewhere she was dimly aware that her fascination with all things medical was rescuing her from a debilitating depression. An instinctive curiosity stayed alive even when the rest of her was hibernating, gone so far underground there seemed no sign of reemergence.

Little by little, Sophie felt the earth tipping toward the sun. Maybe it was the vividness of forsythia that brought her back. Maybe it was the scent of lilacs.

MARTIN COULDN'T DECIDE which was less forgivable: having been there helpless on the lake, or the wish to have been blameless somewhere else. In the middle of long January nights, he was tormented by a fraction of relief that Henry was dead. All those times he had tolerated the choice Sophie made, and all the ways he'd deliberately made his own choice not to be anyone's competition.

A few times just before dawn, waking from yet another nightmare of paralysis—whispered voices calling *Help Me, Help Me*—Martin visited the shale-strewn cliff edge overlooking the Mohawk, pushed by the longing to find refuge in a place high above the frozen water.

Frozen almost frozen.

He had missed the signs.

Even by the end of February, separate in their grief, Martin found that he and Sophie still didn't have the heart to be near one another. After nearly two months of distance, he made attempts to reconnect them, inviting Sophie to meet for hot chocolate or to take a walk through the scattering of naked birch and oak and maple behind the high school. But their once-companionable silence felt strained now, full of thick absence.

Sitting side by side at the diner's counter, they ordered by pointing at the menu; they exchanged no more than a few words before leaving their ceramic mugs of cocoa half-finished and then parting wordlessly on the sidewalk out front. The walk in the woods was another abandoned effort: both kept slowing their steps as though tranquilized, and Martin kept wishing that he was alone under the trees instead of listening to Sophie's labored breath nearby.

Even Bear lacked the power to distract or sustain him. School was never a place Martin cared about in the best of times. Standing for the pledge was beyond excruciating. When all of March went by without seeing even the back of each other's heads in homeroom, he was sure that Sophie realized something was up.

"I did," he said, when Sophie called to ask if he had dropped out.

"What will you do?" she asked.

Martin shrugged, tossing his hair around, though Sophie couldn't see him.

"I've got a full-time job downtown," he said. "At the plant." *The Company, of course. Where else.*

"Did you already start?" she asked.

"Got my first crappy paycheck yesterday," he said. He guessed she could feel the acceptance in his voice, just alongside the resignation.

"I don't know what to say," she admitted. "I didn't realize you wanted to give up on graduating."

"Konnorónhkwa." He spoke too quietly for her to hear. *I show you that I care.*

"What was that?"

He waited, deciding. "You're the one with big plans," he said, instead of the other things. Time was curving itself between them, sending them in separate directions.

"I mean it," he said. "Someone's got to get out of here alive."

G RADUATION DAY, JUNE 17, was heavy with humidity and the threat of rain. As she tried her best to smile, posing for the same photo over and over again, Sophie doubted this was the best moment of their lives. Miriam had managed to persuade David to attend the ceremony even though it was held on a Saturday and required him to ride in a car, violating the Sabbath. Sophie appreciated the significance of his gesture, and stood in time for her name to be announced among the students graduating with highest honors; she hoped this made her father feel that his exception was worth the trouble.

In truth, the communal air of celebration seemed not quite to reach the surface of her skin, remote as the syllables of a foreign language or the view from a passing car through a sealed window. Every time she saw one of her classmates with a boyfriend's arm around her waist, a flash of pain streaked through her solar plexus. Fingering the gold chain that rested on her collarbone, Sophie touched the empty place where a charm might have dangled.

Turning down invitations to two graduation parties, Sophie kept thinking of Martin, punching his time card in and out; their high school was some distant country he no longer lived in. She had reached the point at which he was the only person she wanted to see, but every time she called, his phone rang into empty space. It occurred to her that he was working night shifts and sleeping during the days, avoiding her, avoiding anyone. But then he called Sophie's house three days after graduation and asked her to meet him at the place across the street from Henry's house. The Steinmetz property.

"Now?" Her heart thrummed so hard she was sure he could hear it through the phone.

Martin cleared his throat. "Eleven tonight."

Sophie hesitated only for a moment, then said, "I'll be there." All day she kept seeing the fox's flaring red tail like some sort of beacon, pointing to a memory from when Henry was alive. She felt as much as heard the cicadas at sunset, and when the first fireflies winked on, she imagined she could hear their invisible wings. The evening air vibrated.

Finally, when it was time to meet Martin, she left the house quietly, carrying her sandals in one hand and a sweatshirt in the other. She passed the dining room table where her father had all of his belated income tax piles spreading like a map of the year. Her parents were in bed watching the news, and she let them think she'd gone to bed too, getting onto her bicycle so she could ride toward Martin in the damp night. It was still hot at 11 PM, and all of her senses were alert to the ripeness of the earth. She pedaled fast and felt wisps of her hair lifting away from her neck; her bike tires hummed on the warm pavement.

Hardly any porch lights were on. In nearly every house she passed, a window leaked flickering blue light from a television set. The same blue light was filling rooms all over town, all over America. Overhead, the moon glowed in a blurry sphere, reminding her of the Company logo. She studied its face while she rode, and what came to her was the idea that the moon looked bewildered. For a moment, she prayed that Henry's death might float quietly behind them, with Iroquois Lake almost restored to its innocence.

Sophie's elongated shadow appeared before she did, an animated sketch of arms and legs on the sidewalk. Then Martin struck a match and took a deep drag of the tightly rolled joint he'd brought along.

"Want some?" he said, holding it toward Sophie.

She blushed into the darkness, feeling like a little girl afraid of a dangerous game. "No thanks," she said.

Martin shrugged. "Helps me think," he said.

She joined him cross-legged on the sidewalk, leaning against a rocky wall at the edge of Henry's family's undulating lawn, their backs to the hill that led up to his house. There was an especially dense pool of darkness at the center of the Steinmetz property, as if the space once occupied by the house had swallowed the night sky. She couldn't help searching for movement at the base of the pine trees, beckoning to the fox with an unspoken request.

The cicadas had suddenly gone to sleep, along with the rest of the neighborhood. It seemed Martin and Sophie were the only ones still up, the moon a distant spotlight for their small stage. He had something to tell her but she had no idea what it would be.

"I've been drafted," he said, and the last word was a gunshot, a cracking sound splitting the silence.

"No," Sophie whispered.

Martin inhaled again, held his breath, and then released a blue-gray plume of smoke into the night air. *It's true,* the smoke said.

Sophie looked over at Martin's bare feet, the bottom edge of his jeans frayed with white threads touching his brown skin. She thought his toes were the most elegant shapes she'd never noticed before, and she studied them for a long moment, seeing how the second and third toes were the same length.

"I'll come back eventually," Martin said, and at first Sophie didn't understand what he was talking about, thought he meant he would serve a tour of duty and come home on leave. But then her head cleared.

"You mean Canada?" she whispered, and Martin released another ghost of smoke.

"Where else?" he said. The effort in his voice had become audible, one flat note in a symphony.

Sophie wasn't surprised by his choice not to become a soldier, a choice to stay alive and also not to kill. But draft dodging meant it was possible he could never come back to America, or else risk being thrown into jail. That very day, Muhammad Ali had been convicted of evading the draft and sentenced to five years in prison. He was one of the more famous ones, amidst a rising tide of refusal. But a crime was a crime.

To lose Henry under the ice and then say goodbye to Martin too: Sophie didn't see how she would be able to continue. A pair of losses bigger than any container she could hope to hold them in, her head, her heart.

"I don't believe you," she said, not looking at him. "I don't believe in eventually."

Helpless, she couldn't even guess how the underground was organized. When she pictured Martin climbing into some anonymous car, watched it like a movie in slow motion; there was no role for her at all. They had told him how it would go, and he told it to her so she could envision the scenes in order, frame by frame. But she wasn't allowed to be anywhere near the pickup point, and there was no plan for her except to stay all the way out of it.

Before they separated that night, Martin had one last thing to do. Reaching into his canvas shoulder bag, he carefully removed a cluster of four feathers that had been tied together with silk thread.

"Eagle," he said simply, and wrapped her fingers around the place where the feathers were knotted into one. Four directions scattered and joining, dispersed and reuniting.

"For my sake," he whispered, daring her to love him at least that much. "Just promise you'll keep moving forward."

Sophie nodded, tears welling, but he said that wasn't good enough, he said she had to put it in writing and sign it. She had to make it real. Martin pulled out his notebook and turned to a new page, but she was shaking too much.

"I can't," she said.

"Swear to me out loud then," he said, when her fingers gripped hard around his Eagle's gift. "Say you'll go on."

He gazed at her without blinking, refusing to look away.

"Promise you'll come home," she whispered.

MARTIN SINGING. BREATH of his grandmother inside him, and the grandmothers before her, ancestral spirit pouring through. Certain notes expanded his chest until he felt broad as a mountain, and the melodies stayed so fully present he awoke to them and fell asleep with them. This was how he left Electric City, how he prepared to say the rest of his goodbyes.

Like the movement of his blood, pulsing and flowing, present behind his closed eyelids and in the tender spot below his jawbone.

A river. The only one he had left.

Being "sealed" was how Annie described it. Ancient energies stored in rhythmic packages, cellular memories, and the body would never forget it for the rest of its life. He wondered what kind of music might bring him closer to the full story of Martine's death, the mother who had vanished before they ever knew each other. And although he supposed she must have known more than a little of him while he had floated inside her body, it seemed possible that even her ghost wouldn't want to be found.

"Umbilical connections aren't necessarily the ones that last," that's what Robert would probably say.

Strange and yet not strange to find himself about to head so far north. Maybe his great-uncle's restless spirit, long-drowned in Canadian water, was looking to attach itself to Martin's edges. Maybe this was simply a way to practice stretching his own reach across greater and greater distances. It was Sophie's absence he expected to miss the most, but in the pause between songs, Martin couldn't stop feeling particles of Henry holding a place inside. Matter, which had never been created or destroyed.

The unlikeliest of friendships remained like some broken bone that resisted healing. A name carved into the skin of a branch.

"This war will end and you'll find your way clear of it," Annie said to him, kissing the top of her grandson's head when he bent low for her blessing. "I'd rather see you a tormented ghost than an obedient ghost."

"I'd rather not be a ghost at all," Martin replied. "Not just yet anyway."

Bear would stay with Annie, and cousin Isaiah would keep an eye on both of them, and those were the pieces of his life Martin had to surrender in the name of staying free. It made no sense and it made perfect sense. *Brother Beware.*

At Midge's house just after sunrise, he stood with his hand on the canoe that still hung from the rafters of her shed, asking her not to mind saving it a while longer. She knew better than to try talking him out of this departure.

"We have to cure ourselves," she said, not bothering to tell him she was quoting Joseph and Steinmetz both.

When Martin turned away, not wanting to see her tears, she placed her left palm between the wings of his shoulder blades, letting it rest there for a long moment. By chance, that was the same way he settled both hands on Bear's solid ribcage, thanking him for every breath they had shared on this earth.

He would learn the names of trees and rocks all over again, record his footsteps in an altered landscape. The residue of everyone he loved could be saved in his own body without regret or pain. If he traveled with just enough weightlessness, the air itself could keep him aloft.

T HE CAR WAS a Plymouth, dusty green and with New York license plates, several years old but in decent shape, only a couple of rusting dents in the chrome of the left rear fender, and a web of hairline cracks in the windshield. A twenty-something woman was driving. She had short brown hair and sunglasses and a forced smile; she wore a white scarf tied loosely around her neck and a navy blue cardigan over a T-shirt and blue jeans.

An orange tin lunchbox took up space on the seat beside her, and a cocoa-skinned baby slept in a car seat in the back, mounded with pastel blankets. The woman seemed surprisingly calm, her hands on the steering wheel and her smile betraying nothing.

You've done this before. Martin was surprised to see the baby but didn't say a word. The woman got out of the car so that Martin could take the wheel, and she climbed into the passenger side after double-checking on the baby.

"He's such a good sleeper in that car seat," she said. "Lucky."

"Okay," Martin said. "Are we all set?"

He had tossed a duffel bag into the trunk, nothing large or bulky in case anyone checked. *We're just visiting relatives across the border,* they would say. *An overnight is all.*

*T*HERE HAD TO *be a balance,* thought Proteus, *between morbid imaginings and a genuine sense of death's imminence.* Not even doctors could predict the timing of the Grim Reaper's arrival, but this profound weakness in his legs, the night sweats, and waking dreams—these were symptoms impossible to misconstrue. Long-suffering Corinne Hayden had pleaded with him for decades to create some order out of his chaos; if this was indeed an illness from which he would never recover, there was no more room for delay.

While the majority of his collection of glass-plate photographs had been carefully sorted into albums, his more recent work—that is, after he switched to film—were prints piled into boxes, awaiting further catego-rization. With shaky handwriting, he began labeling envelopes, to make a start: *Aqueduct, Erie Canal Skaters, Streetcar, Ferris Wheel, Portrait of Sir, Camp Mohawk.* Here was an entire group of images he wished to give to Joseph Longboat, a necessarily incomplete visual record of their several decades together, their overlapping stories.

Frequently he had to rest from the effort of breathing. During one of these pauses, to Steinmetz's astonishment, Joseph himself appeared at the bedroom door, holding a finger to his lips.

"What's the secret?" Proteus whispered. His friend leaned in close to say they had to slip away from the house, just for an hour.

Nobody knows. Joseph silently mouthed the words.

Steinmetz understood that they had to avoid being seen by any of the Hayden household, who would surely try to stop them. And for good reason. How would he find even a fraction of the energy required to make it all the way down a flight of stairs, much less into the chill of a late fall afternoon, and not to mention wherever Joseph planned for the fugitives to go.

"I'll carry you," Joseph said. And lifted Proteus into his arms.

He might have been dreaming. Wrapped in a quilt warm as fur, Steinmetz allowed himself to be cradled while Joseph serenely walked them away from the house and along the wooded path. Half dozing, he occasionally looked up to observe leaves drifting toward the ground in shafts of filtered sunlight. There was a timeless hush surrounding them, a hesitation between the warning frost and the first snow. Joseph's stride was even-paced, limber-jointed, and smooth; there was no sense of burden but merely a determined momentum. The river wasn't far now, and the canoe was waiting.

Lighter than ever, once again easily mistaken for a child, Proteus floated on water the way amber floated. The geode whose beauty was hidden until split open. The two-row wampum belt, flowing in both directions; the exchange between spirit and flint. Always echoing and repeating: lightning-shaped and fox-shaped, mirror-splintered and time-bent.

Joseph guided the canoe by walking beside it, thigh-deep, tracing the shoreline. No need to go far—just beyond the reeds so Steinmetz, as if alone, could lean back and gaze at the sky, spot an eagle's distant pinpoint. A farewell view from the water, looking up to the sweet sanctuary of Camp Mohawk.

"Grandfather. Thunder Chief, Hinon," Joseph said softly.

The light was leaving so fast. Joseph pulled the canoe back to its resting place on the slope and lifted his friend into his arms again to carry him home.

THE CASSETTE TAPE Sophie received from Martin was so richly layered with sound she could close her eyes and feel they were together in the same room. She sensed how close the walls were, and she could hear which floorboards creaked along with the scrape of a chair pushed back from the table. She heard him fill a glass of water from the tap, and even his inhalations were audible before he spoke. In her mind's eye he was carrying the microphone as though it were a long-stemmed rose. Or a branch of berries.

Woven into the electrostatic ribbon, someone was playing piano in the next room or maybe another apartment, practicing "Für Elise" the way Simon used to all those years ago when their parents made him take lessons. Piano for him and ballet for her, though neither of them stayed with it. Hearing those familiar faint notes in the background on Martin's tape, she felt their old childhood worlds were blended again, at least for a while.

"It's just another September up here, Sophie. One of those perfect fall mornings that's like someone warning you not to miss out on the light because it's about to disappear for a while."

The piano player paused on the other side of a thin wall. Martin swallowed from his glass.

"The neighbor's cat left a dead mouse on my doorstep late last night, ears and tail quite delicately chewed off, and I'm trying to figure out what it means. An offering, maybe. Some cat wanting me to know he's ready to make friends."

He laughed, a soft sound.

"This cassette is my offering to you, Sophie. A voice in your ear so you won't forget me."

"How could I forget you?" she said back to the tape player. *Anything but that.*

"Für Elise" started over again imperfectly, keyboard notes under some stranger's fingertips, someone who lived audibly close to Martin in a nameless city in Ontario or Quebec, a place kept secret from her. She was grateful anyway, telling herself that not knowing meant extra safety for Martin, protection from jail, or worse: from war. She'd rather he stayed in Canada for good if it meant he didn't have to kill anyone, or get killed himself.

"You know why there's no return address on this, right?" he whispered at the end.

There was a bittersweet melody in his long-distance voice, a song she wanted to memorize. And then the tape hissed into her ear, empty of voice and piano, full of magnetic dust.

Much of the time she couldn't differentiate between losing Henry to death or losing Martin to the northern lights. On Friday nights with her parents, Sophie prayed aloud to the holy god of her ancestors; silently, she prayed for help from the dead left in Europe, the ones who *didn't* make it out alive.

Although her first year at Union College had begun, she was still living at home, struggling to keep her gaze on the future. Simon's choice of cross-country distance seemed impossible to consider. Union's eight-year program would relay her straight through college and into medical school, relieving her of the decision-making that paralyzed her in advance. Instead of a shimmering uncertainty, Sophie could yield to the river closest to home, the one already in motion.

T HAT SEPTEMBER 1967 audiotape from Martin was the only one he ever sent, even though he had intended for it to be the first of many. Every time he sat down in the blank-walled kitchen with the coiling microphone cord attached to a new cassette player, his mouth wouldn't open. Hopelessness caught in his chest and tightened his jaw, convincing him he had no right to whisper into Sophie's ear. Not with all those miles between them, not without anything palpable to share. If he couldn't hold on, he was supposed to let go.

He imagined Annie saying, "You can't be the tree trunk for anyone until you can be your own."

By October he had found a job with the phone company, climbing telephone poles all day and listening to the wires humming, subtle messages being sent back and forth, faster than thoughts. On a Saturday morning in early November he struck up a conversation at a truck stop diner with a woman named Lucy Justine, whose weathered face and chapped hands reminded him of nobody.

He found out that she'd been living for a dozen years in a remote cabin where she raised huskies and trained them for sled-dog races, pulling teams hitched to her pickup on the snow-covered back roads of Northern Ontario. Each of them seemed surprised to be willing to talk about themselves at all, a pair of hermits looking into the wary eyes of a mirror. They'd ordered the same meal, cheese omelet with hash browns and toast, black coffee and bacon on the side.

In the diner's parking lot, when her truck wouldn't start, Martin in his Ma Bell 4x4 came to her rescue, and surprised them both a second time by following her home on a black-iced road. He found himself invited into a bed that she admitted hadn't held a man in years. She didn't apologize for the indoor outhouse-style toilet or the fact that she hauled her water supply once a week in her pickup.

He was confused to see that Lucy Justine's dogs slept outside the house, in sheds she had built herself.

"They're animals and I'm not," she explained, utterly serious. "Other people have pets, but I'm not other people."

Martin didn't bother trying to describe what his life with Bear had been like. In the morning, he watched her train her best team of blue-eyed dogs, seeing that she used a vocabulary of tasks and skills, never playing favorites, never being overtly affectionate. Nothing like the way Bear had anticipated his every move, always awake when Martin opened his eyes in the morning, happy to be alive and in each other's company.

Bear had stayed behind in Electric City with Martin's grandmother, a separation as brutal and necessary as saying goodbye to Sophie. Now twenty years old, Martin had begun imagining this was what his own father had done, staying gone one year at a time, practicing solitude as a kind of penance for being alive. The idea of being motivated by so much guilt made Martin furious as well as mystified, but even if he could have asked Robert if any of it was true, Annie would have shaken her bony fist at him.

"You don't need to ask favors from the ones gone missing," she had told him. "They do what they please."

He hoped that his father had reconciled with loss more completely than his son had been able to. After a while, the ghost of Martine must have drifted away like smoke, leaving no residue at all.

With minimal discussion, Martin and Lucy agreed he could move in for the winter. They joked it was a way to cash in on body heat, reduce her need for cord after cord of firewood to make it through the longest nights.

Trudging deep into the snow wearing thigh-high boots, Lucy used a rifle for target practice with a row of old beer bottles. She tramped through the drifts to shovel snow off the woodshed, propped a row of new green-glass targets. She loaned Martin a gun to use too, but it never felt quite comfortable in his arms.

"You could improve a lot more if you cared to," Lucy pointed out.

"I know," Martin said. It was the one-year anniversary of Henry's death, and once again Sophie's birthday. He was farther than ever now, beyond a mountain range of pines.

The truth was Lucy had always preferred to live alone with the huskies outside and the open space all around; the time she spent with Martin was an experiment. Exactly four months from the day of his moving in, she told him the whole thing wasn't right for her after all. She just wanted the dogs for company, she said. She knew their language best.

Martin tucked his long braid under the collar of his coat, gave her a rough hug that in his mind translated into something like mutual relief.

He would probably miss the rasp of her voice calling commands to the huskies, her whistles and shouts. He would miss watching their speed and grace. But he was content to see for all of them that parting was so effortless.

From that spring onward, he took to wearing his braid inside his shirt, the flannel collar resting just where the braid began at the nape of his neck. It was a reminder that he preferred to keep himself to himself, not giving anyone else the right to see his private body. For some reason this felt similar to the way he had reclaimed his left-handedness after so many teachers had tried forcing him to use his right.

"You'll be thankful later on," they insisted, but his right hand said *No* and his left took back the pencil with simple defiance, because it knew better. *There is no point*, he had said to himself, relaxing his tormented right hand and feeling the blood come back reluctantly into his tense fingers. When he told her about it, his grandmother had nodded and said nothing, just took both of his hands and folded them into her own, brown to brown, strong and tender.

Things Martin kept with him:

One blue-inked sketch of Sophie and Henry, from that Lake George weekend out of time.

A strand of knotted gray rope he used as a toy when Bear was a puppy. Coiled into a fist-sized shape and no longer used for anything except remembering.

A Blackstone cigar box that once belonged to Steinmetz, with its time capsule of aromas: spicy, ashy, sour, and sweet.

The memory of the "anonymous" American GI on the radio explaining: "We had to destroy the village in order to save it."

His handmade canvas bag, torn and repaired over and over. Martin's own scent woven into its fibers. The smooth leather tobacco pouch, always.

His molecular history, not visible to the eye.

After nearly two years of construction, a new bridge appeared on the Mohawk River. One day everyone crossed the river using the old bridge, and the next time they crossed there was a slightly confusing diversion around some traffic signs, a battered orange plastic cone or two, and they were on the new bridge, with the same old river down below.

The sounds were different: Sophie sensed someone had adjusted the dial on the radio station or turned the volume way up. The wooden slats and metal roadway had been replaced by asphalt over concrete and steel. They played a new tune now, car after car, trucks and buses and delivery vans. She wondered if the pigeons and ducks noticed. Maybe the slow-moving fish gliding silently through the shadows cast by the steel trusses and the wires—maybe all of them were listening. Maybe not.

Sophie watched for a second package from Martin that never arrived. Returning home at the end of a long day of classes—molecular biology, organic chemistry, anatomy, statistics—she would reach for the mail, hopeful and hungry. Month by month, she pretended not to care that the letters were never from Canada.

New Year's Eve was a landmine, an explosion waiting to happen. *You could have at least called from an anonymous pay phone,* Sophie thought. *Or you could have invited me to visit, even for a day. I would have used an alias, climbed on a northbound bus in a heartbeat.* She blamed Martin for losing track of the difference between courage and cruelty.

Simon told her he had tried hitchhiking to Electric City from California, but turned around again almost immediately, claiming that the West Coast was the only sanctuary he wanted.

"I'm never coming back," he confided to her. She couldn't help feeling that the sentence might have been Martin's too.

When the wet spring of 1968 bloomed in silence, not even a picture postcard with a pretty stamp, she grew convinced he must be happy to have disappeared. Giving up one home for another: people did it all the time.

One Friday night after dinner with her parents, her father said that the only way he knew to avoid despair was to put himself to work in the service of something greater.

"Apply the gift of your mind," he said.

She touched the lacquered edges of the sign on the wall of David's study, the one that said THINK. There was a small fluorescent desk lamp that her father always turned on before the Sabbath began; he left the light burning throughout the night. Standing close enough to touch it, she had to resist the urge to switch it off.

"I thought that's what I've been doing," she said. "Mind over matter."

David sat down on the cot that was used for overnight guests, causing a complaint from the springs. "Edison always kept a couch in his office," he said. "He believed naps were necessary for problem solving."

"Maybe I should try sleeping in here," Sophie said, only half kidding. In fact, she had finally begun looking for a studio apartment within a block or two of Union, a long-delayed decision to move out of her parents' house. They could all stop pretending it was convenient and inexpensive for her to keep living at home. A change of scenery might shake off the stupor of inertia once and for all.

Miriam stepped into the study, handing an orange to her husband and another one to her daughter. She had her own beliefs about problem solving, usually involving the taste of something sweet.

"I just heard on the local news," Miriam said. "Instead of being torn down, the Van Curler Hotel is being redesigned as a community college."

Sophie's belly tightened at the mention of the name. She had always assumed that one of these days she would bump into Gloria or Arthur somewhere in town—but so far, nothing. Once she was supposed to attend a dance performance at the Unitarian Society, a gleaming white building located alongside the Steinmetz property and nearly opposite the Van Curlers' house. She planned on arriving early and sitting on the stone bench under the trees, waiting for a sign. The performance had been canceled due to a blizzard, and Sophie never saw the fox again.

"You see?" Miriam said, while Sophie deliberately avoided her mother's eyes. "The world goes on."

A week after the death of Robert Kennedy, whose assassination followed too close on the heels of the death of Martin Luther King Jr., Sophie made a decision to talk to the river.

If Martin could make a new life, so can I. If my parents could do it, so can I.

She sat on a slab of shale at the edge of the water and gave herself a stern lecture as though Martin were admonishing her, cheering her on.

"Get yourself through premed, then medical school, all of it. There are always going to be sick people and you might as well be one of the healers."

She chanted words like *photosynthesis, leukocytes, autoimmune system. Electrocardiogram.* As if the syllables themselves could keep her from giving up.

In her blank new apartment on Jay Street, for the first two nights in a row, Sophie dreamed that Martin was climbing steel towers while she was the one on the ground, holding someone's life in her hands.

S OPHIE WAS ASSISTING a research project in Ellis Hospital, wired on caffeine and too little sleep. It was a late July afternoon in 1969, when everybody in Electric City was talking about the Apollo space mission. Late that night there would be an astronaut landing on the moon.

Following a stainless steel trolley being pushed down the hall on the fourth floor, Sophie watched the candy striper move so slowly that the five vases were shivering but not toppling. Roses and daisies and plenty of ferns, not original in the slightest, but designed to add something representing nature within these otherwise sterile and bland walls. She saw the way the volunteer's cheerful silhouette promised comfort, and flashed back to that brief phase of her own life, viewed from a vast distance, as if through a telescope instead of a microscope.

The entire floor was eerily quiet. Even the nurses' station was in a kind of stasis, no code reds or blues on the intercom. Just a steady beeping from several monitors, and Sophie's rubber-soled shoes on the waxed floor, the hushed wheels of the cart ahead of her. In each room she passed, visitors were sitting bedside with televisions turned to low. In place of war images, the screens were all depicting the anxious hopeful faces of the team at NASA, who were in turn mesmerized by their own screens tracking the path of a fragile capsule in space.

For a moment, Sophie perceived the brick hospital building with its numbered wings and hallways, its beige walls and fluorescent lights, as though it were the entire planet. Someone was giving birth and nearby someone else was dying. Strangers lay asleep in identical beds, while others lay awake in pain. X-rays and bandages, blood and saline. Machines were pouring light through bones and extracting toxins. No wonder people brought flowers when they visited this place, an attempt to bring reminders of life inside. And maybe to remind themselves that they were the ones who could step back outside the elevators and return to the world.

In the neuropsychiatry ward, most of the patients were sleeping. With special permission arranged by her psychology professor, Sophie was allowed to read charts as long as she didn't disturb the silence. It was the fourth room that startled her. A sad woman in a lavender nightgown, IV pole on one side of the bed, its thin line disappearing under the sheets. Her wide open blue eyes didn't blink when Sophie walked into the room. The volunteer placed a vase of six pink roses on the nightstand and left without a word.

Though much older and paler, mouth downturned as though wearing a mask, she was unmistakable: minus pearls and makeup, minus cashmere sweater and elegant upswept hair.

"Hi, Mrs. Van Curler," Sophie said gently, and the woman's expression seemed to snap into focus, some shift of thought or emotion bringing her back to the present. She looked at Sophie and smiled, but it was more like a question than an acknowledgment.

"Hello," she said, and then, "Do I know you?"

Sophie was embarrassed now, for both of them, and regretting her awkward use of Henry's mother's name; after all, she was just a premedical student with a chart in her hands. She tugged at her nametag and leaned a bit closer to her bed so it could be easily read. Gloria shook her head and lifted one hand out from beneath the sheets to wave it weakly in the air.

"No reading glasses, my dear."

"Sophie Levine," said Sophie.

Gloria waited, giving no sign of recognition.

"I'm—I mean, I was—a friend of Henry's." Speaking the words out loud, her cheeks felt hot, and she wanted to grab the sentence out of the air. Nothing to do but keep going now.

"You gave me my first glass of champagne. I was seventeen. It was my birthday." Then her throat constricted. She couldn't say it had been the day before New Year's Eve, not to Henry's mother.

Gloria shut her eyes, and a long moment passed. Sophie feared that the stricken woman might actually want her to go away, and she looked toward the door where the cart had already moved on.

"I remember," Henry's mother said, her eyelids fluttering but still closed. "Of course I do."

The IV bag dripped so slowly, like the end of a rainy day. A call button beeped from the room next door.

"Sophie Levine," Gloria said, and then whispered something to herself, far too softly for Sophie to understand. She looked toward the ceiling. "Can I ask you a favor?" The one free hand waved again, and Sophie saw her veins through her nearly translucent skin. She gestured toward the closet. "My bathrobe?"

Sophie retrieved it, lavender silk that matched her nightgown, filmy and soft and exactly what she would want Gloria to have, even here in the hospital. The IV made it impossible to put on the sleeves, though, so the robe draped like a shawl across her shoulders, and she winced a bit when Sophie fluffed the pillows. Her sparse white hair floated about her. There was a deep purple bruise on her chest, spreading in an oblong just below the neckline of her gown. No complaint, however, just that glimpse of pain, followed by her smile, restored.

"Such weak hearts we have," she said.

Sophie's own heart pounded fiercely in reply.

"Your heart seems fine," Sophie said, pointing first to the monitor's steady rhythm and then at the chart she held in her hands.

"On Arthur's side," she began, and then paused in search of the missing detail while the equipment beeped into the empty space. Here was a woman who had lost both of her children, first and last. What chart could make any sense of that?

"When the cardiologist located Arthur's blockage," Gloria said, "he discovered that my husband's heart had repaired itself."

Sophie felt her pulse racing, as she suddenly pictured the four of them seated around Henry's dining room table. The large chandelier. The color of the lobster bisque with saffron. The somber-faced paintings on the walls and the linen napkin twisting into a knot between her hands.

"Repaired itself, like a bypass?" she said.

Gloria nodded.

"I didn't know that was possible," Sophie said.

Gloria lifted her colorless hand again. "It can only happen at a certain age," she said. "That's what the doctors explained. The heart has to have enough time—"

Sophie's breath caught again, and Gloria's mind seemed to turn a corner.

"I need to ask one more favor," Henry's mother said. She paused, held Sophie's gaze with her own. "Will you stay with me?"

MARTIN WAS UP high on a telephone pole, canvas vest full of pockets and tool belt so familiar after almost two years that he could hardly remember wearing anything else. There was heavy weather visible on the eastern horizon, far enough not to be dangerous but dark enough to observe. Wires stretching in both directions against the pale sky looked like sheet music waiting for notes.

He remembered the time his entire freshman class had made a simulated thunderstorm in the high school gymnasium. Everyone sat on the polished wooden floor, arranged in a circle so they could see each other, and the phys ed teacher at the center turned with open arms to gesture and guide the transitions. A few hundred students rubbed their palms together, snapped their fingers, slapped palms on their thighs, stamped their feet. From sprinkling to dropping to pounding to rumbling, and then reversing their way to hushed calm. Conducted like a choir, hands and feet as instruments, becoming a force of nature, imitating—as if they could summon it—rain.

He tried and failed to recall if his grandfather had ever shown him how to do a rain dance.

Now it was July 20, the night of the moon landing. Out on the remote road with a partner, having worked overtime on storm-wrecked telephone lines, both of them were too far from home. When the truck's static-filled radio voice said, "In a few minutes we'll all be witnessing history," Patrick called up to Martin that it was time to go.

Within moments, Martin was beside him and Patrick in the driver's seat had sharply steered them onto a dirt road leading up to a shack serving as both convenience store and local bar. An unmistakable blue glow shivered in its window, just below neon letters sarcastically announcing *The Office.* Martin noticed a promising TV antenna teetering on the shingled rooftop.

"This is it," Patrick said, as he jogged up to the front door and pushed. Inside the dim space, maybe two dozen adults and children were squeezed together, everyone barely glancing away from the set when the two newcomers sat down on a pair of folding chairs.

All eyes were aiming at the same screen, and Martin felt a surge of sympathy rising in his chest. This was exactly how it had to be: everyone around the world discovering they were connected by way of a space-suited man looking back at the earth. Tears sprang to Martin's eyes, but he didn't say a word. Later, the astronauts would struggle to find an adequate way of describing their view of home from so far away. The sun only a star among billions of others.

Martin, far from home himself, wondered who would care that Neil Armstrong's silicone boots had been manufactured by the Company? The logo that now he could see only in his dreams was high above them, carrying the message that Steinmetz must have heard when he harnessed lightning. Electricity's power not only to light the world, but to change the world's view of itself.

Martin decided to memorize not only what was on the television but also this single room and the echoes of it all around the planet, a current flowing in all directions, the antidote to wars and everything that caused them.

We are all electric cities, he thought. *Separate and together.*

THE BUZZING LIGHT inside the treatment room was fluorescent, and it did not change or flicker.

First the IV dripped an anesthetic, and Gloria counted backward, only getting as far as ninety-six before her voice went blurry and then silent. The hand holding Sophie's loosened its grip as the muscle relaxant was injected—to prevent broken bones and cracked vertebrae. A nurse inserted a rubber block between Gloria's fine white teeth to spare her tongue, then placed an oxygen mask over her nose. Sophie willed herself not to look away when they rubbed jelly onto Gloria's temples and connected the electrodes.

The toaster-sized machine was called a Konvulsator, its switches and dials marked in German words Sophie couldn't make out. The temperature of the treatment room seemed suddenly much too cold. She clenched her own jaw when the doctor pressed the button, watched his fingers turning up the voltage. Sophie held her breath, watching spasms shudder through Gloria's legs.

The nurse counted to twenty in a monotone; the doctor's face stayed blank. In part of her awareness, Sophie realized that this was how you detached yourself from your patients, how you practiced your profession in the gear of neutral. She stared so hard she saw Henry's mother's forehead muscles tighten, and a tiny tear formed at the corner of each eye.

What stunned Sophie most was how invisible it all was. Not just the electric current itself but also the change it was causing, the supposed cure for Gloria's "intractable depression." Somewhere deep inside the brain where it couldn't be fully understood, a pulsing electric shock was rearranging this person's thoughts, feelings, recollections. So much hidden power. So little to see.

When the button was switched off, Sophie exhaled.

"That's all for now," the doctor said.

Gloria's face softened, and the nurse peeled away the electrodes, pressing a bit of gauze to wipe away what remained of the conducting jelly at Gloria's temples. The tears dried by themselves.

"And the side effects?" Sophie kept asking, as they wheeled Henry's mother into the recovery room. Because the nurses and doctors seemed to dislike talking about this part. Entire periods of recent memory were being deleted. Sophie pictured a blackboard at school, fine particles of chalk floating free in the still air, vanished lines just barely decipherable afterward. Ghost words, shadow equations. After a few more strokes of the felt eraser, even those faint remnants were gone. Covered over? Replaced? Gone for good?

Nobody knew if the losses could be restored or resurrected; nobody knew if this was a temporary forgetting or a more permanent amnesia.

Sophie sat by Gloria's bed as her eyelids twitched and quivered, opening and closing and opening and closing.

Will her memories come back? Will I be the only one left to remember him?

Gloria opened her eyes once more, reached up to touch Sophie's nearby face. Then she rested one fingertip on Sophie's collarbone.

"I want to give you something," she said. "Promise you'll keep it safe."

Two years later, when Sophie began, along with her medical school classmates, to wear a brand-new stethoscope around her neck, she imagined what it might have been like to inherit the one that had been used in Europe by her vanished grandmother. Nestled in the hollow of her throat and balanced on that delicate strand given to her by Henry was this gift from his mother: a gold-rimmed antique oval holding a portrait of a blue eye that once belonged to some long-lost Van Curler. It now made a quiet counterpoint to the silver-and-black symbol of her life as a healer, each a talisman of a particular kind. Erasures transforming themselves inside her, as promised.

NNIE VISITED MARTIN in a dream, informing him that she was preparing to leave the earth. She stood in the center of her garden, her thick braided hair reaching down almost to her knees. When she held out her hands toward her grandson, he saw that her bare fleet floated just above the soil, and that her palms were filled with pebbles.

The following morning he woke before the sun and prayed, something he hadn't consciously remembered how to do. The gestures were simple. Out in back of his small apartment, he burned a fistful of tobacco in a white ceramic bowl, watching the smoke rise in a spiral toward the barely lightening sky. He made sure no one was watching, though there might have been an owl.

Let her wait for me, please.

After calling in sick and leaving the radio turned on in the bedroom, he filled his canvas bag with some beef jerky, a couple of tart apples, and a thermos filled with water. His knife stayed in its usual place deep in his jeans pocket; he wore both of his best pairs of wool socks. Once he had hitchhiked as far as the roads could take him, he waited in a grove of dense pine trees until the sun dropped well below the horizon.

Martin walked through moonlight along the hidden path that crossed reservation land. There wasn't any good reason to tell anyone his plans, and if he did everything right, he would return before there were signs he had ever left. It was the last week of September 1976, just over nine years since he had gone into exile.

He stepped carefully yet swiftly across the wide fields that included the Canadian border, certain he had no choice except this risk of everything, even prison, in order to see his grandmother one last time. Not for Bear, not even for Sophie, but for the woman who had shaped his life, the one who braided feathers into his hair more times than he could count.

The crickets reminded him of the evening he had climbed the tree on the Van Curlers' property at Lake George. Hitchhiking south not far from that same lake, the shrill sound rose and fell along with the temperature of the air. Martin felt the solid presence of the mountains observing his journey.

Three rides later, he was dropped off at an abandoned gas station just blocks from downtown. It was two in the morning. An owl was definitely following him now, its muffled wings parting the air overhead. He listened for its call and then the distant response of its mate.

Was Sophie still living in Electric City?

Martin couldn't allow hope for seeing her, not if he was going to leave town as quickly as he came. After nine long years, he felt almost sure she had left long ago. The only comfort he could envision rested in the dry warmth of his grandmother's hands. And in the chance of receiving one last blessing from her.

The first piece of shattering news was that Bear had run away less than a week after Martin's departure, never to be seen again. And before that could be absorbed, his cousin explained that their grandmother hadn't spoken a single sentence for days.

"She's more than halfway out of here," Isaiah said, when the two of them hugged briefly in her kitchen. Martin noticed but didn't comment on Isaiah's substantial weight gain. In return, his cousin didn't ask any questions about how Martin had managed to slip back into town, or where he had been living and working all these years.

"Any word from my father?" Martin asked.

"Nobody knows," Isaiah said.

His wife Debora was giving Annie a sponge bath, and the two men stood patiently just outside the bedroom door. Through a crack in the door, Martin could make out the back of Debora's plaid shirt and blue jeans, and in the overheard murmuring, he appreciated the gentle way she spoke to his grandmother. There was a noticeable fragrance of sage in the house, which underscored the fact that the scent of Bear was long gone.

Martin kept this additional pain to himself, hoping Bear was tucked into the warmth of someone else's world. When he did the math in his head, he realized it was probable Bear had already died. Would Martin have felt that death in his heart? Somehow the unanswered question convinced him there was no point in searching for Sophie. She was better off elsewhere anyway, better off in the arms of a living city.

Losses were the exact size of sorrows left unspoken. Martin was a ghost in a town already filled with them.

When finally he was given some moments to be alone with his grandmother, Annie could only keep her eyes squinting open for a few seconds at a time, just long enough to register his presence.

"You're right not to waste your strength with words," he said to her. "Just let me hold your hand." Her child-sized body astonished him, as though already her soul needed less space.

"Her feet are growing cold," Debora whispered, ominously. This was how a body began to depart: from the ground upward.

For the rest of the night he sat beside the bed, stroking Annie's gnarled fingers, softly singing to her some phrases from his childhood. This chance to study her face while it still retained some trace of her was to be her parting gift.

"Akhso," he whispered to her. *Grandmother.* "Konnorónhkwa." *I love you.*

He saw her smile as he bent to kiss the hollow of her cheeks.

Before dawn glinted on the horizon, he suddenly considered dialing Midge's number, with the thought of simply inviting her to sit with him and bear witness. Annie's breathing had slowed almost to nothing. *We wouldn't need to talk*, he thought. *Just listen to the wind.* He stood to wake Isaiah and Debora, to ask their opinion, but in that very instant he felt something shift inside the room, inside his bones.

He waited.

No more miniscule movements of her eyes beneath the lids, no more delicate rasp of inhaling and exhaling. This vessel, emptied of her spirit, was completely and finally still.

Smoke. Incense. The chanting of blessings for her soul's great journey.

And for his own journey yet again. There was only enough time to get back across the border before anyone at work could question his absence. Midge would hear the news from Isaiah and Debora; they would be the ones to wash Annie's body for the last time, to lower her into the earth.

So Martin headed north once more toward the place he now lived. Steinmetz had built himself a fully expanded existence in a new country more than once, and Martin thought he could retain the will to do that too. But so far Canada still felt like an accidental refuge, a borrowed place.

Crossing to the other side, Martin dreamed a silent song.

All in motion flickering on and off and on again, bursting fast in the darkness and then extinguishing, brief but insistent, flashing like stars against the infinite night sky. What if the sun chooses never to come up again? What if those lights are trying to tell you something you can't understand? What if it's Bear calling you from beyond, trying to make sure you know you are still loved, even now?

Maybe this is all anyone can ever understand about time or the future or electricity or being. Moonglow on moving water. Rivers, oceans, the passing of molecules back and forth, darkness into brilliance and then gone.

Like Steinmetz. Like Henry and Sophie and you.

G RABBING AT THE first medical internship she was offered in Manhattan, experimenting with a life beyond Electric City, Sophie monitored the stubborn layer of numbness inside, resulting in a performance of herself that was almost but not quite convincing. The relentlessness of New York City traffic blotted out most of her dreams. She studied her face in the mirror as always, except now she had the eye portrait Gloria had given to her, dangling on that slender gold chain. It was as if someone were gazing back at her who knew more about the future than she did.

She visited Electric City only once in her first year away, to spend the Jewish New Year with her parents. Observances still meant more to her father than to the rest of the family, but that was enough of an excuse to take the train ride alongside the Hudson River, watch the dance of leaves and water as she headed north. She sat on the left side of the train as it pulled out of Penn Station, saw the grays and browns of urban decay eventually give way to vivid blue-green nature. This time of year, the extra gift came wrapped in reds and golden yellows.

She gave herself permission to do nothing except stare out the window. Just a thermos with some tea, a sandwich purchased in the station, a solitude that soothed her completely. She pretended she didn't even speak English, ignoring any conversation drifting too close.

Arriving at Rensselaer Station where her parents waited to meet her, she noted the unmistakable evidence of their aging—not just the silvering hair and weakening eyesight, but the way they walked a little more slowly, repeated certain questions, and seemed to have mislaid words. They mentioned moving to Florida or at least buying a small condominium there. Simon was living in Berkeley with a woman Sophie hadn't yet met, but they were about to have a baby together, which was why he didn't even consider coming "back east" for the High Holy Days.

In fact Simon had stayed mostly true to his word about not returning, at least for more than a few days' visit. As for Jewish holidays, he told his sister he'd become an atheist, but their parents didn't hear about this.

"Better leave them out of it," he had said to her on the phone. "No need to hurt anyone's feelings."

The baby was due just after Rosh Hashana. In the car on the way back to the house, David told Sophie that Miriam jumped every time the phone rang. Excitement aside, her mother was clearly hurt about the idea of being a long-distance grandmother.

"Do you really think they'll stay in California, even with a child?" she asked her daughter and her husband with undisguised sorrow. "Isn't her family somewhere on this side of the country too, after all?"

"You'll be able to visit them whenever you want," Sophie said, though she doubted this was entirely true.

She spent the night in her old bedroom, in a twin bed with the same sheets she'd used as a teenager, pastel-flowered and extra soft from being laundered so many times. Even with the door closed she could hear both of her parents snoring. They had been married for nearly thirty-five years, a stretch of lifetime that seemed unimaginable to Sophie, who had never spent more than ten months in an adult relationship with anyone. She was twenty-six. It had been nine years since she'd heard from Martin, nearly ten years since Henry's death.

In the late spring of her graduation from medical school, when her father had been alarmed by shortness of breath, she and her mother had taken him to the emergency room at Ellis. The ER doctors sent David home with reassurances about the condition of his heart and lungs, prescriptions for blood pressure medication and encouraging words about exercising more. Sophie's father had nodded soberly at the advice, as though giving it serious consideration.

"I walk to synagogue once a week," he told Sophie when she asked now if he was taking up any regular physical activity. "Remember? I take the shortcut through the parking lot of the country club."

"That's a good start," she replied.

Her parents had once upon a time known how to cross-country ski, or so they claimed. Yet she couldn't recall anything athletic about them except what she'd glimpsed in rare photographs from their arrival in America. Before Simon was born, while they'd lived in Sheridan Village, an ice storm had stranded everyone for a week. "We got around without cars for the entire seven days," David had proudly recalled.

Sophie wondered if he had ever seen the images Steinmetz had taken of skaters on the Erie Canal, yet another echo of her parents' Dutch life superimposed on New Amsterdam. But now her father was talking about plans to retire from his research projects. The Company was still keeping its promise to light the world, but its headquarters had gone skeletal. Several manufacturing structures for the plant now stood empty, glaring evidence of the "neutron" approach of management. Wipe out the people but leave the buildings standing.

School enrollment was down by half, David told Sophie. The neighborhood surrounding once-glorious Proctor's Theatre was seedy-looking and grim. When she stopped by to visit the library, Sophie found a diminished and weary-looking staff. No one knew what had become of her old boss, Mrs. Richardson.

While her father attended synagogue, Sophie invited her mother to drive out to the orchards across the river to buy apples. McIntosh, Cortland, and Golden Delicious. They would slice the fruit and dip it into honey for a sweet new year. She steered Miriam's dark blue Chrysler along their favorite back roads, felt its smooth ride across the bridge and the newly repaved asphalt. The colors of leaves and sky splashed onto the water.

"I miss apple picking with you kids," Miriam said. The car wheels' music changed notes after getting off the bridge.

"I remember," Sophie said.

"Your father doesn't even like to visit California," Miriam said, jumping to a topic she was evidently brooding about nonstop. "He thinks everyone out there is a little crazy."

Sophie laughed, but her mother did not. "It's true," Miriam said. "He said as much to Simon and by now he's talked himself into it completely." She turned toward Sophie in her seat, allowing a glance at the worried look on her face. "Did you know that Simon's wife, I mean, his girlfriend, is going to have the baby at home? Without a doctor? What do you think about that?"

Sophie hesitated, keeping her attention on the road, watching for signs marking the orchard entrance. Hardly anything looked recognizable after she crossed the bridge. There were brand-new houses along the road flanking the river, oversize and ugly, with three-car garages on display. She wondered who was moving here, from where, and why. It was a strangely optimistic act, given how everything in town seemed so emaciated.

"Are you sure about their plans?" she asked her mother. Finally, a series of small red arrows appeared, and then the familiar faded painting of a Red Delicious apple, which was still nailed to the same telephone pole. Riverview Orchards.

"A midwife!" Miriam exclaimed. "She's using a midwife."

Sophie had delivered her first baby only two months earlier, a routine birth but with plenty of standard hospital drama nonetheless. There were fetal monitors and epidurals and she remembered thinking there was nothing all that "natural" about it. The mother was twenty years old, her husband had to be escorted from the delivery room when he almost passed out, and the healthy baby boy weighed seven pounds exactly.

After it was all over, Sophie changed out of her scrubs, went home to her apartment, and immersed herself in a bath where she sobbed for nearly an hour. She had no idea if she wanted a baby of her own, now or ever. She was happy for Simon and his girlfriend, happy for the couples whose babies she had helped guide into the world. But some part of her kept mourning for Gloria Van Curler, losing both of her sons.

What courage it takes, she thought, *to become anyone's mother.*

During her four years of medical school, Sophie had fallen mostly in love twice. The first man, named Winston, was a year ahead of her in school but somehow felt like a younger cousin; he lived with two other medical students and an ancient, overweight cat to whom she became increasingly allergic. Alistair the cat was her excuse for ending the relationship, although both knew she wasn't adequately smitten to overrule the problem.

"You just want to be somewhere else," Winston said, on what turned out to be the last morning he and Sophie woke up together.

He was right, and she admitted as much, sliding back into her clothes while he regarded her ruefully from the disheveled bed. Neither of them mentioned the idea that he could have moved into her place, or that they might have found a place together without the cat.

"I'm sorry," she said, and then after sneezing eight times in quick succession, she kissed him goodbye without regret.

The second time, she found herself in something more convincingly serious with a man she met at Roosevelt Hospital while interviewing for her internship in New York City. Paul was French Canadian and Jewish and a visiting specialist in radiology; Sophie was attracted by his accent and his thick head of dark curls shot through with silver. His brown eyes twinkled and his teeth were charmingly crooked. They dated steadily as soon as she moved to Manhattan; two months later, he shocked her by asking her to marry him, and she shocked herself by almost saying yes.

It was when Paul turned stone-faced in response to Sophie's request for a long engagement that she realized the idea of moving with him to Montreal had been a significant factor in her desire. Maybe even more important than she was letting either of them know.

"You know I don't speak French," she said, apologetically and repeatedly in the days following his proposal.

Paul replied the same way each time, frowning. "But you'll learn; you're an exceptionally smart girl."

Sophie flinched at the word *girl*, and began to feel scraped by the edge of superiority in his voice; she wondered how quickly they would grow tired or at least resentful of each other as soon as they crossed the border.

"And my medical training?" she said. "I have to complete it here in the United States."

Paul demonstrated his favorite shrug. "Are you so very certain of your need to be a physician, Sophie? Would we really need two Jewish doctors in the family?"

Which was, of course, the kiss of death. He went back alone to Montreal and she discovered that her weekends filled up perfectly well with long late shifts at the hospital and a half-serious passion for reading mysteries to help her through her solitary nights.

I am waiting while pretending not to wait, she admitted to herself.

Wedding announcements featuring various high school classmates proliferated for a while in the copies of the *Electric City Gazette* sent by her well-meaning parents. Miriam gradually gave up on her practice of asking Sophie if there were any new men in her life.

At the end of Rosh Hashana, Sophie headed back to New York City on the last train, watching the light from the moon on the Hudson. The playful dance of it mesmerized her, moving like time-lapse photography—a city at night viewed from space or at least the altitude of a mountain, the crazy-rapid movement of cars or beings or life inside illuminated buildings. She kept thinking this was some kind of language, a coded conversation between herself and the future, or the past, or everything at once.

Was time sticky like amber? She hoped it was.

MOONLIGHT GUIDED JOSEPH Longboat through the woods surrounding the Steinmetz house: yellow birch, white ash, cherry oak, birch again, pine, pine. There was an owl, then its mate, then silence unbroken by footfall. The melody of Great Creek sang in his right ear, a steady companion.

His friend Proteus was dying; they were the only two who knew how close the moment really was. The Hayden family slept soundly in their beds; they would barely feel his presence in their dreams. Joseph had a key that he rarely used, but tonight it let him open the heavy front door, slowly, slowly, so he could climb the carpeted stairs toward the room whose soft lamplight leaked under the door.

Steinmetz, lying on his distorted back under a goose-feather blanket, was disappearing, shrinking beyond even his smallness. Joseph recalled the first time he saw him and thought he was a child. Now the barely visible rise and fall of his chest assured Joseph he wasn't too late; there was time to say one last goodbye.

The strained heart was tired, and the lungs had compressed too much to sustain; all of this Joseph comprehended without quite knowing the medical facts. The strenuous cross-country journey with the Hayden brood turned out to be more costly than anyone expected. Now the Wizard's eternal spirit was ready to depart its temporary vessel; that's what Joseph understood.

While he positioned himself in a wooden chair next to the bed, Proteus's eyelids fluttered open once, twice, then closed against the exertion. Joseph placed a hand on his dear friend's wide forehead, leaned in to touch his lips there too. Nothing needed to be said anymore. Their decades-long conversation was complete.

Holding the four directions as a cluster of eagle feathers in his left hand, Joseph waved imaginary ceremonial smoke with his right hand, allowing it to remain unlit for the sake of remaining imperceptible to the family. He beckoned forgiveness from the gods who were already waiting, already here to receive.

After Brother Proteus exhaled his last breath, Joseph stayed a little while longer, moonlight shifting its subtle angles in the vast night sky. This agonized body had let go. Matter transformed again to energy, restored to itself.

Joseph Longboat returned the way he came, through the forest of pine, yellow birch, cherry oak, white ash.

ET ANOTHER AUTUMN had nearly come and gone, and Midge
was starting to recognize one or two of the fellow mourners who
visited the cemetery at this season's edge—or at least the ones
who brought flowers and decorations. The bicentennial year of 1976 was
mostly over, but some of the veterans' graves were still being draped in
stars and stripes. She had long ago given up trying to understand why
she readily made this pilgrimage to Daddy Steinmetz's grave year in and
year out, while the graves of her own parents were looked after more
randomly, if not indifferently. Perhaps because their death dates were in
spring, making it easier to treat the anniversary as something more like
a sweeping meditation. She would scrape away the dirty residue of leaf-
mold under snow, nurture the new growth of grass around the headstones.

But it was here at the Vale Cemetery, each 26th of October, that
Midge felt a curious blend of gratitude and loss that resonated with the
extinguishing colors overhead. No one had ever filled the enormous
space this small man had left behind when he died. She held to the
conviction that every person owned a kind of energetic fingerprint—a
wave like light? a molecular portrait?—and when they were gone, this
unique signature disappeared forever. If she closed her eyes and listened, she could almost conjure the strange way Steinmetz pronounced
her name—*Meedge!*—and yet, so many decades on, his dear face could
only be accurately remembered with photographic assistance.

Today the thought once again crossed her mind that her adopted grandfather's presence didn't really need to be visited here, at the cemetery. Surely in the afterlife his ghost would be happiest floating near the river, smoking cigars at his long-vanished cabin; maybe playing poker or entertaining a group of departed friends in the equally ghostly house on Wendell Avenue. And what made people think they could only resume incomplete conversations with the dead at the place where their empty bodies were last seen? The idea made about as much sense as waiting for a garden to seed and resurrect itself, yet still Midge stood at the familiar grave marker, paying her respects.

Chalk it up to habit, she thought, allowing a fleeting smile. *If Martin were still here, maybe we'd take a walk and tell each other stories. Maybe we'd spot an eagle above the river.*

She was pretty sure that Martin had tracked his own anniversaries of loss, at least when he was still in Electric City. But it had been almost nine years since she'd even received a postcard from him, Canadian-stamped and greeting her with deliberately vague descriptions of his whereabouts. The Vietnam War hadn't killed him, that was a blessing, but exile was itself a kind of death, when she thought about it. She hoped that Annie had been able to see her own grandson one last time before she died, even if it meant Martin had managed to sneak into town and out again without Midge knowing a thing. Everyone had to be so careful, it seemed, just to stay free.

After kneeling down to scoop her bare fingers into the soft earth, removing just enough dirt to make room for her offering, Midge settled the single white orchid so that its roots could find purchase. Now adorning the lower corner of the Steinmetz gravestone, the flower seemed to regard her with its own face, as if in quiet acknowledgment of their history.

She returned to her feet and felt a throbbing in her shoulder, accompanied by tightness at the small of her back—her body's usual chorus of minor annoyances. A neighbor had recently told her she ought to consider seeing a chiropractor, but Midge explained that she had tried that once, when she lived in California, and found she greatly disliked the sensation as well as the sound of her own bones being shifted around. She thought of all the years Daddy Steinmetz had lived with his own spine bent into the form of a question mark. The pain must have been unbearable, and yet he never complained.

The chiropractor in San Francisco had asked Midge to help her locate the knot in Midge's upper back, just beneath her left shoulder blade.

"That's the spot," Midge said, flinching beneath the woman's fingertips.

After deftly proceeding to snap something rather alarmingly into place, the young woman had commented, with tenderness, "It can be sensitive there, behind your heart."

Midge remained on the table for a few minutes after that, feeling her body try to find its new arrangement. "Thank you," she said, with genuine appreciation for the experience, though she instantly decided it would never be repeated. That had been a long time ago, on the other side of the country from where she belonged.

"You wouldn't believe how fast cars can travel these days," Midge spoke aloud to the air, not minding if anyone alive might overhear her. "But the pollution's a pretty wretched price to pay for modern life. You'd be the first to agree about that, I'm sure."

A high-throttling breeze was rising now, yanking leaves and throwing them at the ground. Not far from where she was standing, Midge could make out the shape of the tragic angel grieving on top of the

Van Curler mausoleum. *More boys who died too young*, she thought, unable to imagine what it would be like to lose not one but two of your children. It happened all the time in other centuries, in other countries. *But weren't we supposed to be protected from all of that now, in the Great Age of Modern Medicine, in the New World?* Then she wondered what Steinmetz would have said about transplants and dialysis, keeping bodies on life support even when the brain was never going to come back.

"I miss you," she said. The wind blew her words among the leaves, which scattered across the cemetery, until they piled along the wrought iron gates framing the garden of the dead.

WHEN IT WAS no longer a rumor but a fact, no longer hinted at underground but declared out loud and made official on both sides of the border, the Amnesty became part of Martin's consciousness and then settled there for a while, fermenting. He hesitated to be sure this wasn't a ploy; if anything had ever been learned by an Indian it was to be deliberately mistrustful whenever it came to governments and documented promises. Extreme wariness was required regardless of so-called party affiliation or what kind of man President Carter appeared to be on television, what his words looked like on newsprint or even sounded like on the radio.

This was simple history: vows broken like the smallest of twigs, a flick of the wrist or a twitch of an eyebrow, snap of a camera lens or a pulled trigger. Martin owed it to himself and to his ancestors not to take any assurances for granted, not to believe something just because he wanted to.

So he waited. President Ford had tried an Amnesty in 1974 but there were strings attached: obligations to work in service organizations, and who knew what else. With Carter inaugurated at the start of 1977, this Amnesty seemed genuinely openhanded, not a trap door. Others returned to the United States ahead of him, and the news stayed good, and there were no repercussions or arrests, no backstabbing or reneging.

Weeks passed, months. The days lengthened and temperatures rose; earth sent its moisture and fragrances into the heavy air. Insects traded messages, and birds lined up on the telephone wires. Martin watched for signs of danger and saw that the river remained calm; clouds passed across the sky and didn't rain down damage or loss or death.

Patiently and methodically, he began making arrangements, giving away nearly all of the little he owned, trusting a local charity to figure out where his belongings could do the most good for someone else. A mattress with platform, a couch, a desk, a kitchen table and chairs: his small apartment emptied itself easily, until it began to resemble the impersonal space it was when he first rented it.

Without self-pity or blame, he knew that nobody would miss him.

He bought a one-way ticket on Greyhound and crossed back over.

Electric City entered from the vantage point of the bus station appeared particularly grungy and desolate, a lost place for lost souls. Martin knew that bus stations couldn't be counted on for representational accuracy, but still the obviousness of the bleak mood gave him pause. Whatever the Company planned for keeping the few remaining thousand local men gainfully employed, downtown where the plant used to sprawl was looking more like a place where a plague had struck. Buildings still stood but they were as empty as cardboard boxes. The end-of-workday siren wailed into the void and Martin jaywalked without seeing a single car.

"Where is everybody?" he asked the empty street. The glowing letters above the factory headquarters seemed almost a mockery.

All around, Martin saw trash-filled parking lots and broken-glassed storefronts. Illegible graffiti stained the pitted outer walls of warehouses;

even Erie Boulevard wore an exceptionally depressed air. He knew from scanning the headlines that the Company, having moved so many jobs into the South, was now moving even more jobs to Asia, wherever labor was cheapest. Martin had no trouble imagining the snaky length of the unemployment line, his own fellow assembly-workers undoubtedly among its ranks.

So much for Steinmetz and his Socialist ideas. Electric City was being disconnected, unplugged from its own socket.

The farther he walked from State Street, the deeper he listened for birdsong as the mapping of territory. He had taught himself so many names for each North American species, not just the Latin designations of phylum and class and genus but the Mohawk words too, the ones that spoke of wingspan and nest shape. Familiar seasonal music could be found in every arabesque overhead, every gesture and pause. Now, almost as though he had never left, he walked along the river's edge, his own patterned footsteps harmonizing with the sky language, even with birds he couldn't see.

Like before, even Martin's cousin Isaiah didn't know he was coming back. It wasn't as though anyone needed an exact date for his arrival, and hadn't that always been the way of his family? To listen for the season's invitation, the changing intensity of sunlight as a beacon of homecomings. July's sticky heat pressed against him, softening his clothing and moistening his skin.

He knew that Bear could not possibly still be alive. It used to be that even if Martin was miles across town, across the river, in Bear's universe, when Martin's footsteps were heading closer to the door, molecules alerted his ears and his nose. A tingle in his nervous system making the fur on his back rise up, a thump of his tail in the midst of a dream.

And Sophie?

When Martin tuned inside himself, focusing on a pair of points beneath the cage of his ribs and at the center of his abdomen, he felt absolutely sure she didn't reside here anymore. Unfortunately that also meant she could be pretty much anywhere, in another state or even another country. He'd so thoroughly forced himself to imply no claim on her while he was in Canada, he didn't dare allow himself to question whether that silence had been a mistake. When his parents had left him—first Martine in death, and then his father in faraway work—he learned not to take abandonment too personally. Much more benevolent to keep his eye on what *wasn't* missing.

She would have learned her own ways of living with loss by now. But for the first time in his life, he began to imagine what it might be like to choose to stay connected, to keep even the frailest of cords from snapping apart.

He considered wandering past Henry's house, to search for the fox and interpret the wind. He could look between the stacks of books in the library, ask questions between the pages. Somewhere within miles or maybe days of distance, Sophie could be a wife and mother, a research scientist, a professor.

Did she even want to know him now, so many years gone?

He would have to find out.

MONDAY, MONDAY, SOPHIE sang under her breath, trying to invite optimism into the July morning. *So good to me.* She was late for work, waiting too long for the delayed subway line to get her to the ER for a shift she should never have agreed to take. She'd impulsively agreed to extend herself as a favor to a colleague not quite back from a long weekend in East Hampton. Another morning of stepping through the automatic ambulance doors of Mount Sinai Hospital, never quite knowing what she'd find awaiting her. Sometimes she felt her entire life had been like this: a doorway with some enigma on the other side, a spectrum from chaos to paralysis, crowded to evacuated, cacophony to deafness.

Her skin itched every time she imagined saying goodbye to her emergency life, a choice that would require forcibly resisting the urge to look over her shoulder in case she was needed for one last procedure. As an intern, she had envisioned going into family practice. Taking time to sit with her patients and find out about their lives, calmly listening to their fears and responding to their questions in lengthy detail. But instead she kept discovering how much she loved being the woman in motion, the one with the stethoscope and a scalpel-sharp mind for triage, balancing intricate lives in her grasp.

"Things go wrong," her chief resident had repeatedly said. "No matter how skilled we are, doctors just like everyone else have to stay humble, with all the same limits and imperfections. The key is to know almost everything, to be prepared and then to surrender. Having the tools is as close as you can get to having control, but the outcome still doesn't belong to you. I'm not talking about God but just about reality and life and death. We are almost but not quite in charge."

"Time of death: that's your job too," she was taught. "Pronounce it."

For Sophie that was the dazzling paradox at the core of her world. Getting to take responsibility for the losing and the saving, both.

MARTIN HAD IMAGINED himself sitting with Sophie on a bench in Electric City's own Central Park. The lost years would rise and fall between them, substantial and irrelevant. Where they'd lived and with whom, lovers and friends, jobs, vacations, happiness even. The rest of it. Stories now, as if a decade could be reduced to a simple narrative, episodes illustrated by photographs or scars, each wrinkle an event, a moment of sorrow or worry. And was any of it any less real than that summer on Lake George? Or that winter they didn't all survive?

He had been dreaming again of his great-uncle falling from the bridge, falling over and over, splashing into the green-black water. Other men were falling too, more than he could count, losing their footing on the bridge—which transformed into a cloud-piercing skyscraper he was working on with Robert, elaborate arrangements of steel beams and rebar.

Whenever he awoke from one of these nightmares, Martin told himself that these were fears about building a new life for himself. This terrifying desire to climb toward the future—with or without the one woman he hadn't seen in so long.

It wasn't Electric City that could reunite them, he understood now. It would have to be something new. Another city, a place free of memory. A place they would each have to discover, just like stepping off a ship and onto an unfamiliar shore. Steinmetz taught them that, but Martin was deciphering truths of his own. Sometimes you had to journey across continents and oceans; sometimes you had to reach across a border and back again. In order to become yourself. The new New World.

I T WAS JULY 13, 1977, and Sophie was halfway through back-to-back shifts in the ER. By now she knew the necessity of pacing herself, mastering the tricks of slowing down during the occasional lulls in the action, finding empty spaces to sit down while reviewing charts instead of leaning on the counter at the nurses' station. She could swear she'd seen doctors fall asleep standing up, but was determined as often as possible to prove her fortitude and stamina, wouldn't permit herself any state less than alert and on duty.

For a Tuesday, this sequence wasn't out of the ordinary: a car accident with excessive bleeding but no broken bones, a false alarm for a pregnant woman who needed to be sent back home, one high-on-something psychotic who thought he was still under attack in the jungle of Vietnam and needed to be evaluated upstairs.

That was the first few hours of the morning and then everything went quiet for a stretch. Sophie took her chances and sneaked a nap in one of the unused lounges, pulling the heavy beige drapes and locking the door after checking to be sure her beeper was on.

When she was startled awake by sharp rapping on the door, she pulled her hair back into a loose knot and patted her cheeks twice for extra blood flow.

"Unconscious six-year-old in Exam 1," the nurse said. "We need you."

"On my way," she answered, opening the door and trotting to keep up with the blond ponytail. The hallway was bright and polished, all the marginal sounds thick with urgency, and she found herself running a little ahead of the nurse now, no time to waste.

The girl was blue when Sophie got to her, slack in the muscled arms of a paramedic kid with a crew cut and tears in his eyes.

"No pulse. I tried everything," he groaned.

The nurse dragged a crash cart though the curtains and Sophie instructed the paramedic to lay the child on a gurney while they got the paddles ready. This was the part she'd only done with other doctors in the room, but she was on her own and there was no hesitation allowed. A heart had stopped in a six-year-old body and without pausing Sophie opened the small mouth and reached in with her fingers, making sure there was nothing in the airway.

She knew about seeing the light go all the way out, the voltage of the body shutting itself off. This was what had happened so invisibly to Henry on Iroquois Lake, his burned-out heart in the heart of dark water. Now would be the second instant of an absolute Before and an absolute After.

In a flash of detachment, she had a view of herself on translucent ice, with Henry's glittering ghost skating by. Standing now at the side of the gurney with the defibrillator paddles in her hands, she was just like the doctors she saw in the movies, the ones saying "CHARGE." Like a general leading an army. Like the one out front, with every atom of energy illuminated and armed.

And no matter what they prayed or hoped for, everyone knew that the flow didn't always find its target. Sometimes the current turned aside, or stopped, simply failed to do its magic. Sometimes the dead stayed dead, and the living had to move on.

Sophie motioned for the medic to stand back.

"Charge," she said, and that crazy thing happened where time slowed to a shimmering viscous thing. The girl's body jumped under the shock, but the monitor showed its same straight line.

"One more," Sophie said, her voice so clear and steady it didn't seem to belong to anyone.

The shock almost threw the child off the table, but it worked.

Her young heart was back in its proper music now, and the line on the black screen drew jagged angles where it should, up and down, up and down.

"Her name's Linda," the medic said, his voice cracking a little.

"You did a good job," Sophie told him.

She didn't know if the parents were anywhere nearby, but hoped they'd been spared this sight. Nurses were already removing the crash cart and double-checking for the leads staying hooked up to the right places. When Linda's eyes opened, Sophie caught her breath, placed her hands gently on each one of Linda's bony shoulders. Her expression was unnaturally calm, pale blue eyes regarding Sophie as though they'd been through this dance before.

Is it you?

"You're okay," Sophie said. "Everything is okay."

Seeing the Vietnam vet in the Mount Sinai ER had sparked a cascade of thoughts, surfacing hours later when Sophie had space in her head to review them. The idea that it could have been Martin, if he hadn't disappeared into Canada, or even Henry, if he had lived long enough to be drafted too. She'd heard in the recent news about the Carter Amnesty, but hadn't heard a word from Martin in years.

So many absences. First Henry, then Martin, and even Henry's mother, whose obituary Miriam had sent to Sophie from its page in the *Electric City Gazette*. Sophie still wore the eye portrait every day, and in her Lower East Side apartment, in a small crystal vase on a windowsill, she kept the collection of eagle feathers Martin had given to her when he said goodbye. Flanking the vase were two of her grandmother's medicine bottles.

The girl's eyes had made her think of delft blue, the paint she had layered onto her kitchen walls. The color linked to cascading images of Haarlem/Harlem, then Amsterdam Avenue and Brooklyn, on and on, every reminder of the Dutch. Henry's lost ancestors and her own. Her curiosity about Holland as a place somehow overshadowed by its New World echoes. The paintings of ice skaters she often visited at the Met, Brueghel and Vermeer, restless voyagers from a perfectly flat landscape.

The Hudson River flowing to Manhattan from Canada, fur traders and tobacco and beads. A beaver dam seen from the train window on her way alongside the river. One home and another.

When the power failed, Sophie was in the break room on the surgery floor, so the outage barely registered before the emergency generators kicked in. She was sitting on a lumpy couch in one of those dazed states with a cup of lukewarm coffee that she depended on to get her through the last hour of her thirty-six-hour shift. Absentmindedly, her fingers pressed a switch turning the nearby table lamp off and on, off and on.

The fluorescent bulbs of the room and hallway flickered as if in warning, and the microwave's digital clock flashed 12:00 before going blank altogether.

Residual daylight came through the windows along one wall of the room; in the waiting area, another merciful window meant the families who had some poor relative in the OR weren't plunged into total darkness. Sophie thanked the gods for not placing her with a scalpel in hand when the electricity paused, and then she offered up another silent prayer when the generator's backup power restored itself.

Still, beyond the hospital, the blackout lasted. She could see only dead traffic lights from the third-floor windows, nothing blinking, and she predicted as the evening gave way to complete darkness that the lights of the city would stay asleep. They'd already been having record temperatures, with the heat rising off the pavement in waves, tar-melting heat, the kind that seemed to triple itself inside high-rise offices and stores and apartment buildings, inspiring an overwhelm of usage from every power source. She was hurtled back into her memories of November 1965, recalling the candles and her parents and the phone calls from all of their friends, the way everyone came together in the dark.

Now, the Company had relocated thousands of families so that entire neighborhoods had dispersed in less than a decade. Among Sophie's parents' tribe, most had semiretired by now to Florida or North Carolina; her parents had purchased their Boca Raton condo. If she could ever relieve herself of the daughter's obligation to stay close by, she wondered for the hundredth time if she could move cross-country to California. Become reacquainted with Simon. Create a family of her own, in some other place.

At the edges of reverie, she heard her name being called, not on the intercom, she realized, but out in the hallway, from the nurses' station.

"Dr. Levine," over and over, not with urgency but with something like kindness, or so it seemed. "Are you all right?"

"The power's out all over Manhattan," said Alice Matheson, RN. Sophie took a second to read her badge. "Maybe the other boroughs too, not sure yet."

"Oh," Sophie said, and realized that for several minutes she'd forgotten she wasn't in Electric City but in New York City, which scared her a little, to see how her exhausted mind had lost its geography, how it reverted so quickly to the place she used to live.

"But we've got our generators," Alice said proudly, as though she were at least partly responsible. "Anyway, you're needed downstairs in the ER waiting area."

She studied Alice's face for a moment, her wavy red hair clipped back with gold barrettes, her wire-rimmed glasses framing a face scrubbed pink and young. Sophie thought she looked like that other Alice she had known from high school, which seemed so long ago.

"Thank you," she said. "I'll just check on things in the OR before I go downstairs."

"They've just finished up," Alice said.

Sophie turned to see the surgeons in their scrubs coming through the swinging DO NOT ENTER doors, looking at once haggard and relieved, peeling off their paper hats.

"Good lord," one of them said. "Tell me that didn't really happen."

Sophie smoothed cool water onto her face in the lounge, dried herself with stiff paper towels, and did what she'd been doing all her life—looked into the mirror for an image that might reveal clues to the mystery of herself. Faint suggestions of lines at the corners of her eyes, bruised shadows of her sleeplessness, and the future impression of an older woman. She saw her girl face too, persistently hoping toward joy, with layers of sympathy and sorrow etched between her eyebrows.

When she stepped into the hallway and saw the back of his head, that unmistakable sleek hair in a braid down the center of his denim jacket, she knew he felt her looking at him. She was well past ordinary fatigue and could later forgive herself for framing the scene in a cinematic blur. But this was not about sleep deprivation or dreamy sleepwalking or anything other than a surreal day of waking up from an elongated nightmare she didn't even know she was struggling through.

He turned around.

Here was all she had learned about the heart as an organ, the chambers and valves and ventricles, how it functioned as a pump and a motor, with its ebb and flow. An electric machine too, that could miraculously be shocked back into motion. She knew so much and so little.

Here was his smooth skin, the obsidian gleam of his eyes, the carved shape of his cheekbones and jaw, the beautiful astonished wave-breaking smile, and her once-tentative heart leaped up. It flew.

"You're here," he said, and she would have said it first if she'd been able to speak.

They stepped closer, and their arms folded around one another as though they'd been doing this all their lives, except it had been almost ten years since they'd had the chance.

Time bending.

Sophie felt utterly calm and crazily jangled, her breath caught by the edge of release. Moths at an illuminated window. Leaves in the wind. Every promise returning to the truth.

Their bodies pressed tight, then tighter together. Cascading breaths, in and out, blending them.

She didn't want to let go, not ever again. But he stepped back to take another look at her, and he touched the cold disc of stethoscope in her pocket, smiling, and she grinned back, wider than she had known she could stretch. When she placed a fingertip on the surface of the eye portrait at her throat, her pulse throbbed underneath the gold.

"Dr. Levine," Martin said, without a trace of irony, and she'd heard it so many times but never quite this way, in the voice she'd missed for so long.

"Martin Longboat," Sophie said. "Welcome home."

AUTHOR'S NOTE

I OWE MANY DEBTS of gratitude to anecdotal as well as scholarly sources for this novel. My own childhood in Schenectady was certainly the initial point of origin for the emotional backstory, but when I began to focus on the Great Northeast Blackout of 1965, I realized I needed my characters to be a decade older at the time than I myself had been (I was five). That decision further led to a chain reaction of invention and fictionalization, including treatment of the characters loosely based upon my parents and their friends, as well as my own school friends, and beyond.

The character of Martin Longboat was inspired by a Mohawk dancer whom I happened to meet in Central Mexico; the simple fact of his existence (and the discovery that he was exactly my age) revealed to me in a heartbeat how little I knew about the Native American history of my birthplace—and about the indigenous people who were my contemporaries. I began to consult books like *Indian Voices* by Alison Owings and *Myths of North American Indians* by Lewis Spence. I listened to some rare audio recordings and did my best to imagine my way into the ghostly residents of my hometown.

As with most writers of fiction, I took liberties with the facts I learned, when it suited the purposes of my narrative.

It was my father who encouraged me to consider using Charles Proteus Steinmetz as a character in my novel. In order to research his significant role in the development of electricity, I consulted documents and photographs held by the Schenectady County Historical Society and the Schenectady Museum, including videos in the Schenectady Museum Film Series called "Charles Steinmetz: The Man Who Made Lightning" and "Thomas Edison Visits Schenectady." I visited the Edison Tech Center (formerly called the Edison Exploratorium); I read *Nature's Electricity* by Charles K. Adams, along with some of the essays and articles written by Steinmetz himself. Extremely informative was the biography of Steinmetz by John Winthrop Hammond. I pored over the images and texts of *Schenectady, A Pictorial History*, and *The General Electric Story*. What seemed so remarkable was how Steinmetz has been so nearly erased by time, even though during his lifetime he'd been considered as famously important as Thomas Edison. The recent video about Steinmetz (*"Divine Discontent: Charles Proteus Steinmetz"*) reinforces my conviction that this man, overlooked by history, is being restored to the giant-sized status he deserves.

ACKNOWLEDGEMENTS

F OR LISTENING TO me through the darkest nights, lifelong thanks to beloved friend Maia Newman. For healing of body and soul, a deep bow of gratitude to Dr. Garrett Smith and your band of angels. For inspiration and abrazos, near and far, Ana Thiel. For countless exquisite dinners, Constance Holmes and John Van Duyl.

For sanctuary, sustenance and solace: Ragdale Residency, Lamu Artist Residency. And with special thanks to Susan Hall, Dorothy Jacobs, Mark and Nancy Jacobs.

For fellowship on the path, Carol Lopes and Harry Stark; for opening the door, Julia McNeal. For peaceful companionship, doggie care and graceful space-sharing, Brooke Deputy and Chris Malcomb. For long walks and longer talks, Lori Saltzman. For musical interludes and much more, guitar hero and impresario Joe Christiano.

For each and every one of my writing students who keep me humble and well-distracted, my sincere thanks. May the muse be with you.

For reading drafts of these pages (early and sometimes often), for generous encouragement to persevere, and for your wide hearts, thanks to Lynne Knight, Saint Rosner, Harriet Chessman, Wendy Sheanin, Steve McKinney, Meredith Maran, Larry Grossman, Michael Dales, Elizabeth Stark, Andre Salvage, and Lauren Reece Flaum (in blessed memory).

For seeing what some others could not, thanks to brilliant agents Miriam Altshuler and Reiko Davis. For commitment, teamwork, and leaps of faith, thanks to Counterpoint Press. For immeasurable wisdom, humor, patience and insight, a song of eternal joy to editor Dan Smetanka. Shine on.